ELIXIR

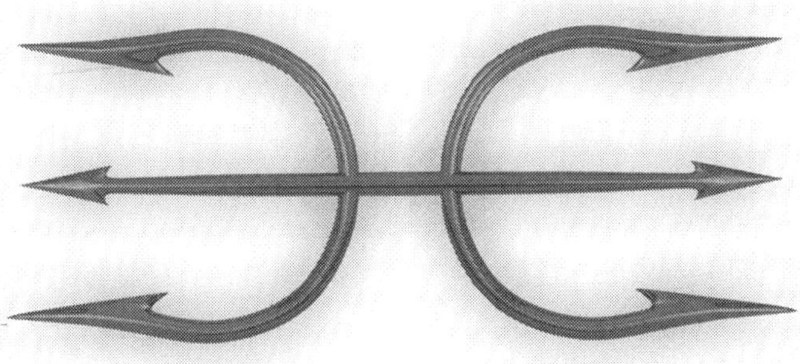

PHIL CLEARY

ISBN: 1466389257
ISBN-13: 9781466389250

To Gran

Merry Christmas

Phil Cleary

Phil Cleary is a former police officer and specialist in covert operations. On leaving the police force, he used his experience on the front line of crime fighting to help create SmartWater, a unique forensic coding system that has become one of the most powerful deterrents in the world. He is now the CEO of a major international company of the same name.

Phil is a Fellow of the Royal Society of Arts, a media personality with countless television appearances to his name, and one of the Security Industry's most in-demand gurus.

He lives in Shrewsbury with his partner, Melanie, her two children, Emily and Alicia, two dogs, Lily and Maisie, two cats Sid and Pixie and the rabbit, Poppy. (Phil would like to apologize if he's failed to mention any other living thing that may be currently residing with him that he's unaware of).

For my beautiful daughters,
Leigh, Chrissie, Emilie and Katie.

ACKNOWLEDGEMENTS

The number of people who helped me with this book is legion but I would like to single out for special thanks Dr Jo Greenwood, Head of Technical Services at SmartWater Technology, who advised me on some of the laboratory processes and my sister Cath for her pharmaceutical insights which I was able to weave into the story line.

(I hasten to add that all the liberties and inaccuracies in terms of the 'science' within this book are totally down to me).

Special mention should also go to the staff at The SmartWater Security Group HQ who had to listen to my endless gibbering rants, which would occur at any time during their working day, particularly when I was struggling with the plot line – other than feigning illness, there was no escape for them.

Finally, I would like to thank my partner, Melanie, for providing useful snippets of historical trivia which I plagiarised mercilessly and for her endless patience in helping me with the proof-reading of the many, many iterations of the book as, without her help, undoubtedly, *Elixir* would have withered and died.

Men fear death as children fear to go in the dark.

—Francis Bacon

The greater the continent of knowledge, the longer the shore of mystery.

—Huston Smith

PROLOGUE

'Coffee, regular!'. The cafe assistant looked him square in the face as she passed over the polystyrene cup full of steaming liquid but showed no sign of either recognition or alarm..

Strange, the man thinks to himself. Strange to know you're about to kill someone. And strange to know that nobody – really, *nobody* – can tell.

But then, Tom Shaw had grown used to strangeness.

Take the people he passes as he walks south along 6th Street. Most of them are too busy to give him a first glance, let alone a second. Too busy with the minutiae of their day to notice other people. Some of them, however, recognized him. They performed a double take. They stop and stare and whisper to their companions. 'It's him. It's *him!*' Tom has spent the whole of his life being unknown, and he wonders if he'll ever grow accustomed to this. He supposes he will, given enough time.

And after all, he has all the time in the world.

Tom doesn't *need* to walk, of course. His driver could take him straight to his destination in minutes. But Tom insisted on being dropped two blocks back. 'Mr Shaw, sir,' the driver had said, 'is this a good idea? They're waiting for you. Midday, Mr Shaw. It's already ten to...'

'They can wait a little longer,' he'd replied as he climbed out of the vehicle.

Yes. They can wait a little longer.

He likes being in the street, even with the glances and the whisperings. He likes to feel a part of things. A man in the crowd. It won't be long, he knows, before even this will be impossible for him. He stops outside a noodle bar, breathes a lungful of monosodium glutamate and looks in. An Asian guy is flambéing something in a wok. Tom's reflection stares back at him from the restaurant window. A well-cut business suit. A sober tie. A leather briefcase. And his face: not young, not old. A little grey around the temples. An ordinary face, but with a look in the eyes that is somehow a shock every time he sees it. Is this, he wonders, what all people contemplating murder see when they look in the mirror? The definition of murder in California requires 'malice aforethought'. Does he harbour malice towards his intended victim, he wonders. Oh yes. He has it in spades.

A diner in the noodle bar has recognized him, so he turns away and carries on walking. At the end of the street he turns right into Pennsylvania Avenue. Four hundred yards along he passes the J Edgar Hoover building and he wonders how much the Feds would give to learn what he was about to do.

He keeps walking. The White House is only 500 yards away. He sees the famous white dome and the manicured lawns. It's a beautiful day, and the dome is impressive framed by the blue of the sky. Funny, Tom thinks to himself, how the powerful construct buildings to demonstrate their Might. But time will always turn them to dust. A building can't last forever.

He walks calmly in the direction of the White House. And as he walks, he thinks of men who have done something similar before him. He thinks of Lee Harvey Oswald. What did he feel in the hours before he squeezed the trigger. Fear? Excitement? Rage? Tom wonders if he himself should be feeling these things. He doesn't. He barely feels anything. Just a vague sense that what he is about to do is right.

At the entrance to the White House, he quietly tells the security personnel his name. He is expected. The tall security guard is polite but firm as he asks Tom to remove his wristwatch and walk through the airport-style arch. Tom complies. There is no sound from the security gate. On the other side, a second guard frisks him down, searching for hidden weapons. A knife. A gun. A sharp object. Anything deemed to be a threat to the President. They find nothing. Tom opens his briefcase without even being asked. The guard looks inside. He sees a sheaf of documents and a large brown envelope. Otherwise the briefcase is empty.

'Would you like me to remove them?' Tom asks.

The security guard shakes his head and smiles. 'I hardly think a few slips of paper represent a clear and present danger, Mr Shaw.'

Tom smiles back.

'You can go through now,' the security guard tells him. 'Have a nice day.'

'I will, thank you.'

The President's Chief of Staff is waiting for him just beyond the security gates. Don Jackman – hawk-nosed and hawk-eyed. But charming with it. 'Mr Shaw.' He shakes Tom's hand warmly. 'The President has been very much looking forward to today.'

'As have I, Mr Jackman,' Tom replies. 'As have I.'

They walk the corridors of power. How many individuals of note, Tom wonders, have been led along these carpets? Heads of State and captains of industry? Heroes, and villains? Yet, as he passes the offices and the meeting rooms, he senses everybody stopping their work to watch him. Even these White House workers, their appetites for powerful men and women jaded, want to catch a glimpse of him.

How strange it is, Tom thinks to himself once again. How very, very strange.

Then he is being led into the Roosevelt Room. This is the second time Tom has been in here. The first time, under very different circumstances, he sat at a long, polished table. Today, however, in addition to the TV cameras, he sees three rows of chairs, lecture-theatre style. An audience of about 50 people, mostly the great and the good from the scientific world, and a few journalists.

Witnesses, I suppose, thinks Tom. But witnesses to what?

The President walks in, accompanied by black-suited Secret Service personnel. There is a blinding cluster of flashes as the President approaches Tom with a smile.

'Welcome to the White House, Mr Shaw,' he says, and he offers his hand.

But Tom declines to take it. Two Secret Service officers, having witnessed the very obvious slight, automatically take a tense step forward, but the President waves them away and tries again.

It is difficult to be a man of honor in the world he now inhabits, but Tom sees no reason not to make an attempt. And it would be unseemly, to say the least, for him to shake a man's hand just before he takes his life.

'Shall we begin, Mr President?' he asks.

The President clearly doesn't know what to say, or how to respond. But the cameras are rolling and the eyes of the world are upon him. He dare not show his displeasure, or his confusion. He watches as Tom takes one of the two seats set out for himself and the President, places his briefcase upon his knees, opens it up and takes out a large brown envelope.

For the first time, Tom feels a sense of anticipation as, literally, he holds the life of the President of the United States in his hands.

'Yes,' the President says. 'Yes. Of course. Let's begin.'

PART ONE

SIX MONTHS PREVIOUSLY

I

Friday, 11.30 p.m., Pacific Standard Time

'Coffee.'

It wasn't a question. It was a statement. And a disgruntled one at that. Clint wanted to get home and the coffee in the cup he was holding was burning his hand. .

Who could blame him? This was his third night in a row working late. He'd been in the lab for fifteen hours. He was only twenty-three and it was Friday night. His friends were drinking beers in a sports bar downtown. There was this girl he had his eye on and his buddies were no doubt hitting on her right now. Clint had lanky hair, pockmarked skin and thick-rimmed glasses. He crumbled in the presence of the opposite sex, but he still liked to imagine that he'd be uncharacteristically charming if he was there. And it wasn't even like he was being paid overtime for these extra hours washing conical flasks and microscope slides. It wasn't like he was being paid much at all.

He placed the white cup down on the epoxy resin worktop. It was scratched and, although scrupulously clean, looked threadbare and worn. Truth to tell, this whole lab was shabby.

The equipment was old and the walls – bare, except for an old poster of the periodic table – needed painting. But it was obvious to anyone who worked for Pure Industries that this place wasn't getting a refit any time soon.

'Dr Leo?'

Only now did the woman crouched over her microscope look up. 'Thanks.' The woman gazed around vaguely. More so than usual, her mind was clearly on something else. 'What time is it?'

'Just past eleven, Dr Leo.' Clint tried to keep his voice level.

Dr Leo glanced at the clock on the wall and, with a slight shake of her head, said . 'What are you still doing here? You should have gone home hours ago.' She picked up her cup, took a sip and winced. It was a strong exotic brew which was not really to her taste. And drinking it in her office was strictly against the rules, rules she'd created herself after a accidental spillage the previous year. Clint had been badly scalded by hot drinks, causing him to knock over bottles of various chemicals and other materials in the Lab. The decontamination process had taken weeks, time they could ill-afford. Dr Leo had enforced the rule more strongly after that, but she became less strict about it after hours when there were fewer people around.

Secretly, Clint quite liked the way her nose wrinkled when she tasted a particularly pungent blend. His immediate boss was a beauty by anyone's standards. She had pale blue eyes and clear, tanned skin. Her hair was naturally a bleached blonde color and cut into a neat, fashionable bob. She looked tired, but somehow that didn't spoil her appearance. You didn't have to spend much time with her, though, to realize that she was a 'look but don't touch' kind of girl. Dr Rachael Leo was married to science. There wasn't much room for a third person in that relationship.

'Honestly, Clint,' she said, still sounding distracted. 'Go home. I can manage here.' She turned back to her microscope.

Clint stood there for a moment, shuffling from one foot to the other. 'You look like you could use a break yourself,' he said suddenly, surprising himself with his own boldness. 'Maybe we could... I don't know... grab a beer or something?'

He waited anxiously for a reply. None came.

'Right...' he stuttered. Was she ignoring him? Or was she so lost in her work that his offer hadn't even registered? 'OK... well... whatever. I guess I'll call it a day...'

If Dr Leo had heard him, she didn't let on. She just remained hunched over the worktop while Clint, his skin flushing slightly with embarrassment, stepped backwards in the direction of the door, removing his lab coat as he went.

'Well... goodnight then,' he said. 'Don't work too late.'

He walked out of the lab, shut the door and exhaled deeply.

Idiot, Clint, he told himself. Can't you tell when someone's out of your league? He walked down the antiseptic corridor towards the exit, his footsteps echoing as he went. His heart was racing, and his mind was turning over. It was no surprise Dr Leo had ignored him, but he couldn't help wondering what was so important that she seemed practically to be living in that run down old lab.

Two minutes later he had stepped out into the humid Californian night. A storm was coming. His battered old Ford was one of only two cars parked in the Pure Industries car park.

As he opened it up, he looked back towards the lab. The lights were still on inside. Clint couldn't help wondering how long they'd be burning.

Sometimes, Rachael Leo thought to herself, she felt as if she spent her waking hours with one eye shut. It was the only way she knew to see further than everybody else.

She had one eye shut now, and one eye pressed to the eyepiece of her microscope. She could see two things. The first was an air bubble. You often got them when you dropped the slide cover on to the damp slide, but she generally elected to put up with it rather than waste any more time preparing the slide again

The second item was a tiny organism. *Caenorhabditis elegans*. The nematode worm. It was no more than a millimetre long, but now that it was magnified 100 times Rachael could see the textures and contours of its tiny body. One end of its body had spiralled round in a helix shape. Pretty enough, but it was the other end that held her attention, and her fascination. It was moving. Wriggling.

Alive.

Rachael stood up and ran one hand over the small of her back. It felt like she'd been bent over a microscope or a computer for half her life. Tom, her CEO, was forever telling her that she'd be hunchbacked before she reached fifty and he was only half joking. She walked purposefully to the other side of the lab.

There were white lab mice here, scores of them kept in Perspex cages. They scratched around in the sawdust, their noses pink and wet, their eyes bright and their fur lustrous. Rude with health. Rachael smiled. As a kid in Arkansas she'd been crazy about animals. There was a rabbit hutch in the yard, two dogs and a cat that ruled the house. The young Rachael Leo had begged her mom for a pony. When her mom pointed out that their tiny yard and tiny income made it impossible, she set her sights a little lower and asked for a mouse. Her mom had shuddered at the thought, and Rachael's menagerie never expanded.

It was in her first year at college that she dissected her first rodent. The stench of the formaldehyde had made her want to vomit even before the scalpel had pierced the gristle of the animal's belly to reveal its neatly packed innards. She'd wept that night and wondered if she really had what it took to be a scientist. Two days later, however, her mother was diagnosed with an aggressive cancer of the brain. *Glioblastoma multiforme*. The most cursory glance at the medical literature told Rachael her mother didn't stand a chance. And so she'd taken time out from college to nurse her. She'd held her thin hand, and changed her soiled sheets when she became bedridden. The horror hadn't lasted long. Her mom was dead in a month.

When Rachael returned to college, her resolve had hardened. If she had to dissect ten animals a day to expand the frontiers of medical knowledge, a *hundred* animals, that's what she would do. She'd lost count of the number of bloated, stinking and dismembered lab-mouse corpses she'd shovelled into incinerators in the name of science. The process no longer disgusted her. Dr Rachael Leo, beneath her professional exterior, was a kind-hearted young woman, but you didn't want to be an animal in her lab.

These mice, however, bucked the trend. Prime specimens, all of them. And it was mice that had first alerted her to the anomaly.

Pure Industries was struggling. Nobody had said it in so many words, but everyone knew it was true. The four members of the executive board had perpetual frowns on their faces, and Rachael knew of at least one ugly rumor going round the more junior staffers about Pure's 'great white hope': an herbal remedy to be marketed under the name Legum. Legum was designed to ease muscle pain after exercise. The idea was a good one: the fitness market was ripe for tapping, but Pure Industries wasn't pinning all its hopes on selling pills to a few muscle-bound knuckleheads. Tom's idea – the idea that was going to turn around the company's fortunes – was more ambitious: to sell Legum to the US military to increase the energy levels of front-line troops. As an herbal product it could go to market without approval from the FDA. Rachael's team were testing it thoroughly nonetheless. Tom had insisted on that, and she respected him for it. The lab staff had noticed, though, that Dr Leo was spending much more time trialling the compound than she needed to. They had started to whisper. There was a problem with Legum, they said. It was serious. A rumor had spread that it was killing a significant proportion of its subjects...

Rachael knew the rumors. She also knew the truth.

She wasn't party to the board's private discussions. She didn't know what was really going on in the company's account ledger. But she did know that her research budget had been cut by a third which meant that, for a while at least, as much of her time had been spent examining her departmental finances, as conducting the actual research she and her team were employed to carry out. It was tedious combing through a year's expenditure and deciding what could be trimmed back and what could be discarded entirely. She'd felt more like an accountant than a scientist. It was disheartening, too. Prices always went up, not down; and the quantities her team required of the key sundries that kept any lab going seemed to increase every month.

All of them, she realized, except lab mice. Their numbers followed an inverse trajectory and she couldn't understand why.

Rachael had the soul of a scientist. She hated not knowing something. It was like an itch she couldn't scratch. Worse than that. A sore she couldn't salve. Why were they incinerating fewer rodent corpses? Was this a statistical blip? It didn't seem to be. The anomaly was statistically significant – it had taken her half an hour of high-school mathematics and an Excel spreadsheet to see that. The research that followed had taken a lot longer. Months of working late and in secret. She'd had to become an expert outside her own specialist field of the plant life of the Amazon, branching out into the study of light spectra, thermal dynamics and the biology of Sarcopenia. She was drained and exhausted, but the more she learned, the more she had to carry on. It was like a narcotic.

A crack of thunder outside. Rachael blinked. How long had she been staring at the scurrying mice in their cage? She looked at her watch. It was a quarter to midnight. She cleaned her glasses again, then walked out of the old lab, along the corridor, past the common room, where the lab technicians would all hang out during their breaks, and into her little office on the left-hand side. In truth, office was a grand word for what was really a glorified closet: a tiny desk, piled high with papers, a beige PC barely powerful enough to run the modelling software she needed for her work. And a telephone.

Rachael sat at her desk and for a moment stared at the phone. It was Friday. Nearly midnight. Hardly a sociable time to be calling anyone, least of all her boss. But after months of work, of checking and rechecking the results, of replicating her experiments and convincing herself that she was right, what did one broken night matter?

It didn't. She picked up the phone and dialled a cell number.

The cell rang. Four times. Five. The voicemail clicked in. 'This is Tom, leave a message.'

Dr Leo hung up immediately and redialled the number. Voicemail again. Once more she hung up and dialled. This time, it was answered immediately. 'Hello...' the voice was only half awake. '*Hello?*'

Rachael closed her eyes.

'Tom, it's Rachael Leo,' she said. 'I'm sorry it's late, but I'm at the lab and I really think you ought to get over here.'

A pause.

'Now?'

Rachael felt her skin tingle with excitement. 'Yeah,' she said. 'Now.'

2

11.58 P.M., PACIFIC STANDARD TIME

When the phone had vibrated by his bedside for the first time, Tom Shaw had clenched his eyes and desperately tried to stay asleep. Sleep was good. It made him forget about everything else. He clung to it like a drowning man clinging to a piece of driftwood.

When it had vibrated for the second time, he had not only opened his eyes, but realized with a familiar sense of desperation where he was. The small room was dark, the only source of light a green glow by the side of one of the two single beds. Tom slept in one, his wife Jane in the other. The sound of her shallow breathing filled the room. He could just make out the silhouette of the drip stand containing an antibiotic serum to combat her latest bout of infection, and the winch at the head of her bed. She didn't need it now, but they both knew it was just a matter of time. Tom found these beds incredibly uncomfortable. He knew, though, that Jane lived for Friday and Saturday nights when he could sleep in her hospice room. Tom had learned that it's a lonely business waiting to die. He couldn't do much to help his wife, but he could relieve the monotony.

When his cell vibrated for the third time, he was wide awake. And when he heard Rachael Leo's voice at the other end, a tiny, guilty part of him was grateful for the excuse to get away, if only for a few hours. He could be back by the time Jane awoke, and she need never know that he'd gone. He slipped out of bed, pulled on his jeans and Averett University sweatshirt and headed for the door.

'You off to paint the town red?'

Jane's voice was hardly there: a thin, reedy, wheezing gasp. But somehow, through the filter of illness, it still retained some of that quality that had first attracted Tom to her back in their college days: that knowing, twinkling quality, like she was always on the verge of laughing fondly at him.

Tom stopped still, winced in the darkness and turned back towards her bed. 'Hey,' he said softly. 'How you feeling?'

She didn't answer. She never did when the reply was something she thought he didn't want to hear.

'I just got a call from the office,' he told her. 'But I don't have to go. I'd rather st...'

'Go,' she said. 'I'll be fine. Just make sure you kiss me when you get back, even if I'm asleep.'

'Hey, just try and stop me.' He brushed his lips against hers. They were dry and cracked, but he pretended not to notice. 'I'll be back before you know it,' he told her. Jane just smiled, but it was clearly an effort and she closed her eyes again almost immediately.

The Canyon Valley Respite Home was in a northern suburb of Laguna Niguel, Orange County. It was less than a mile from

Tom and Jane's modest family home, where their son Jack was being looked after by his favourite local babysitter; and five miles from the estate on the southern edge of the town where Pure Industries had its headquarters. Tom drove carefully through the heavy rain that reduced his visibility to only a few yards, but at this time of day it was still only ten minutes before he was holding his magnetic swipe card up to the electronic entrance gates and driving in. The premises – a series of bland, single-storey prefabs – were deserted, apart from a single vehicle in the car park and a tell-tale light shining from the window of the lab. Tom parked up in his usual spot – the space reserved for the company's CEO, though there had been no shortage of parking spots available since the redundancies of a couple of years ago – and turned off the engine.

He sat in silence for a moment, staring at the rain on the car windscreen. When he'd first arrived here four years ago, the challenge of the place had excited him. Diversify, they'd told him. Find new markets. Even when things started to go wrong, he'd relished the prospect of getting the company back on track without resorting to the underhand tactics of his more ruthless competitors. When they'd started developing Legum, his enthusiasm was total; and when the US military started making encouraging noises, the CEO's optimism had noticeably filtered down to the rest of the company.

And then came Jane's diagnosis. Funny, Tom thought, how things can change overnight.

Now he was just going through the motions, playing the part of the conscientious CEO. But he knew that the other members of the executive board were exasperated by his apparent lack of concern about the precarious state of the company's finances; by the way the army deal seemed to be slipping through his fingers. Truth was, Tom had other, more important, things to occupy his mind these days. One of them was lying on a hospice bed, wasting away on account of a rare form of muscular dystrophy. The other was being looked after by his babysitter, and would need all of Tom's love and attention when his mother finally left them.

He caught sight of his reflection in the rear-view mirror. Tom had never looked anything other than unremarkable – he'd never *been* anything other than unremarkable, despite what Jane tried to tell him – and he had to admit to himself that he wasn't aging well.

He tried to shake these thoughts as he exited the car. The flashing orange locking lights reflected in the puddles as Tom ran into the building.

He found Rachael in her office. Her face was bathed in the light of her computer screen which she was studying with a characteristically serious face. She was so immersed in whatever she was reading that she didn't notice Tom standing in the doorway. He coughed gently. She startled.

'You know, Rachael,' Tom said with a half smile. 'I really don't pay you enough to work these kinds of hours.'

Tom was fond of Rachael Leo. He wasn't much more than ten years her senior, but he felt kind of fatherly towards her. And while he prided himself that he was a pretty benevolent boss – especially compared to the hard-nosed standards of US big pharma – there were certain of his employees for whom he had a special likeness. Rachael was one of them, and not just because she'd stayed loyal to the company despite its ailing fortunes. Tom knew she could walk into any research post at any pharmaceutical company in the world. She hadn't, and he was grateful for that.

Rachael blinked. She looked surprised to see him.

'You asked me to...'

'I want to show you something,' Rachael interrupted suddenly. 'It's in the lab.'

She stood up. Moments later, Tom was following her along the corridor and wondering what the hell this was all about.

Tom tended to avoid the lab as much as possible nowadays. There was something about the smell of the place and the antiseptic surfaces that reminded him of hospitals. He reckoned he'd seen enough of those to last him a lifetime.

'Rachael,' he said as they walked along the corridor. 'You know I'm not a scientist. Can't you just tell me what this is all about?'

Rachael didn't reply. She just opened the door to the lab and ushered him in.

'If there's a problem with Legum, I need to...'

'Just look,' Rachael told him. She pointed towards the microscope. 'Please.'

Tom sighed, then approached the microscope and bent down to look in it. The image was blurred so he adjusted the focus. Even when it grew sharp, he wasn't much wiser. He was looking at some kind of organism. A bacterium, maybe? No. He knew that the magnification needed to be stronger for that.

'*C. elegans*,' Rachael announced, as if that explained everything.

Tom stood up. 'Very pretty,' he said. 'What is it?'

'A nematode worm.'

Tom gave her an exasperated look. 'And?'

'And it's alive.'

'I'm very happy for it.' Tom's knowledge of the nematode worm was limited to the fact that one strain could only survive on a particular German beer mat. As this knowledge was gleaned during one alcohol-fuelled evening while at college, the whys and wherefores were lost on him now.

Now it was Rachael's turn to look exasperated, at her boss's evident lack of understanding. 'We study *C. elegans* for good reasons,' she explained. Her voice had taken on the tone of a college lecturer. 'It's a very simple organism, which means we can study it in detail. We can examine individual cells, measure their rate of decay. And its cellular responses are remarkably similar to those of complex mammals. Even humans.'

'Thanks for the biology lesson, Rachael. But it's kind of late, so if this is going somewhere...'

'*C. elegans* had a mean lifespan of 20 days. Standard deviation, 2 days either side.'

'And in words we mere mortals can understand?'

'If one of these organisms lives to Day 23, it's bucked the trend.' She pointed at the microscope again. 'That little guy is 103 days old today. Still going strong.'

Tom stared at her.

'What are you telling me, Rachael? That it's undergone some kind of mutation? That happens, right?'

'Sure,' Rachael shrugged. 'It happens. But I have a hundred specimens of *C. elegans*. Each one from a different batch and therefore a different family. Every single specimen is displaying the same symptom. The chances of them all spontaneously mutating in exactly the same way? Infinitesimal. It's just not going to happen.'

Tom looked back into the microscope. The nematode worm was still moving. 'You have a control group?' he asked. His knowledge of the scientific method was better than he liked to let on.

'Of course.'

'And?'

'All dead within the expected timeframe.'

Tom stood up again. Rachael Leo's face was earnest. 'I've measured their new mean lifespan,' she said. 'A hundred days, standard deviation ten days. They're living five times as long, Tom.' She nodded towards the other side of the lab. 'Come and look at the mice.'

Seconds later, they were standing by the Perspex cages. Tom had no love of rodents, but he could see that the lab mice looked well. 'I've been measuring the cellular degeneration of these mice compared to a control group,' Rachael told him.

'And?'

'The rate of decay is slower. Care to guess by what multiple?'

Tom felt a chill. Probably just the lateness of the hour.

'Five?' he asked, his voice little more than a whisper.

'Five,' Rachael confirmed. 'Just like *C. elegans*.'

The lab was almost silent for a moment. Just the sound of the lab mice scratching in their cages, and the electric hum of the bright strip lighting overhead.

'I think you'd better tell me more,' Tom said.

Rachael Leo passed one hand over her eyes. All of a sudden she looked exhausted, and for a moment she didn't speak. She was clearly trying to gather her thoughts. When she finally spoke, it was slowly and deliberately.

'About six months ago I noticed an anomaly in our purchasing records,' she said. 'We were buying fewer lab mice. Now, we've been using these mice to conduct our trials on the Legum compound to make sure it has no unexpected side effects.' She smiled at him. 'You know all this, of course.'

Tom inclined his head. 'Carry on,' he told her.

'We monitor the animals' health, and of course record any instances of premature death. But *extended* lifespan has never been on our radar. We didn't expect to see it. That's why it only came to my attention when I started going through the paperwork.'

'Are you trying to tell me,' Tom interrupted, 'that Legum is making these animals live longer?'

Leo shook her head. 'It's more complicated than that. We've been testing Legum for a long time. Only one batch has exhibited these properties. When I first noticed the purchasing anomaly, I had to do a bit of detective work. About a year ago there was an accident in the lab. Nothing serious – at least, I didn't think so at the time. One of my technicians, Clint…'

'Young guy?' Tom asked. 'Glasses, bad skin…always seems to have a coffee cup in his hand?'

'That's him, sees himself as a coffee expert and brings in all sorts of exotic blends for us to try, most of which I find undrinkable. Anyway, Clint was offered a cup by another of the lab workers. He was working on the Legum master batch. He reached out for his drink and burned his hand on the cup. He pulled his hand back, knocked the master batch over and smashed another jar of additives that was on the bench. It was all in powder form so got everywhere. We immediately started the decontamination process and entered the episode into the accident book. To be honest, I didn't think much more of it. I just banned them from bringing hot drinks into the lab. Most of the time, anyway. If we hadn't entered it into the accident book, I'd probably have forgotten all about it. It was just one of those things. Happens all the time.'

'I'll take your word for it.'

Dr Leo didn't look like she'd even heard him. She just carried on talking.

'When I started digging, I was able to correlate the reduced incidence of mouse deaths with the contaminated batch of Legum involved in the accident.'

'I thought you said the lab was cleaned thoroughly after the spillage. How come we still have contamination?'

Rachael smiled. 'Yes, that puzzled me too so I looked into it further. It seems that you can blame Queen Anne and George Washington.'

Tom pinched his forehead. 'Alright, give in. Explain, please.'

'When the US was a British colony, we used their measurements for weight and length, which were last amended during the reign of Queen Anne in 1706. After independence, we retained the same measures but the Brits changed to the Imperial system in the 19th century, which made their pint of liquid considerably more than ours. We have an exchange student from Europe working in the lab who was involved in the clean-down after the spillage. We used a diluted solution of bleach to clean the benches. The ratio is two pints of water to one capful of bleach, but the pints she used were Imperial, not 'Queen Anne'. The cleaning solution was overly diluted, and therefore ineffective. We thought we'd cleaned the benches and equipment thoroughly, but in fact the contamination was still there.'

Tom stared at her. 'I still don't understand how this thing *works*,' he said.

'We understand the aging process very well, Tom. There are more than a hundred labs in the US alone researching the subject. The basics aren't hard to understand. Organisms take in nutrients from the food they digest, right?'

'I guess.'

'That food undergoes a process called oxidative phosphorylation, which converts it into chemical energy in the form of a molecule called ATP. ATP is the currency of a cell. It's essential for all cellular functions. ATP production takes place in parts of each cell called the mitochondria. If the cells stop being able to create ATP, it would lead to the dysfunction of an organ, and eventually the organism.'

'And that's what happens when we get older?'

'Right. Reduced gene expression means the production of proteins essential to the process slows down. The muscles find it harder to convert chemical energy into the mechanical energy they need. This, in combination with depleting mitochondria, makes muscles weak and impairs their ability to perform. It's called Sarcopenia – age-induced muscle wastage. As it develops, it sets the stage for further physical complications of aging. Researchers have known for a long time that if you can delay Sarcopenia, you can delay the aging process, but they've never been able to do it.'

'Until now,' Tom breathed.

Rachael nodded. 'Until now. I've found that the Legum compound stabilises production of the proteins necessary for ATP creation. It's the Holy Grail, Tom. It's what every researcher in this field has been looking for.'

'And we've stumbled across it..by accident?' Tom couldn't help a note of scepticism entering his voice.

'Lots of scientific breakthroughs happen by chance,' Rachael replied, her voice suddenly a little defensive. 'Penicillin, radioactivity. Evolution is all about accidents. This is no different. And it's *right*, Tom. There's no doubt about it. It's a hundred per cent. The data are clear and I can replicate the results. The adulterated Legum compound increases life expectancy by a multiple of five. So, if you were destined to exist for eighty years and took Legum from birth, you'd live for four hundred years. And I'm sure that we can improve on that, although it will need more research.'

Tom stared at her for a moment. Then he turned and started pacing the lab, avoiding Rachael's eyes. Everything she'd said was tumbling around in his brain. He approached a window on the far side of the lab. The rain was a torrent and he stared wordlessly at it, how long for he couldn't have said. He was vaguely aware of Rachael still talking. 'Do you know what this means, Tom. For us? I mean, not just us, but for... for *humans*...'

He didn't reply. He just stared out into the rain as the image of a thin, weak woman lying in a hospital bed flooded his mind. When he turned again, the smile had vanished from his face as he considered the potential impact of the discovery. Rachael was staring at him. She looked like a kid waiting for the approval – or otherwise – of their parents.

'These results are worthless, Rachael. You know that as well as me.' The time had come for him to drop all pretence of scientific ignorance.

She glanced momentarily at the floor. 'What do you mean?'

'You *know* what I mean. The Legum compound might give positive results under laboratory conditions, but you can't extrapolate those results to humans. Lots of drugs work in the petri dish. It doesn't mean they work on people.'

Rachael continued to avoid his glare.

'It works on people, Tom,' she said quietly.

'You can't *know* that. Not unless you've trialled it. Not unless you've...'

He stopped. Rachael had raised her head and was defiantly jutting her chin at him. He suddenly knew what she was saying, even though she wasn't saying it.

'You've trialled it on yourself,' he breathed. 'Jesus, Rachael, that was *incredibly* dangerous.'

'It's ethically sound,' she snapped back. She seemed genuinely aggrieved that Tom might have thought anything else. 'I'm perfectly within my rights to test this compound on myself. There are hundreds of precedents.' Her eyes flashed, and she inhaled deeply as she got control of her temper. A moment later, she slowly put her hands in the pocket of her white lab coat and pulled out a small pill bottle made of brown glass.

'It was the only way to be sure,' she said, calmer now. 'I've examined my rate of cell decay. It's practically zero. The compound doesn't just work in a petri dish, Tom. It's working in me. Now.'

She walked across the lab and handed him the little brown bottle. Tom swallowed hard. He held the bottle up to the strip lighting. It was half full. He opened it up and poured a small portion of the contents into the palm of his left hand. Ten or fifteen tiny pills tumbled out. Each circular pill was tiny – no bigger than three milliyards in diameter.

'Are you seriously telling me,' Tom asked, 'that now you're taking these things, you can't die?'

'Sure I can die. Stick a knife in me, make me bleed, poison me – I'm dead. But failing any kind of major physical trauma, and assuming I continue to take the compound... My body won't deteriorate, provided I look after it. My core strength will remain.' She took a deep breath. 'Tom, think of the advances we can make. If we live longer, we can do so much more research. Improve the compound. A multiple of five is just the beginning.'

Tom dropped the tiny pills back into the bottle. 'What's the dosage?' he asked. It seemed like a trivial question given everything Rachael was telling him.

'I'll need to conduct more tests to be sure, but the data suggest that one of those pills taken yearly is the optimum dose. Stop taking it and the cell decay returns to its usual rate within a couple months.'

'Who else knows about this?'

'Nobody. You and me. I haven't told a soul. The lab techs think I'm working on something else. There's a rumor going round that there's a problem with Legum. I haven't done anything to quell it.'

Tom wasn't a suspicious man by nature, so with his next question he took himself almost by surprise. 'Why me, Rachael?' he asked.

'What do you mean?'

'You know what I mean. You could have taken it to anyone.' He looked round the shabby lab and remembered examining himself in his car mirror and being unimpressed with what he saw. The hair that needed a cut. The unremarkable features. 'Why me?'

Rachael chewed on her lower lip. 'Look,' she said. 'You'll want to take this to market. I'm not stupid – I know that. I'm a scientist, not a business person. But this discovery, it's about more than money. It has to be handled responsibly. Ethically. And I trust *you* to do that. I'm *right* to trust you, aren't I?'

Tom looked at the bottle of pills in his hand. *Was* she right to trust him? Could *anyone* be trusted with information like this?

He avoided the question. 'You can replicate the adulterated Legum compound?'

Rachael nodded. 'The Legum powder was contaminated with another substance in the lab at the time. Additionally, I've conducted tests on the process equipment we use on it and found anomalies with one of the ovens and the UV curing box. As well as the composition of the original Legum, these are the three details we need. Without them, it's impossible to make the compound.'

'But as soon as we patent it...'

'We *can't* patent it. If we do that, we have to reveal the composition and the processes. They'll be making the compound by the ton in India. All sorts of charlatans will crawl out of the woodwork, some of them selling a genuine copy, some of them selling snake oil instead of the real thing.'

'But can't another researcher just analyse it? Work out what you've done?'

Rachael shook her head. 'Think of Coke. Their formulation has been secret for years. Hundreds of scientists have tried to discover it and not been successful. We're using far smaller quantities of key components. Even if the someone works out what they are, the processes involved are very specific. Reverse engineering simply isn't possible.'

'So what's in it?' Tom asked. 'What was the Legum batch contaminated with?'

A mysterious look crossed Rachael's face. 'Tell me, Tom,' she asked. 'Do you believe in Dragons?'

'Of course not. What are you talking about?'

'Well...' She hesitated for a moment. 'Maybe you should start believing.'

She passed a tired hand over her eyes. 'I'm sorry. Look, I can't tell you the components. Not yet. You'll understand soon.'

There was a silence between them. It lasted for two minutes. Tom started pacing the lab again. A small part of him didn't even believe what he was hearing. It was too fantastical. But he knew that Rachael Leo – petite, hardworking, serious Rachael

Leo – wasn't the type to make things up. Why would she? If this compound went to market, a fraud would be uncovered in weeks as soon as somebody taking the pills dropped down dead. No, at the very least Rachael herself believed what she was saying. And Tom trusted her. If she believed it, what reason did he have not to?

It wasn't doubt that was creeping through his mind. It was something else. An emotion he didn't recognize. Somewhere between hope and fear. His thoughts had turned to a hospice bed uptown. A thin woman lying on it, her eyes sunken and her lips cracked. As he continued to pace, he tried to formulate a question he didn't know how to ask. There was no need.

'It won't cure her, Tom,' Rachael said quietly. 'That's not what it does.'

He stopped pacing and inhaled slowly.

'Although we're still testing, we know now that the compound slows down the aging process, but it doesn't reverse it. If you give it to somebody who's' – Rachael hesitated, and Tom could tell she was avoiding the words 'terminally ill' – 'who's very sick, they'll just stay sick for a very long time. Their quality of life will be worse, not better. It wouldn't be fair to prescribe it. It wouldn't be ethical.'

'Isn't that a choice they should make for themselves?' Tom was aware that he sounded belligerent. It masked his lack of conviction. What would Jane say if she was here? Would she be begging him to keep her alive with nothing to look forward to except the regular infections that were a consequence of her wasting disease? Or would she want nature to take its course, for one of the infections finally to steal her from him and Jack?

It was Rachael's turn now to stare out of the window at the hammering rain. 'These are things we have to decide,' she said. 'And we have to make the right decisions.' She spun round. 'Tom, don't take this the wrong way, but I think you should give me those pills back.'

Another silence, but after a moment Tom stepped towards her and handed back the little brown bottle.

'You're going to have to share the components,' he told her. 'Sooner or later.'

'I've thought about that,' Rachael replied.

'And?'

'And I'll explain it to the board when we meet. We *will* be meeting, right?'

'You doing anything in the morning?'

'Funnily enough, my diary's clear.'

'I thought it might be. You should go home. Get some sleep.'

'You sound like my dad.'

Tom put one hand on her shoulder. 'If I was your dad, I'd be proud of you. I'm proud of you anyway. If you're right about this, you've made a discovery greater even than Penicillin or, a cure for cancer. But you know that already, don't you?'

Rachael nodded. She looked remarkably unruffled, Tom thought, for someone in her position. 'You know?' she said. 'I really am quite tired. I think you're right. I should get some shut-eye. I've spent a lot of time in this lab and it kind of feels as if the walls are closing in on me.'

Ten minutes later the lab was dark. The mice still scratched in their cages; the nematode worm still curled and uncurled on its slide. But nobody was there to hear or see them. The premises of Pure Industries were deserted.

Except for one man.

Tom sat behind the wheel of his car and watched in the rear-view mirror as Dr Rachael Leo's vehicle drove out of the parking lot. He waited for the lights to disappear, then sat in the darkness with his eyes closed, listening to the rain. He didn't feel like a man who had just been handed the gift of immortality.

Was it always like this, he wondered. When some great discovery was made, did those in the know find it difficult to understand how the world around them could continue as if nothing had happened? Did the moment seem unreal to them? Did they worry about how their life was about to change, or if they were up to the task of presenting such a discovery to the world?

Did they feel the heavy weight of responsibility on their shoulders?

And what did Rachael mean about believing in Dragons?

Tom opened his eyes and slid his hand into the pocket of his trousers. He removed five small, white pills and stared hard at them. The voice of Dr Rachael Leo echoed in his head. *It won't cure her, Tom. That's not what it does.*

But if the drug could keep her alive until a cure became available…

It has to be handled responsibly. Ethically. And I trust you to do that. I'm right to trust you, aren't I?

Was she? He caught sight of his reflection in the mirror again. For some reason, he found himself unable to hold his own gaze.

Tom returned the pills to his pocket. Moments later, the CEO of Pure Industries was driving away from the company premises, heading north into Laguna Niguel and back towards the tiny hospice room where his wife lay dying.

3

Pat Dolan. *Detective* Pat Dolan. It had been a long time since he'd been allowed to use that title. Eleven years since DC Dolan had left the Royal Ulster Constabulary to live in LA with his father, a retired LAPD cop, after his mother had died. He missed the RUC to be sure. Of course, if its disbandment was a condition of securing the Peace Treaty and ending the Troubles, it was worth it, but he missed it all the same. And he missed detective work too. Now, however, since his recent promotion, things were looking up. And if that wasn't worth a drink, he didn't know what was. He nodded at the barman, who took his glass and replenished it from the bottle of Jameson's behind the bar.

Taking US citizenship and joining the LAPD had been a no-brainer for Pat. Police work was all he knew. It had only taken a short time for him to assimilate himself completely into the LAPD – proving his theory that police officers and their work were the same the world over. He'd spent more than ten years in uniform, but his detective skills had shone through. He was now the proud owner of the distinctive gold badge that came with the promotion.

Not that he was wearing it now. The only fellas walking into LAPD headquarters dressed like he was were the ones heading down to the cells. Pat had three days' growth on his chin. He wore a black donkey jacket – the kind of garment the workers on the Lagan docks might have worn back home – sturdy boots and a pair of tough old jeans. The garments were shabby, but that didn't mean they hadn't been chosen with care. The rough clothes matched his rough, grizzled face: the nose broken from a rugby injury as a lad, but which made him look like he'd seen a fight or two; the uneven stubble of a shade slightly lighter than his copper-brown hair. Pat Dolan was no fashionista, but he knew the look he was after.

He checked his watch. A quarter past midnight. His contact was late. Fair enough. Contacts like this were always late. But he couldn't stick around too much longer. Look desperate, and he'd make himself suspicious. And that could prove terminal, especially if everything the spooks had told him was true.

They'd briefed the members of the Special Operations section of the Detectives department two weeks previously. Pat had been assigned to the SO section on account of his distinctive Irish accent – useful in undercover ops because who would suspect a Mick in the upper echelons of the LAPD? It had been his first briefing as a detective and it had felt like coming home. During his time in the Province, he'd had more of such briefings than he could count. Back then his targets had been the boys and girls of paramilitaries from both sides of the divide. His father's family might have come from south of the border, but for Pat picking sides was easy. Regardless of your color, creed or politics, if you set out to deliberately injure or kill innocent people, you were a scumbag and had to be dealt with. He'd been unable to help wondering, as he'd made his way through the bustling office, receiving and responding to nods of acknowledgement from his new colleagues, what kind of scumbags he'd be turning his attention to this time.

The briefing room, just off the main corridor, had already been filled with detectives, analysts, surveillance specialists and a number of others whom he believed to be Special Agents from the FBI. Windowless with steeply banked seats facing a lectern at the front and containing a full suite of AV equipment, it had more of the feel of a lecture theater in an eminent University than a downtown police facility. Pat had only just managed to find himself a seat near the front when the door opened again and Lieutenant Walker, head of Special Operations, had walked in, followed by two strangers: a man and woman.

Walker was a thick-set African American, as was the man who followed him in a black double-breasted suit. He commanded a lot of respect. The buzz of conversation in the room died down the moment he entered. There was no ceremony from him. No welcomes or thank yous. It was straight down to business.

'The code name for this operation,' he announced, 'will be Jaguar. As normal, all information passed on today is for the benefit of the people in this room only and not for disclosure to anyone else, regardless of status or rank. Any enquiries from senior officers about this operation should be referred to me. This is Secret with a capital S. Does anybody in this room *not* understand that?'

Walker's voice reverberated around the room with everyone listening intently, not wanting to miss a word.

'I would like to introduce two agents from the Central Intelligence Agency. You will refer to them as Agent 1 and Agent 2. Agent 1 will now provide you with the background information you need.'

The woman who had followed him in, tall, blond, in her mid thirties, stepped forward. 'For the last few years,' she'd announced, 'we've been working with the Colombian authorities, helping them keep their foot on the throat of the drug cartels who, despite the recent high-profile law-enforcement successes, haven't gone away and are simply re-grouping. Of particular interest is a group called the Black Hawks. These are a right-wing paramilitary organisation who have, in the past, provided muscle for some of the cartels and who have close links with similar organisations in Venezuela. We have credible intelligence sources about their medium- and long-term planning, and it is apparent that they've established links with Hispanic gangs in the USA. At this point, I'd like to pass you over to Agent 2.'

The black-suited man had taken the floor and nodded at someone at the back of the room. 'I'm going to show you some slides,' he'd said in a southern accent, 'which will explain in more detail why this situation is now of relevance to LAPD.' The lights had dimmed, and a map of Colombia had appeared on the projection screen at the front of the briefing room. Using the red spot of a laser pointer, he'd highlighted one area of the map. 'The Black Hawks operate out of the city of Cúcuta, close to the Venezuelan border. US relationships with Caracas are still strained after the failed coup in 2002. This means the Black Hawks can rely on corrupt officials in local, regional and even central government who help them in transporting cocaine consignments by turning a blind eye or – worse – providing genuine transport documents.' The slide had changed to show lines on the same map extending north to various US cities, including LA.

'We've received information,' Agent 2 had continued, 'that the Hispanic gangs in Los Angeles are prepared to receive large consignments of cocaine from the Black Hawks via Venezuela. If these deals go ahead, the Black Hawks will have a significant level of liquidity. Frankly, we in the Bureau don't much care about there being a few more junkies on the streets of LA, but the Black Hawks are a terrorist organisation with plans to make their mark. We won't let that happen. We know that these drug deals will require a significant amount of funding. We've identified the man we believe will provide this funding. He's one of your locals, and we're pretty sure he's unlikely to be on your radar at the moment.'

The slide had changed again to show a photo of a good-looking, well-tanned man in his late 30s. The image had been taken with a telephoto lens, but Pat had clearly been able to make out an immaculate Bentley Sports convertible.

'This is Theodore Croft. Former hedge-fund manager and super-rich. No police record. It's an open secret that he was a bit of a rogue trader in his day, but the Securities and Exchange Commission have never been able to put their hands on the right evidence. He's a slippery customer, ladies and gentlemen, and pretty much without scruples. Our intel suggests that he's now trying to muscle in on the drug trade by befriending a number of well-known gang leaders from downtown. Other than that, he currently has no other connections to organized crime which is why we – *you* – know nothing about him. This needs to change. Operation Jaguar is designed to do that.'

Agent 2 had sat down again, leaving Lieutenant Walker to continue. 'That's where we come in, ladies and gentlemen. Croft might have no police record, but all the anecdotal evidence we have, show us he's a nasty piece of crud. Plus, he's surrounded himself by people who *are* known to us for one reason or another. Mostly, but not exclusively, suspects for outstanding homicides. Our working theory is that this lot do his dirty work for him, so Croft himself stays lily white. One of you will be required to infiltrate Croft's inner circle, get close to him and feed back what he's up to. This operation carries an extremely high level of risk – if our mole is busted, it's over for them – so the selected agent will be known only by his CIA handler and by me. He, or she will, however, be supported by the resources of the Special Operations section, and you'll be expected to work up any intelligence that gets fed back to us as a result of Operation Jaguar. Any questions?'

Detective Pat Dolan had none. Just an intuition that caused a cold sensation down the back of his neck, somewhere between excitement and fear. If *he'd* had to select an agent to blend in to gang like that, who would *he* choose? A tough, hard-bitten LAPD cop who might be known to any number of the criminal fraternity in that crazy city? Or a Northern Irish immigrant, whose history was much easier to blur and who could pretend to have spent his formative years in the Provos' nutting squads? The choice practically made itself.

Which was why he found himself here, now, two weeks later, in the middle of the night at a bar his handler had told him was frequented by one of Theodore Croft's men, a sinister piece of work who gave his name as Tony Foreman. And who knows – maybe Foreman was even telling the truth about that. He checked his watch again – 00.25 hrs – and ordered himself another whiskey.

'You want to be careful, Mickey,' a lazy American drawl said from behind him. 'Too much of that stuff, you'll be falling off your bar stool.'

Pat turned to look over his shoulder to see a man standing just half a metre behind him. He was in his mid to late thirties, had balding black hair and was dressed very smartly. To this guy, Pat was Mickey Connor, former IRA lieutenant and a man whose CV would make people's kneecaps twitch just looking at it.

'I've never met a Yank yet who I couldn't drink under the table, Tony.' Pat was aware that he was exaggerating his Ulster accent a little. He turned back to the bar, picked up his replenished glass and knocked it back in one. 'I didn't see you come in.'

'You weren't supposed to, buddy.' Tony looked up at the barman. 'Gimme me a beer,' he said, and took a seat next to Pat.

They sat in silence. Pat had to stop himself smiling. Silence was good. It was comradely. He'd expected it to take months to get this close, but Tony Foreman was treating him not as a friend, exactly, but as someone he could do business with.

And Tony Foreman was just a step away from Theodore Croft himself.

Tony sipped his Bud.

Pat sipped his Jameson's.

Don't push it, he told himself, reminding himself of the first rule of undercover operations. Don't make yourself obvious. Let them come to you.

'So, I might have a bit of work for you,' Tony said finally. 'If you're interested, that is.'

Pat Dolan shrugged. On the inside he was punching the air. On the outside he just looked bored.

'Could be,' he said. 'Could be. Tell you what, my friend. Why don't you buy me another drink, and tell me all about it?'

4

Saturday morning, 6.00 a.m., Pacific Standard Time

Ruth Adams was sleeping soundly. When the alarm clock beeped, however, her eyes pinged open immediately. She lay in a single bed. In all her 58 years she had never shared a bed with anyone, and she saw no reason why she should waste money on anything larger than she needed.

Her apartment was nothing to speak of: one bedroom on the third floor of a condo in the eastern part of Laguna Niguel. Small. Immaculately neat. Ruth despised clutter almost as much as she despised dirt. Disapproval oozed from her every pore.

The brash American DJ announced that it was going to be a beautiful day and his voice grated on her nerves. Most things about America grated on her nerves, but that was equally true of her native England. At least in the twenty years since she'd emigrated, she'd had the benefit of the West Coast sunshine. Not that you'd know it to look at her. Her wrinkled skin was pinched and pale, and she wore a perpetually sour look as though she had taken deep offense at something.

She switched off the radio and climbed out of bed before padding, in her shapeless cotton nightdress, to the tiny adjoining bathroom. There were no feminine accoutrements here. No lotions, or creams, or perfumes. Just a toothbrush, a toothpaste tube, a flannel and some coarse soap. What else did she need?

Ruth was in the middle of brushing her teeth when the telephone rang. Somehow she managed to scowl even with the toothbrush in her mouth. Who on earth could be calling her at this time on a Saturday morning? If it was a prank caller, she would give them a piece of her mind. In her head she was already rehearsing her waspish response as she walked back across the bedroom and picked up the handset on her bedside table.

'Yes.' The word wasn't framed as a question; more as a challenge.

'Good morning, Ruth,' a soft American voice that she recognized very well replied. 'It's Tom. I'm very sorry to call you so early in the morning.'

Ruth felt her lips thinning as she forced her mouth into the smile she always wore to disguise what she really thought about her boss. As Tom's PA, she was expected to be on call any time of the day, or night, but she had never once been summoned at a time like this. Not that 'summoned' was a very good word to describe the way in which Tom spoke to his members of staff. He was unfailingly polite. To the point of weakness, in fact. Ruth Adams was a curt, abrupt woman. She saw anything else in others as a failing.

'Mr Shaw,' she said in her clipped, British tones. He had long given up trying to persuade her to use his Christian name.

'I wonder if you could do me a favour, Ruth.' He paused for a response, but she didn't give him one. 'I need to call a meeting of the Board. An urgent meeting. Every member. Ten o'clock this morning.'

Ruth prided herself on being unflappable, so she was glad this was a telephone conversation and not face to face. It meant she could more easily hide her surprise. 'You'll require minutes to be kept,' she stated.

'Ah, no, Ruth. Thank you. That won't be necessary on this occasion. Thank you very much for offering.'

Ruth Adams's eyes narrowed slightly, but she didn't voice her displeasure at this rebuttal. She simply replaced the phone in its cradle, retrieved the numbers she needed from the old-fashioned leather notebook in her spinsterish handbag and went about making her calls. Only when she had informed the various members of the Pure Industries executive Board that their presence was required, did she go about preparing a cup of Twinings. And only then did she start getting dressed into clothes suitable for work: a tweedy suit, chiffon blouse and a gold brooch. Her boss was naïve and incompetent. Ruth was quite certain that he only held on to his position because she was there to ensure that things ran smoothly.

She wasn't well enough paid for the duties she performed. Not *nearly* well enough paid, nor did she receive sufficient recognition for her contribution. But something important was clearly happening, and if Tom Shaw thought that he could keep her ignorant of the proceedings, he was very much mistaken.

7 a.m. The early morning sun was already bright. It shone through a chink in the curtains of Jane's hospice room, creating a narrow sunbeam that illuminated the dust in the air and lit up a small patch of pillow to the left of her face.

Tom stood by his wife's bedside, staring at her. He thought about opening the curtains. The view from here was pleasant: an open vista towards the Saddleback Valley, where they'd loved to walk together in happier times. But he knew Jane couldn't bear to look at it now. She couldn't bear to be reminded of the things she couldn't have.

Her breathing was steady but noisy. Her chest barely moved. He often gazed at her when she was asleep and remembered the woman she used to be. He remembered her hair, shining and sweet-smelling on the day they'd married 16 years ago when he was only 22. He remembered her skin, slightly plump. Now it clung to her bones like kitchen film. She looked old, but there were no wrinkles on her face because her flesh was not sufficiently slack.

He had one hand in his pocket. The five pills were still there. It would be so easy to do it. Jane was obliged to swallow an untold number of medicines throughout the day. To add one more tiny pill would be simple.

Jane's eyes opened and Tom saw what he always saw when she awoke: a fleeting expression of horror as she remembered where she was, and why. But she soon mastered it, and even managed a weak smile at the sight of Tom looking down at her.

'Is it morning?' Her concept of time was shaky.

Tom nodded. 'I have to go out again,' he said. 'Jack's coming today. He'll keep you company.'

'He shouldn't have to. He's only ten. It's not a childhood.'

'He wants to see you.'

'And I want to see him. But still…' She closed her eyes again. 'It won't be for long.'

'Don't talk like that, Jane.' Tom could hear his voice cracking.

'It's alright,' she breathed. 'It won't be so bad. At least you and Jack will be able to get on with your…'

'Don *talk* like that.' He sounded sharper than he intended and immediately regretted it. But the thought of him and Jack alone without her, was almost unbearable. What would they do? How would they manage? It wasn't just the prospect of loneliness that horrified Tom; it wasn't just the fact that their son needed a mother and that he could never hope to be the many things that Jane was to Jack; it wasn't just the horror of it all. There were practical things to think about too. Would he be able to continue in his job? Someone needed to look after Jack and, with the way the company was struggling, money was tight…

Jane didn't look like she'd even noticed his abruptness. Tom realized she'd fallen asleep again. What would she tell him to do, he wondered. Perhaps he should just ask her, but he knew he wouldn't do that. He'd kept his troubles to himself ever since she'd been ill – half because he didn't want to worry her, half because he knew he had to get used to dealing with these things by himself. Would she beg to have her painful life extended? Or would she encourage him to make a success of this miraculous new drug. To do some good in the world and, while he was at it, make the money he needed to ensure that Jack had a life worth living…

Tom knew which was most likely. He bent over, moved a strand of hair from her forehead and lightly kissed her. Then he left the hospice room and made his way back to the car.

It was a few minutes past eight o'clock when he arrived back at the Pure Industries premises. He made himself a coffee in the small kitchenette used by the admin staff. Tom never really felt comfortable being waited on by his PA, but Ruth was a stickler for that kind of thing. He could sense the waves of disapproval coming off her whenever he did anything she considered to be unworthy of a CEO, but in truth Tom had never felt comfortable lording it over his staff. Maybe Ruth was right. Maybe it meant he wasn't true executive material. Maybe it was one of the reasons Pure was struggling.

As he sat in the comfortable leather chair of his office, however, and stared at a picture of him, Jane and Jack on the beach in San Diego in happier times, he realized that the days of this company's money concerns were numbered. It didn't take a genius to understand the financial implications of Rachael's discovery. But he also agreed that there was more to this than just money. The question was, would the rest of the executive Board feel the same?

They all arrived within five minutes of each other, dressed in casual clothes instead of the business suits in which Tom was used to seeing them. Peter Wright, VP Finance. He was a tall man with a slight stoop in his shoulders and thin, greying hair. If he had anything approaching a sense of humor, Tom was yet to see it. Peter had been with Pure Industries longer than anyone – twenty years – and he knew where every last cent was being spent. Meticulous and dour, Tom knew very little about his personal life, and he suspected he never would. He did know, however, that Peter had no fondness for the CEO's management style, for his laid-back attitude towards his staff. More than once he'd told him that you couldn't run a business with a bleeding heart. More than once, Tom had ignored him.

Nor was it a secret that Peter had very little time for Silvia Lucas, Head of Marketing. Certainly the elegant good looks of this attractive Chilean forty-something made no impact on him. But Sylvia wasn't the kind of woman to let the withering glances and silent disapproval of a man like Peter worry her. She dealt with him with the brusque efficiency that only a woman who had juggled motherhood with a demanding career could manage. Tom knew that Sylvia felt a personal responsibility for the poor state of the company, and that her efforts to reverse Pure Industries' fortunes had led to tensions at home. She had two kids of school age and a husband who'd sacrificed his own career for hers. It was obvious that she hardly ever saw them, and that Sylvia's long eyelashes and fashionable hair masked the personal anxieties that she hid from the world.

And then there was Kyle. Calm, sensible Kyle. The company's young VP Business Development was in his late twenties and reminded Tom of himself in so many ways. He'd spent a brief stint out of college on a trading floor in Wall Street, but the cut-throat nature of that environment hadn't suited his altogether milder temperament. He'd headed out west to be back near his family, and Tom had seen something in the young man the first time he met him. He'd taken Kyle on with a view to nurturing him to Board level, and Kyle hadn't disappointed him. If anything, Tom felt guilty that his young protégé had shown such loyalty to a sinking ship. He was imaginative and full of ideas, and Tom quietly knew that he'd walk into any executive post he cared to choose. But like Tom himself, he had remained loyal to the company. He was ambitious, but not at any cost. A rare quality, Tom realized. One to be cherished. Kyle had repaid Tom's faith in him with more than hard work. When Jane had been diagnosed, it was Kyle who was there to offer him support over a cold beer; and to little Jack he had become more like a favourite uncle than some stuffy guy from his dad's office. And now, as he stood with the other two Board members, he had a suspicious glint in his eye.

'So what's up, Tom?' he asked. 'Last time I saw you in work on a Saturday...'

He didn't finish. The door to the office opened and Tom's PA, Ruth, walked in. Unlike the others she was dressed smartly in her usual business clothes.

There was an awkward pause. 'Ruth,' Tom said. 'I didn't expect to see you...'

'I wanted to be here in case you changed your mind, Mr Shaw,' she said, entering the room as she spoke. 'A meeting of the Board without adequate minutes would be very unusual...' She turned to the three Board members and smiled a thin smile.

'There will be no minutes, Ruth.'

The skin round the PA's eyes tightened, but she inclined her head in acceptance. 'No, Mr Shaw,' she said quietly. 'Of course.'

Tom turned to the others. 'I'll meet you in the Board Room,' he said, then waited for them to leave his office, closing the door behind them.

'I'm sorry, Ruth,' he said. He worried that she felt humiliated, and that was not his intention. 'You'll understand what's happening soon enough.'

'Is there anything else I can do while I'm here?'

'Dr Rachael Leo will be here any moment,' Tom said. 'Would you be so good as to ask her to join us in the Board Room? But Ruth, I really don't want you to sacrifice your weekend, so do go home. I won't be needing anything else.'

He left her standing there and walked out of his office, along the corridor and into the Board Room.

As Board Rooms went, Pure Industries' was one of the less glamorous. There was an overhead projector gathering dust on a stand at one end, and the windows looked out on to the car park. The lights hummed, and so did the water cooler in one corner. The table in the middle was large. It could easily have sat fifteen, so the three other members of the Board sitting round it, with plastic cups and expectant faces, were rather dwarfed by its size.

'Thanks for coming, everyone,' Tom said as he walked in.

'What's the problem?' Peter asked. He looked genuinely worried. 'What's so important this morning that wasn't important yesterday afternoon?'

'A lot can change in one night, Peter. I'll let Rachael explain.'

'Rachael?'

'Dr Rachael Leo. She'll be joining us any...'

At that moment, the door opened again and Rachael walked in. She had changed since last night, abandoning her white lab coat in favour of a pair of slim-fitting jeans and a plain jumper.

Her hair was still damp from the shower, and she looked slightly anxiously at Sylvia and Peter. When her eyes met Kyle, she gave a nervous smile and looked away again quickly.

'Ladies and gentlemen,' Tom continued. 'You all know Rachael Leo. Rachael's in charge of our research lab and she… well, Rachael, I think it's only fair that *you* explain.'

Tom took a seat next to Kyle and watched as Rachael walked to the head of the table. She cleared her throat. 'What I'm about to tell you has been checked, double checked and triple checked,' she said. 'We scientists don't say this very often, but so far as I can tell it's beyond doubt.'

The Board members glanced at each other, clearly wondering what the hell was going on.

'There is a mystery in science,' Rachael continued. Tom sensed that she had been preparing this speech for some time. 'Some of the most brilliant minds in history have wrestled with it. Isaac Newton, Nicolas Flamel. None of them had any success. In the USA alone there are 130 labs working to solve this mystery. They've spent billions of dollars on research, because they know that the person who wins this race will change the course of human history, let alone become wealthy beyond their imagining.'

'What have you done, Rachael?' Kyle asked with the flicker of a smile on his face. 'Found out how to turn lead into gold?' He chuckled slightly.

Rachael didn't seem to share the joke. 'Transmutation?' she asked. 'No, not that. To be honest, Kyle, I don't think that would be a very fruitful line of enquiry. If we could turn lead into gold, gold would become as worthless as lead, right?'

Kyle looked amused. 'Right,' he replied.

'What I've discovered is how to mine a different commodity. A commodity whose value never depreciates. A commodity *everybody* wants.' She paused and looked at each member of the Board in turn before continuing. 'That commodity,' she said, 'is life itself.'

There was a silence in the room. Tom could feel himself holding his breath.

Peter was the first to respond. He scraped his chair back and stood up. 'Tom,' he stated, 'I haven't had a day off in three weeks. If you really think we have time to fool about with idiotic practical jokes...'

'Sit down, Peter,' Tom said quietly.

'Absolutely not. I don't have time to listen to this ridiculous... alchemy. I'm...'

'Peter. Sit down. Listen for another five minutes. If you still want to leave, I won't stop you.' Tom could see that that his CFO was taken aback by his uncharacteristic insistence.

Silence again. Peter took his seat.

'Carry on, Rachael,' Tom said. 'Explain to everyone what you explained to me last night.'

And so Rachael did. The Board listened as she told them about the accident in the lab, the anomaly with the mice and her subsequent research. They listened to her technical description of Sarcopenia, and heard about *C. elegans* and its unnatural lifespan. As she spoke, Tom watched the other Board members closely, trying to determine their reaction. Kyle looked wide-eyed. Innocent, almost. Like a kid in a dinosaur exhibition. Sylvia appeared troubled. Already, he could see, the implications of what she was hearing were at the forefront of her brain. And Peter? Peter's face was unreadable. A stone mask.

The only noise was the hum from the water cooler. Rachael's anxiety was clear when she admitted that she'd tested the Legum compound on herself, but no one applauded, or criticised her decision, and she stumbled on. 'At present,' she said once she had finished her detailed explanation, 'I estimate that the adulterated Legum compound can extend life to approximately 400 years. But we'll keep on researching and I feel confident that we can increase that even further.' She took a seat at the board table next to Sylvia, looking exhausted. So did all the others.

Nobody appeared to know what to say. How to act. When Rachael removed a small brown pill bottle from her pocket and placed it in the middle of the table, they all stared at it. They didn't need to ask what it was. That much was obvious.

Tom cleared his throat. He spoke softly, as if the medicine on the table was a living thing that he might disturb if he made too much noise. 'I haven't had very long to think about this,' he said. 'Just a few hours, really. Not much time when you consider the importance of what we've just heard.' He looked at each member of the Board in turn. There was something peculiar, he thought, about discussing something so humdrum as business opportunities in the wake of such a discovery. But they *were* a business, and this was a product. And a product needed a strategy. 'Clearly the opportunities this discovery presents Pure Industries are too numerous for us to discuss this morning, but we will need to dedicate all our resources to considering its full potential. If we play this right, for example, we can offer new-style mortgages, pensions and commodities to suit extended lifestyles. That's just off the top of my head. But we need to keep this under wraps so that we can consider all the angles. Are we agreed on that?'

'Agreed,' Peter said. 'But keeping this quiet isn't going to be easy.' All traces of his previous scepticism had fallen away. His brow was furrowed and he spoke slowly, as though he didn't quite trust his tongue to do what his brain said. 'You know what this place is like, Tom. Rumors flying around like fireflies. Half the workforce thinks there's a problem with Legum anyway. And the moment we register this–' he pointed vaguely at the pill bottle in the middle of the table. '–this *thing*, the whole world's going to...'

'You don't need to worry about that,' Rachael said.

Peter raised an eyebrow. He wasn't used to being interrupted, and Tom could tell he didn't like it, even now. But he kept quiet and let Rachael speak.

'We can't rely on patents,' she said. 'If we do that, we have to reveal the components of the compound and the processes involved in creating it.'

Peter opened his mouth to speak, but it was Sylvia who held up one hand to stop him. 'Go ahead, honey,' she told Rachael. 'We're listening.'

Rachael gave her a grateful smile. 'There are four key pieces of information required to create the compound. The first is the make-up of the original Legum. That's a matter of record – we've already submitted a draft material safety datasheet. The second is the substance with which it was contaminated. The third is the temperature at which the components need to be baked and the fourth is the level of UV radiation required to cure the finished product. Each of these pieces of information are crucial to creating the compound, and it's the anomalies with the heat and UV that will protect Elixir from being reverse-engineered. Guessing the correct combination of temperature with frequency is as good as impossible, as the permutations run into billions. Without one of these pieces of information, the rest are useless. I'm the only person that currently knows all four. I propose entrusting Pete, Sylvia and Kyle with one part of the formula each. You should secure the information somewhere safe. On your death, the details will be passed on to your successor on the authority of the surviving three.'

'Absolutely not,' Peter stated. 'It's risky and unworkable. Dr Leo, do I have to remind you that this discovery was made entirely using the resources of Pure Industries? It *belongs* to us. You have a legal obligation to reveal every detail of your research to the Board.'

Rachael gave him a cool look. 'So sue me,' she said. 'I won't have it any other way.' She caught Tom's eye, and he gave her a brief, encouraging nod.

'As CEO, Tom should know everything,' she continued.

Tom butted in. 'Actually, Rachael, I think it's better if I don't know anything.' Everyone around the Board table looked surprised. 'I'm the face of this company,' he explained. 'If the purpose of this strategy is to keep the formula secure, it makes sense to keep it from the one person who's most likely to be targeted by anybody with unscrupulous motives.'

There were nods of agreement from Kyle and Sylvia. Rachael, however, still appeared anxious.

'Look,' she said. 'I'm not naïve. I know what this is worth and I know it has to be commercially viable. But I also know that it's not just about money and profit. This isn't Pure Industries' discovery. It's mine. And I need to make sure it's handled ethically, and not used for the wrong reasons.'

'Ethical?' Peter retorted. 'You think it's ethical for only one person to know the formula?'

'Peter,' Tom said. He'd been silent long enough. 'This is how it's going to be. I support Dr Leo in this. Kyle? Sylvia?' He looked askance at the other members of the Board, who nodded their heads. Peter's eyes narrowed, but he said nothing more.

'OK,' Tom continued. 'We'll spend more time on that later. I have my own thoughts about how we might market this, but first I'd like to hear your views. Kyle?'

Kyle looked uncomfortable. Tom noticed how his eyes flickered in Rachael's direction before he spoke. 'If it were any other product,' he said quietly, 'I'd say we cream the market first. Make it a high-end product for those who can afford it.' Peter nodded approvingly. 'We charge mega-bucks, then invest our profits in developing bespoke lifestyle packages for those who are going to be active four times longer.'

Sylvia shifted in her chair. 'I have difficulty with that,' she said. 'It could cause massive resentment for all those deprived of the compound. Are there any production limitations in terms of meeting demand?'

Rachael shook her head. 'No. We make a core batch from which we can create millions of doses. Supply of the core components is limitless. One dose, to be taken orally once a year, would cost us a couple of cents.'

Sylvia turned to the others. 'So the margin is small and the profit is unimaginably huge, whether we make it high end or mass market.'

'Agreed,' Tom said. 'Let's postulate for a minute. How many clients do you think we'll have worldwide after a couple of years. Ten million? A hundred million? A billion? If we charged, what, 200 bucks a month we'd be turning over–' He did a quick mental calculation '$1.2 trillion. I'd say that gives us a bit of wriggle room, wouldn't you?'

'We're not a charity.' Peter was clearly unhappy with the way the conversation was going.

'No,' Tom said, 'we're not. And we're not going to act like one. But like Rachael said, this isn't just about the money. We have a broader moral responsibility to make this product as widely accessible as we can. Kyle, I understand your argument, but I want you to start thinking of this in terms of the drug costing about the same as an average family saloon car. I think that's fair, and I hope you do too.'

Kyle inclined his head. He looked like he was going to argue. 'All *I* want to know,' he said, 'is what about Lily?'

Tom frowned. 'Lily?'

'Yeah, Lily. My dog. Does it work on dogs? I'd sure like to keep *her* around a bit longer.'

The Board members smiled. All except Peter, who was still staring hard at the bottle of pills on the table. Tom sensed that he was trying hard to avoid catching his eye.

'Can *we* take it?' the dour older man asked.

The room fell silent.

Everyone was now looking at the bottle of pills.

'Eventually,' Rachael said.

'And why not now?'

'There are some final trials I need to do. Confirmation tests. But when it goes to market, you'll be able to take the compound along with everyone else.'

'And how long do you think that will be, Rachael,' Tom asked quietly.

Rachael shrugged. 'Six months. Max. That will give us time to get production up and running.'

'It's not a long time,' Tom said. 'We'll have to work fast.' A thoughtful look crossed his face. 'I suggest we take a risk.'

'What kind of a risk?' Peter demanded. He wasn't a risk-taking kind of guy.

'Rachael, you need to continue your trials. I understand that. But you're certain about the efficacy of the compound, right?'

'Right,' said the young scientist.

'I propose we start production now. Stockpile the compound ready for the moment when you give us the final go-ahead.'

'Tom,' Peter interrupted, 'that's a massive financial outlay. If something goes wrong, it could ruin...'

'The company's on its knees, Peter,' Tom snapped back. '*You* know that, *I* know that. We can be meek and out of business in a year, or bold and make this thing work. Rachael, talk us through the production process.'

Rachael nodded. 'I need to make a master batch of the Legum compound. The dose is very small, so a little goes a very long way. It won't take me more than a few weeks to produce a sufficient quantity of the master batch to make, well–' she shrugged '–tens of millions of doses. Once I've made the master batch, I instruct our technicians to add the extra substances and perform the final processes that it needs.'

'How do we keep the substances secret from them?' Sylvia asked.

'They won't know what they're adding,' said Rachael. 'I'll instruct our supplier to remove all reference to the actual substance and replace it with a unique reference number. As far as the technicians are concerned it could be anything. I can stockpile enough of the compound for you to launch – at least in the US – in about a month.'

Silence all around as this sank in.

'We need a name,' Sylvia said. 'Something punchy. Something nobody will forget.'

'Already dealt with,' Rachael told her. Everyone in the room looked at the scientist, who stretched out and picked up the pills again.

'Well?' Peter said.

But Rachael shook her head. 'Not yet.' She seemed nervous again.

'What is it, Rachael?'

She looked at her lap. 'I... I didn't carry out this research in order to make money,' she started to explain. 'But I... I...'

'You need to know what *you're* going to get out of it?' Tom asked quietly.

Rachael nodded.

'What did you have in mind?'

She spoke quickly – as though she wanted to get the words out before she changed her mind. 'A seat on the Board. And shares.'

'May I remind you,' Peter interrupted, 'that you are an *employee* of Pure Industries. You are legally bound to hand over the details. You can forget any grand ideas about holding this company to ransom, young lady, or we *will* see you in court.'

Rachael's expression changed; she fixed Peter with a fierce glare. 'Don't make the mistake of underestimating me, Peter. I will not be bullied by you or anyone like you. This is *my* discovery and all I want is proper recognition for what I've achieved. Send me to jail if you want, but you can't force me to talk. Honestly, Peter – I'd rather die than allow this to fall into the wrong hands.'

Peter looked taken aback by the steel in Rachael's voice. He looked like he was about to respond in kind, but was cut short by Tom, who gently raised a hand to silence him.

'I think what Rachael is suggesting is more than reasonable. Sylvia?'

Sylvia nodded.

'Kyle?'

Kyle did the same.

'Peter, I think we have a consensus. Do you have anything to add?'

'Nothing. For now.'

'Then welcome to the Board, Rachael. I'll have it formalised in the next 48 hours.'

He gave her a reassuring smile, and Rachael visibly relaxed. She stretched out her hand and held up the little bottle of pills.

'In that case,' she said, with a charming little smile on her face, 'I give you: ***Elixir***.'

The members of the Board stared silently at the bottle. It was impossible to tell what any of them were thinking.

'Elixir.'

From Ruth's position on the other side of the Board Room door, the word was muffled. But it was clear enough for her to understand it, just as she had understood everything else.

She breathed deeply, and replayed the conversation in her head. She'd heard all she needed to hear. She knew what was going on. But did she believe it? Did she *really* believe it?

With more than half her life spent already, she *had* to.

$1.2 trillion dollars. The figure seemed to echo in her head. She thought of her tiny apartment. Of the meager salary Pure Industries paid her, and of how little her contribution to its smooth running it recognized. How much of these untold riches would find their way into *her* tiny pension scheme, she wondered. She was fairly sure she knew the answer.

And she knew something else too. There were people in the world who could be trusted to handle events of this magnitude, and those who couldn't. Ruth Adams was in no doubt to which group Tom Shaw belonged. He was weak. Disorganized. Unfit even to head up an ailing vitamin pill company, let alone the behemoth Pure Industries was about to become. The business with his wife was all very sad, she supposed, but a leader should be able to rise above such things. To separate the personal and the professional. The thought troubled her as she walked away from the Board Room.

Ruth's hair might have been grey. Her skin might have been lined. Her joints might have started showing the first twinges of arthritic pain. But her lips were pursed and her mind was as active and sharp as a child's.

Four components, she thought to herself, as she replayed in her head the conversation she'd overheard.

Three people.

What was information like that worth? And how, she wondered, could she make it valuable to herself...

Jack was by his mother's bedside when Tom returned to the hospice. Jane was asleep and their 10-year-old son was sitting quietly, a book open on his lap. His blonde hair was as messy as usual.

'I was reading to her,' he said as Tom walked in. 'But then she fell asleep. Maybe she didn't like the story.'

Tom felt the blood pump through the vein in his temple. 'Hey, champ,' he replied. 'I bet she *loved* the story. It's just this thing she's got. It makes her really tired, right?'

Jack nodded. 'Right,' he said. And then, much quieter: 'I wish she could get better.' His voice wavered and Tom knew what was coming. When the tears arrived he had his boy in his arms and it was everything he could do to stop his own body shaking with emotion. He could cope with almost anything. So could Jane. But Jack's distress was the one thing that destroyed his fortitude.

'I'm going to make it OK,' he whispered through the tears that threatened to well up. 'I promise, champ, I'm going to make it OK.'

All of a sudden, Jack pulled himself from his father's embrace. His cheeks were tearstained, but his face was angry. 'Don't say that,' he whispered. Sometimes he sounded so adult. 'Don't *say* you can do that when you know you can't.' Jack picked up the book from the seat and, not knowing what to do with it, threw it down to the floor. He stormed past Tom and out of the hospice room, though Tom noticed that he closed the door gently behind him.

He wouldn't go far. Tom wasn't cross with his son's outburst. He understood him. Understood how he was feeling. Jack was a sensitive boy and his mother's illness had confused him. Now he was caught between two states: family bliss and the utter devastation that they both knew was to come. Hardly surprising, then, if he could be a little volatile at times. He'd be back though, with a shamefaced look and a meek apology, and Tom would hug him again and it would all be forgotten.

Until the next time. And the next.

And then, when Jane finally went, who could tell?

It wasn't even a decision. More like a reflex action. Something he could no longer stop himself doing even if he tried. The pills were still there, at the bottom of his trouser pocket, gathering dust. He removed one and held it up to the light. It was so small. So insignificant.

It won't make her better...

But it *would* give her time. Give *them* time. Him and Jack, with her. And medicine was always progressing. If Rachael Leo could create Elixir, it was surely only a matter of time before curing Jane's condition was a routine medical procedure.

It has to be handled responsibly. Ethically. And I trust you to do that. I'm right to trust you, aren't I?

A frown crossed his face. Was it ethical, what he was about to do? Was it responsible? Tom didn't know. All he knew was that somewhere in the corridor outside there was a sobbing boy praying for a miracle. In the absence of God, Tom was the only person who could supply it. What father wouldn't do that for his son?

What husband wouldn't do this for his wife?

It would be the easiest thing in the world to slip the single dose on to Jane's tongue. He was even on the point of removing one of the tablets when something stopped him. Hadn't they always discussed everything? Weren't they always honest with each other?

And could he really bring himself to force her into an impossible decision like this?

He took a step backwards and stared at his wife. She looked on the cusp between life and death. Her body was still thin, her face still grey, her lips still cracked, her breathing frail but steady.

Tom sadly let the tablet fall back to the bottom of his pocket. He stepped silently from the room and went to find Jack. He reckoned he'd take him to buy ice cream. He didn't like to spoil his son, but the kid needed something to cheer him up and Tom had the feeling that in the weeks and months to come, he wasn't going to be around half as much as either he, Jack, or Jane would like.

PART TWO

TWO WEEKS LATER

5

MONDAY, 3.50 P.M., PACIFIC STANDARD TIME

Admiral Nathanial H Windlass hadn't been around half as much as *his* wife would like, either. But that was nothing new. The last time he and Lynda had spent a significant amount of time together had been on their honeymoon years ago. Nat had told his new wife that their honeymoon destination would be a surprise, and he was sure right about that. Two weeks under canvas in the wilder regions to the north of Yosemite National Park. At the start of the holiday Lynda's nails had been immaculate, her legs waxed, her hair newly bleached and her bag full of just the right kind of underwear to keep her new husband's attention. By the end she both looked and felt like a savage. She'd eaten nothing other than what Nat had caught; their water came from streams and tasted of chlorine on account of the purification tablets; and the ultimate indignity had been digging a hole in the ground with a shovel to perform more intimate ablutions. By the end of the honeymoon, Lynda had grown to understand why Nat's first wife had left him.

Lynda wasn't going to do that. The former Navy Seal was a man going places and his wife had every intention of reaping the benefit. The very moment they returned to DC, Lynda had checked into the Fairmont Hotel. If Nat expected her to relive his Seal days with him, she told him, then she would. But in return, she would pamper herself as she saw fit. Nat's face had visibly paled when the bill came through for her week of indulgence, but he'd been wise enough to stay quiet.

That had been 15 years ago. Even then, Nathanial Windlass no longer had the physique of a serving Special Forces operative. Some of the muscle had shrunk, leaving areas of loose skin; and the paunch he now sported was already giving hints of its imminent arrival. The years that followed had seen very little active service, and a large number of lunches as Windlass became less and less of a soldier and more and more of a politician – albeit unelected and hardly known to the general public. Now he resembled any other member of the bloated Washington hierarchy, but he still liked to relive his Seal days. Still liked to pretend he was fit and lean and dangerous. At least, Lynda could think of no other reason why a man of his age would insist on these twice-yearly expeditions into the field, scavenging for food like an overgrown boy scout.

And she was very relieved that the latest of these trips was now at an end.

The Windlasses were in a black rented SUV, heading south on Highway 15. They stank. Lynda's face wore the same look of disgust that she'd had on day one of their expedition into the Nevada Desert, and which she knew would remain until she'd been installed in the Four Seasons in Vegas for at least a couple of days.

'Sixteen hundred hours,' Nathaniel announced – more, Lynda thought, to break the silence than anything else. 'I should make the last flight out of Vegas. I'll be back in DC by midnight.'

And I, thought Lynda to herself, will be clean. I'll have drunk champagne. And who knows? Maybe I'll have found someone to keep me company in my lonely old hotel room.

The City of Sin never ceased to thrill her. Each time she arrived in this crazy town was as exciting as the first. When the time came to say goodbye to her husband, she told him she would miss him and he said the same, but they both knew it was a lie. Lynda was here, by herself, out of choice. And as she watched her husband's car disappear down the Strip, she felt the weight of his presence falling from her shoulders. The sooner he was in DC, and the distance between them was extended to several thousand miles, the better.

In the meantime, Lynda Windlass had some serious money to spend.

Vegas didn't thrill Nat Windlass in the same way that he knew it thrilled his wife. It had done once, many years ago, when he'd prized his love of danger above everything else. When he wasn't putting his ass on the line with the Seals, he found the pace of life slow. Small wonder he and a few of the guys had found their way down here for a short vacation. It seemed like another lifetime, that first night at the roulette wheel. And man, the buzz of his first big win. He'd arrived in Vegas with a few hundred bucks and left with the equivalent of six months' pay and confirmation of his belief that it was always – *always* – a good idea to take risks.

Now, though, that thrill was as distant a memory as an alcoholic's first bottle of beer. Unlike an alcoholic, Admiral Nathanial Windlass knew he had a problem. The consequences were there in black and white every time he looked at his bank balance, or shifted a loan from one shark to another. Even so, he knew all he needed was one good run. One lucky streak and he could deal with the best-kept secret on Capitol Hill: that Nat Windlass, war hero and Special Security Adviser to the President himself, was on the brink of bankruptcy.

Nat had winced when Lynda announced she was staying at the Four Seasons. His wife's expensive tastes were not as terrible a financial burden as his ruinous gambling debts, but they sure didn't help. A little part of him, though, had felt a surge of, not excitement exactly – more like anticipation. Vegas to him was a free bar to a drunk. He didn't feel guilty that he'd lied to Lynda about catching the last flight to DC – no doubt she'd be screwing some toy boy before the evening was much older – but he did take care to direct the rented SUV away from the noise of the Strip. He didn't want to risk running in to her, and after all, it wasn't like he was unknown. Easier for him to keep a low profile in one of the smaller, dingier casinos downtown. The kind of place that wasn't for entertainment, and where the hookers were decidedly less appealing. Windlass only had one thing on his mind, and that was the tables.

His anonymous room in the Plaza Hotel and Casino smelt of cigarette smoke and stale sweat. There were bugs in the bed, and the sound of a couple arguing in the room next door. Windlass could have demanded a different room but what was the point? He wasn't here for luxury. He wasn't here for anything much, except a chance to make a dent in his debts. He couldn't shower quick enough. He didn't bother shaving: his few days' growth made him less recognizable, and anyway, he just wanted to get to the casino.

It was just as he was pulling his key card from the light-switch slot by the door that his Blackberry buzzed. Windlass stopped. He turned. The Blackberry was lying on his bed. He'd left it there on purpose, not wanting to be disturbed while he was out. For a moment he stared at it, wondering if he could just leave it there and deal with whatever it was tomorrow. But in the end he gave a heavy sigh, walked back to the bed and checked the screen.

It was an SMS. No words, just five numbers.

'92666'.

Nathanial Windlass's mobile communications devices were encrypted as a matter of course. That wasn't good enough for him. He knew enough about these things to realize that anyone could hack anything given the time and the inclination. Why else had Secret Service banned the President from carrying his own cell phone? For this reason he had developed a code, known only to himself and to his closest advisors. He was looking at this code now.

9: Contact.

2: Windlass's chief aide.

So far, so ordinary. Such a request could normally wait. Only tonight it couldn't, because the three numbers that followed were seldom used, and were the equivalent of his BlackBerry screaming at him.

666, they yelled. Urgent.

Brett Ryder was anxious. This could go one of two ways. He'd either be laughed out of a job, or...

Or what?

It was just gone midnight on the East Coast. His tiny office in a faceless grey building in Washington was tiny and pokey. When Brett had first landed this job, he'd felt like all his Christmases had come at once. Aide to Admiral Nathanial Windlass, one of the White House's most trusted security advisers. He'd secretly imagined himself walking the corridors of the West Wing; the President would know his name; he'd be party to decisions of great national importance.

The reality was quite different.

Unlike the agents he ran, Brett seldom saw sunlight. He seldom saw anything but the four walls of this windowless office, and the bursting folders piled precariously upon it. He had a computer on his desk, of course, but he didn't use it very often. Admiral Windlass didn't trust computers. Too easy to hack. He had an old-fashioned loyalty to slips of paper, especially for the kind of jobs entrusted to what he grandly called his 'A' team. It meant ten times as much work for the hierarchy under him, but that obviously didn't matter to the Admiral. What was it they said about bosses being like monkeys in a tree? They look down to see a crowd of smiling faces, while the people below them look up to see a bunch of assholes.

It was such a relief when Windlass was away. A day without him was like a week in the sun; the Admiral's two-week vacations were like a sabbatical. God knows why he insisted on camping in the most godforsaken corners of America he could find. Brett had met plenty of SF guys. Almost without exception they gave the impression that they were a class apart, but Windlass took that aloofness to a new level. Brett had learned to shrug it off. Normally, he would just enjoy his boss's vacations. Not this time, though. This time, something had come up. Brett knew that if he played it right, it could be his chance to climb a few feet up the greasy pole.

Windlass had only been 24 hours into his vacation when the call came through. Al Templeton was an old college buddy of Brett's. They'd roomed together at Harvard, and when the time came to go out into the real world, they'd both followed a similar path. While Brett had ended up running agents for Admiral Windlass, the FBI had taken Al on. Brett's friend, though, had never really moved up through the ranks. Low-level surveillance, non-sensitive targets and no real prospect of promotion. The dynamic between them had changed. Back at college they'd been equals, drinking the same beer, chasing the same chicks. Now Al looked up to Brett. He was under the illusion that Brett's position as aide to a major player like Windlass was something to aspire to. On paper, he was right. But Brett kept the reality of the day-to-day drudgery of his job to himself.

Brett and Al had met up that night in a bar in downtown DC. A football game played silently on a TV screen behind the bar, and a handful of older guys with check shirts and beer bellies were watching it. Apart from that, it was quiet. A good place to talk without being overheard. The kind of place Brett found himself choosing out of instinct these days.

'So what you working on, Al?' he had asked when they were on their second beer.

Al had pretended to look casual, and Brett immediately knew that this was reason they were meeting. His friend was easy to read. Probably the reason his career was heading nowhere. 'Kind of need-to-know, buddy.'

Brett had shrugged. 'Sure,' he said. 'Whatever.'

There'd been a pause. 'Still, guess there's no harm telling you. Reckon you'd do the same for me, right?'

'Right,' Brett had lied.

'There's a little vitamin pill company on the west coast. Name of Pure Industries. They've been trying to hawk some shit to the military. I don't know – supplements of some kind. Regular DOD procurement guidelines kicked in.'

Brett had nodded and taken a pull on his beer. He knew what Al was talking about. Try to sell anything to the military and the first thing they did was approach the Feds for routine credential checks. So Al had been snooping around two-bit vitamin companies. It wasn't exactly staking out Abbottabad.

'Sounds... interesting,' Brett had said.

Al had given him a sour look. 'Yeah, right. About as interesting as watching paint dry.' He sniffed. 'Until a couple of weeks ago.'

He'd taken a pull on his beer and waited for Brett to say: 'Go on.'

'I'm telling you, man. It's just routine surveillance. The guys intercepting the emails forward them to me at random. I don't even read them half of the time.'

I guess he'll come to the point at some stage, Brett had thought to himself.

'So about ten days ago, I *am* reading one. Financial guy to the CEO. From what they were saying, the DOD procurement deal is dead in the water. Nothing to do with DOD, mind. Pure Industries are pulling out of the deal. The email suggested they had some kind of major scientific breakthrough. From what I could tell, the executives had dollar signs spinning in front of their eyes.' Al had sat back in his seat and pulled on his beer again.

'OK, Al,' Brett had said. 'Why are you telling me this?'

Al's face had grown wary. 'Just shooting the shit with an old buddy.'

'Bullshit. Why are you telling me this?'

A pause. 'Cards on the table?'

'Cards on the table.'

'I need a break, buddy,' Al had admitted. 'I'm standing still with the Bureau. Maybe if something comes of this, you could, I don't know, put in a good word... get me on your team...'

Brett had nodded slowly. So *that* was it. Al Templeton wanted out of the FBI and Brett was his meal ticket. Trouble was, he'd just shown himself up for what he was: unreliable and untrustworthy. The last person on earth Brett would want under him.

'Hey, man,' he'd said. 'You got it. I'll see what I can do.' They'd finished their beers, had one for the road and Brett had split. Chances were, he'd thought as he caught the Blue line back to his little apartment, he'd never see Al Templeton again.

His interest, though, had been piqued.

If Al had anything about him, he'd have investigated further, which was exactly what Brett had done. He had the resources, after all. And he had a team he could trust. It hadn't taken much. A discreet phone tap; one of his guys standing in as a delivery driver and carrying out surveillance on the Pure Industries premises. Textbook stuff. Sometimes, Brett had thought to himself, it was as if these people actively *wanted* their most sensitive secrets to leak out. But then, he reminded himself, not everybody lived in his world.

The intelligence that started to filter through, however, was very far from textbook. It was piecemeal. Fragments of conversations that would make little sense in isolation but which, once collated, told a very different story.

A story almost too bizarre to believe.

But Pure Industries clearly believed it, which meant Brett had to take it seriously. And now that he'd fitted all the fragments together, he needed to put it in front of his boss without delay. He wasn't expecting Windlass back in DC for a couple of days. Hence the 666 call.

Brett Ryder took a sip of cold coffee from plastic cup, then checked his watch. 00.08hrs. He'd sent the emergency SMS to his boss seven minutes ago. Now he had to wait until the Admiral called in. And if that meant sitting here all night…

His cell buzzed. Brett's hand shot towards the phone lying in front of him. Number withheld. He took the call and quickly put the phone to his ear. 'Brett Ryder.'

'Ryder, I told you – that code is only to be used when the situation is urgent. *Urgent*, Ryder. You understand what that means, right?'

'Yes, Admiral. I believe this requires your immediate attention.'

'Jeez… Can't a guy take a vacation? What the hell's going on there that's so damn important.'

Brett's eyes flickered at the file on his desk. 'You ever heard of a small vitamin supplement company out west, name of Pure Industries?'

'What? Of course I haven't. Chrissakes, Ryder. Urgent means life or death. You hear that? *Life or goddamn death*.'

Brett took a deep, calming breath. He was used to the Admiral speaking to him like this, but that didn't make it easier to keep his cool. 'If you tell me where you are now, Admiral, I can arrange for a vehicle to get you to the nearest airport.'

'No,' the Admiral replied, a bit too quickly. 'If it's so damn urgent, tell me now.'

'Negative, Admiral. The information is too sensitive. You need to be here. What did you say your location was?'

'I didn't,' the Admiral snapped back. There was a pause. Perhaps the Admiral thought his sudden retort had been suspiciously defensive. Brett didn't know. But when he spoke again, he was more businesslike. 'I have a vehicle already,' Windlass said. 'I'll be on the red-eye and I'll come straight to the office. You'd better be there.'

The line went dead.

Brett tossed the phone back on to the table. He felt a wave of tiredness. Perhaps he should go home. Get a few hours sleep before the Admiral arrived back in DC. But somehow he knew sleep wouldn't be on the agenda. He opened the file in front of him. It was a short report – it didn't need more than three pages to provide all the salient information – but one which Brett had taken a great deal of effort to ensure he got right. He read through it again. And as had happened every other time he thought about what he'd discovered, he felt a curious mixture of emotions. Excitement, certainly. But also apprehension. Uncertainty. Even fear.

He closed the report and stared at the cover page. It contained only two words, printed in standard type and centerd across the page. The first word was common enough on documents that passed over Brett's desk: CLASSIFIED.

The second word was less familiar. It demanded Brett's attention and magnified his uncertain emotions a hundredfold.

It said: ELIXIR.

6

MONDAY, 10.00 A.M., PACIFIC STANDARD TIME

'Elixir.'

Theodore Croft whispered the word quietly to himself. He liked the way it sounded. Like the Pacific surf hissing gently on the golden sand thirty yards from his beachfront house. This stretch of beach was deserted – uncommon for Malibu – but it was always this way, because it belonged to Theodore himself. Barriers, wire and curtly worded signs warned any potential sunbathers of the likely consequences of trespassing on his little piece of paradise.

He was a good-looking man and he knew it. Of course, the endless procession of silicon blondes with whom he amused himself all *told* him that, but Croft was sufficiently self-aware to recognize greed when he heard it. But he knew he was good-looking all the same. He had the glow of health that so often came with extreme wealth. His sunglasses were propped up on the top of his head, his shorts and golfing shirt were immaculately pressed. In one hand he held a glass of freshly squeezed orange juice, and in the other a piece of paper.

'Elixir,' he repeated, and his tanned face broke into a smile.

Theodore Croft liked a challenge. Always had done. As a kid he had excelled at everything. Like, *everything*. Sport, class, girls. By the time he was a teenager, he was already used to getting whatever he wanted. Now that he was pushing forty, that hadn't changed. He'd made his first million US at the age of 18, shorting 500K of stock that had only cost him 50. That wasn't the biggest deal he'd ever done. Far from it. But the first time is always the sweetest and he'd never forget the feeling of seeing those six magic zeroes and knowing they were his. Life was too short to be poor. Theodore Croft never would be.

His name was known to everyone on Wall Street. He had set up his own hedge fund at the age of the twenty, and it soon earned a reputation for ruthless brilliance. Croft could spot when a company's value was about to leap, or crash with astonishing accuracy. So astonishing that the Securities and Exchange Commission were forever sniffing around him, trying to work out how he could be so prescient. They never found any evidence of wrong-doing, of course, because Theodore Croft was very careful to ensure that such evidence never existed. Insider trading? Such an ugly term. Croft preferred to think of it as using his initiative. He always ensured that his informants were paid above the market price for their precious information. And if, as sometimes happened, they later decided to take advantage of Croft's generosity once again, there were always people who could be hired to encourage them to keep their mouths shut. Theodore sometimes wondered how people could have so little idea of their own market value. Why would he pay a blackmailer an extra hundred thousand, when a couple of hundred bucks would employ someone to break the blackmailer's leg? Christ, 5k would buy you a hit man. It all came down to economics in the end.

Croft had more money than he could ever spend. He knew that. His bank balance was no longer anything to do with making a living. It was just a way of keeping score. A way of reminding himself that he was winning. All this – the beachfront paradise, the penthouse in the Upper East Side of New York City, the yacht moored off the coast of Monaco, the Learjet – it was all very nice, but you soon forgot that your own life was different to everyone else's. Nothing, though, replaced the thrill of the deal. Theodore Croft's hedge fund days were behind him, but he still speculated and it wasn't very often that he did not go to bed richer than when he had woken up.

He'd diversified, too. Tried to vary his portfolio. This Colombia thing, for example. Funny how you could make as much money in a single day on one deal with the Hispanics than some people earned in their whole working life. Gave him a buzz just to think about it; and even more of a buzz to know the authorities couldn't do a damn thing to get to him.

But this? This was something different. It made the Colombians, with their drugs and their guns and their pneumatic women, look like kids in the school yard. And as for Wall Street – it made them look insignificant. Toy people with toy money. This was a whole other ball game and Theodore Croft wanted in.

Crazy, he thought to himself, how your life can change with a single phone call. The phone call had come this morning, and his informant had had the unmistakable sound of greed in their voice. As well they might. This was going to be big.

He walked over to the side of his pool. His Doberman, a well cared-for, shiny-coated beast called Rex, was lying at one end in the warm sun. His tongue was lolling from one side of his mouth and his eyes were open. They followed Croft as he approached, and there was something strangely human about them. Strangely watchful.

A single leaf had fallen on to the still film of the water and Croft felt himself scowling at the sight. He disliked disorder. The pool guy would be along shortly, though, so he decided not to let it worry him as he reclined on one of the sun beds and looked around. The whole of his premises were silent. Alabama – his latest squeeze, more buxom and shiny than any that had gone before her – was still asleep. Not a good sign for her. As soon as they started taking the place for granted, failing to be around to service Theodore's needs, they were out. He gave her four days, maybe five. Certainly no longer, perhaps a little less.

His first call was to his lawyer, Ben Swift. Swift looked after all his legal affairs, and more besides. In looks he was the opposite to Croft. Short, dumpy, so addicted to strong cigarettes that he smelt like an ashtray. He had square glasses with thick lenses, but he'd never look at you directly though them. Almost as if he didn't want you to spot the dishonesty in his eyes. Swift was devious, unscrupulous and almost entirely without principle. Perfect lawyer material, Croft always thought. He liked the guy. They weren't friends, exactly – neither man was the type to offer the hand of friendship to anyone, and Croft didn't doubt that Swift would screw him over if he thought he might profit from the act – but they were kindred spirits.

'Ben, this is Theodore.'

Swift's voice was slow. Careful. But not unpleasant. 'Bit early in the a.m. for you, Theo.'

'Beautiful morning, Ben. Beautiful goddamn morning. Makes you glad to be alive. When you going to come visit, huh? Bring a chick, relax. Hope you don't have anything planned for today, though. There's a little bit of business for you to take care of.'

'Go on.'

'I got my eye on a little company out in Laguna Niguel. Manufactures vitamin supplements.'

'Vitamin supplements?'

'Ah, you know. Fish oil, I guess. Vitamin C for spotty kids. That kind of horse shit.'

'They heading down the pan?'

Heading down the pan? Hardly that. Croft found himself silently recapping what he knew. What his source inside Pure Industries had told him about the peculiar qualities of their new product – this 'Elixir', or whatever the hell they wanted to call it. The steps they were taking to protect the formula. Normally, when Croft made a play for anything, he'd done the math first. But for this, he didn't need to. He knew he was looking at the kind of money that would make even *his* substantial riches look insignificant.

'I said, they heading down the pan?'

'Could be, pal. Could be.'

'What you got, someone on the inside?' Swift sighed. 'I'd sure like to know where you get your tips from, Theo.'

'Ben, I'm very insulted that you think I'd stoop to such a level.'

Swift snorted. 'I ain't never seen a level you wouldn't stoop to, Theo.'

'I want Pure Industries, Ben. Between you and me, I don't much care what price it comes in at. Find out how much stock there is on the market. If we manage to put our hands on enough, we'll force a hostile takeover.'

'And if we can't?'

Theodore Croft sniffed. 'Don't come back to me with "can't", Ben. Not my favourite word, you know that.'

Another pause. 'I'll do what I can.' And then, without waiting for a reply, Swift hung up. Croft stared at his handset for a full minute, replaying the conversation in his head and unwinding a tangle of strategies. If his information was correct – and he saw no reason to believe it wasn't – this would be the deal of his life. And what was more, it would be the deal of a very long life.

He took a gulp of his orange juice, stripped down to his swimming shorts and dived into the pool. When he emerged at the other end, he stretched out one arm and scratched Rex behind the ears. He was right. Today really was turning into a most beautiful day.

Ben Swift stared across his office, out through the floor to ceiling windows and over the skyline of central Los Angeles and the San Gabriel Mountains beyond. He barely moved. Barely breathed. He was like that when he was thinking.

What was Theodore Croft up to? Swift had learned a long time ago that his client had the Midas touch. That he never expressed an interest in anything if he didn't already know, beyond doubt, that he was on to a good thing. Why the hell would he be interested in some no-consequence pill peddlers in Orange County? Surely the guy had his sights set higher than that.

But this was Croft he was talking about. The man never did anything without a reason. In an idle corner of his brain, Swift wondered if he should spin the guy a line and make a play for Pure Industries himself. That thought caused a contemptuous hissing sound to escape his lips. Who was he kidding? Where the hell was he going to find that kind of money? And make an enemy of Theodore Croft? He'd heard the rumors. Were they true? Hard to say, but even though his wasn't much of a life, he'd like to hold on to it a bit longer.

He breathed deeply and his chest rattled. Swift hardly noticed it these days. He knew the tobacco would ferry him to an early grave, but his addiction was too far gone for him to worry about quitting now. In any case, cigarettes were one of the few remaining pleasures in his life. Two divorces gone and the lion's share of his income frittered on alimony, there was always a bit too much month left at the end of the money. He relied on loathsome clients like Theodore Croft to keep his head, if not above water, than at least close to the surface. That was why he pretended to be the same as them. One day, he promised himself, he'd cut the cord, but right now he needed Theodore Croft more than Theodore Croft needed him. Which meant that when Croft called, Swift jumped.

Ben Swift had contacts in this town. The business community was small, and everybody knew someone who knew someone. While it was in theory difficult to check the share structure of a private company, in practise it could be done if you knew the right people. There weren't many companies that didn't have shareholders a hostile bidder like Croft could target. There might be venture capitalists with a majority shareholding, always out to make a quick deal; there might be elderly shareholders, willing to cash in their chips before they cashed in their chips. All you had to do was find them, and Swift was very good at doing that.

The banks were the key. It only took one phone call to verify the banking arrangements of Pure Industries, and another to pin down a contact at the bank in question. Swift knew that Theodore Croft would foot the bill for any financial arrangement he had to enter into in order to get the information he wanted, but in the event there was no need. His contact was indiscreet enough to volunteer the details Swift wanted without any kind of monetary inducement. Heart-warming, or naïve, depending on how you wanted to look at it.

So it was that within an hour of Croft's call, Swift had a list of names. Tom Shaw, CEO. Peter Wright, VP Finance. Sylvia Lucas, VP Marketing. Kyle Byng, VP Business Development. All of them active members of the Executive Board. No consortia, no elderly shareholders. When you'd done this a few times you developed a sense of what you were looking at. Ben Swift's sense told him this was a shareholder structure that it wasn't worth trying to buy out.

He made some more enquiries, then gave it a few hours before calling Croft back. It was his first rule of his business:

always make the client think you've worked harder than you actually have. That way the invoice never comes as a surprise. Croft answered his cell after only a single ring. Swift could tell he'd been waiting for his call.

'Give me some good news, pal.'

A little part of Swift was glad he couldn't do that. Sometimes it was reassuring to know that guys like Croft didn't always get it their own way.

'Sorry, Theo. No can do. Making a move for Pure Industries is going to be a waste of your time and money.'

A pause. When Croft spoke again, it was like the sun going in. 'I want that company, Ben.'

'I've been reliably informed that the current Board have no intention to sell at any price, so it's not going to happen, my friend. Leastways, not by any legal means. And I'm sure you wouldn't think of doing it any *other* way, now would you?'

Theodore Croft hung up.

He was inside now. The afternoon sun was too strong even for him and the marble floor of his beachfront house was pleasantly cool. Which was more than could be said for Croft himself. He managed about ten seconds of calm, before throwing his cell on to the floor, where its casing cracked and the innards spilled out.

'Hey, honey.' Alabama's voice came from the doorway. He could hear her music playing somewhere in the house: a distant but constant thudding that was like barrage to his brain. He didn't care for music at the best of times. 'Why so tense?'

Croft spun round to look at her. She was wearing a colorful sarong, tied halter-neck style, and very little else.

'You want me to help you relax, honey?' A strand of blonde hair tumbled across her face.

Croft didn't even try to hide his sudden disgust of her. 'Get out,' he hissed.

'Hey? What do you mean, honey?'

'Get your stuff and get out. You've got twenty minutes. Any longer than that, I'll throw you out of here myself.'

She blinked at him. 'But honey, I've got nowhere to...'

'*GET OUT!*' Croft roared. A whimper escaped the girl's mouth. For a moment she was motionless, but then she suddenly saw Croft's Doberman Rex standing in the doorway of the room. His tongue wasn't lolling any more, and his eyes were as sharp as any human's. They stared at Alabama, who turned and ran from the room, crying as she went. Her tears meant nothing to Croft. He'd forgotten all about her already, and was pacing the marble floor with a frown on his well-tanned face and a faint tremble of suppressed fury in his hands. Swift was a fool. A damn fool with no vision and no guts...

He stopped. Guts were all he needed. Guts, and a little bit more information. Why hadn't he thought of that before? Pure Industries, major shareholders, takeovers – they were just a distraction. The only thing that mattered was the formula. Once he had that, he had everything.

He ran through the information his source had given him.

Four components.

Four people. Croft knew that the Scientist, 'the Inventor', would be the toughest nut to crack, as there'd be an emotional attachment to 'their baby'. But the other three, the business people, would be easier, they'd would want to listen to reason and 'do deals'. They all do…eventually.

Three people.

Really. How hard could it be?

He was vaguely aware of Alabama sobbing and stamping her way to the exit of the house, and of the door slamming behind her. Peace and quiet, finally. That was exactly what he needed. He took a seat in a comfortable armchair, precisely placed so that it looked through the terrace doors and out towards the ocean. He fixed his eyes on the horizon, pressed his fingertips together, and started to make plans.

Admiral Windlass's office was ten times bigger than Brett Tyler's, and about twenty times more comfortable. There was thick carpet on the floor and art on the walls. He had a mahogany desk and a padded leather chair. Along the far wall was a sideboard with a selection of decanters. Windlass had poured himself a Scotch in a chunky cut-glass tumbler within seconds of arriving, but he failed to offer a drink to Brett. Not that Brett much wanted one. Dawn was just around the corner and he hadn't slept while waiting for the Admiral to get in.

Now his boss was sitting at his desk, sipping slowly and reading even slower. Brett stood opposite him, uncomfortably aware that he was perspiring rather heavily. He watched carefully as Windlass, having finished Brett's short report, went back to the beginning and read it again. When he finally placed it back down on the table, he was silent for a few moments.

'Is this some kind of joke, Tyler?'

'No, sir,' Brett replied. 'No joke.'

'Because if it *is* some kind of joke…'

'Admiral Windlass, sir, *look* at me.' Windlass's eyes widened at his sudden abruptness. 'I haven't slept. I've been on this for days. It's no joke.'

Windlass stared at him. Then at the document. 'I guess you'd better sit down, Tyler,' he said. 'You want a drink?'

Brett exhaled heavily. 'Yeah,' he said. 'Maybe a coffee?'

'What do you think this is? A goddamn diner? You'd better tell me where you got this information.'

'Tip-off, sir, from a friend in the Bureau. I considered it a credible source so I ordered a wire op. The rest was easy – didn't even need to get inside. A laser listening device trained on the window of the boardroom picked up the remaining fragments. I pieced it together from there.'

'Tell me everything else I need to know.'

Brett nodded and took a moment to clear his head. 'They were never *looking* for this compound. There was an accident in the lab, nothing more. Their chief scientist, a Dr Rachael Leo, has tested the thing every which way, and it works.'

'How can they *know* that?'

'My understanding is that Leo tested it on herself and measured the rate of her own cellular degeneration.' He gave his boss an apologetic look. 'Truth is, sir, I flunked biology. All

I know is that the Pure Industries board *believe* this. I've done a background check on all of them. We're not talking flaky new-agers or con artists, sir. These are proper people. Rachael Leo's scientific credentials are excellent. The other members of the Board, straight as a die. They might be deceiving themselves, but I honestly don't think they're deceiving other people.'

Windlass's face was unreadable. 'What do we know about the compound itself?' he asked.

'Not much. It's made from all natural substances, so there's no need to file for FDA approval. One of our guys has managed to get hold of the draft material safety datasheet. Tells us nothing. And they've employed certain security measures to protect the formula.'

'What are they?'

'There are four main components or procedures required to produce the Elixir. Each executive has been entrusted with one of them. The only person to know the whole process is Leo.'

Windlass nodded. 'Basic,' he said. He sounded like he was thinking out loud. 'Fairly effective. Not foolproof.'

'We know from their banking records that they've spent a substantial sum with a company that provides UV curing equipment. It's just an assumption, but I'd bet that has something to do with the Elixir. Apart from that, we're in the dark.'

'Maybe,' Windlass said. 'Maybe not. We can be sure of one thing, though.'

'Sir?'

Windlass stood up. He walked over to the window of his office. It was covered by a thick, plum-colored curtain, which the Admiral pulled back slightly to reveal a panoramic view of DC and, in the distance, the dome of the White House glowing in the night.

'Whoever owns this thing, whoever has the formula...'

'Yes, sir?'

Windlass let the curtain fall closed again and turned to look at him. 'They're going to be wealthier than anyone's ever been before.'

Brett had the strange sensation of acid rising in his stomach. There was something in Windlass's face. He didn't know what it was. A kind of hunger. Desperation, even. The Admiral looked older. Haggard. As if he was struggling under the weight of some terrible secret. For a split second, Brett felt like he was looking at a different person. Someone even less attractive than Windlass himself.

And then this other person was gone, leaving just the Admiral and an eerie, cold sensation at the back of Brett's neck.

'You look awful, Tyler,' Windlass said. 'You need to go home. Get some sleep.'

Brett shook his head wearily. 'I'm fine, sir,' he said.

'No,' Windlass retorted. 'You're not fine. We need to take this to the President as soon as we can get in to see him. Ordinarily I wouldn't even think about bringing you, but I suppose this is different. If you think, however, that a member of my team is walking into the Oval Office looking like a sack of shit, you're very much mistaken. Now get the hell home and start making yourself look human, got it?'

'Yes, Admiral Windlass,' Brett replied. He left the office quickly, shutting the door quietly behind him.

7

Tuesday, 11.28 a.m., Pacific Standard Time

Dr Rachael Leo stood in the doorway of her lab. Seven technicians were hard at work. Two were servicing the UV curing apparatus, two were calibrating an oven to a precise temperature. The remaining three were preparing extracts of various plants. None of them, of course, knew exactly what they were doing – the very existence of Elixir was a secret shared only by Rachael and the other members of the Board – but they were doing it with enthusiasm nevertheless.

There was a new buzz about the lab now. Rachael's team weren't fools. They knew it was significant that Pure was suddenly spending money on equipment rather than cutting corners. They could tell there was a new optimism about the place. Not to mention that Tom had given them all a twenty-five per cent pay hike – much to Peter's dismay. Everyone knew there was something afoot. They just didn't know what.

'Mistress of all you survey?'

Rachael turned round to see Kyle Byng standing there. She smiled. 'It's just nice to be actually doing science,' she said. 'Not accountancy.'

'You want to grab a coffee?'

A mischievous little look played across Rachael's face. 'Sure,' she said. 'Why not.'

Rachael liked Kyle. It wasn't in her nature to give guys a second look, but in the last couple of weeks she'd spent more and more time with him. Strictly business of course, but that hadn't stopped her noticing his boyish, slightly crooked smile. And when she'd taken him aside and explained that part of the Elixir process that was his to know, she'd found herself blushing at the look he gave her. She might not have had much experience of men, but she knew what that look meant.

The little common room where the techies had their breaks was empty. Rachael prepared a couple of coffees and they watched the thick black liquid dribble from the stainless steel machine into their cups.

'Tom's been looking tired,' Rachael said, more to fill the silence than anything else.

'He's got a lot on,' Kyle replied. 'Getting the… getting *it* to market – there's a lot of groundwork. And there's Jane, of course.'

'How is she?'

Kyle shrugged, as if to say: still dying. 'Kind of ironic, what with everything else that's happening. I'm surprised he hasn't asked you about…'

'He has,' Rachael interrupted. She gave him an apologetic smile. 'I'm sorry, Kyle. I don't think I should really talk about it.'

'Hey, of course. Of *course*.'

Rachael turned her attention back to the coffee. 'The techies love this stuff,' she said.

'I bet they do,' Kyle replied. 'The way you work them, I reckon they need something to help them stay awake. You're a harsh taskmaster, Dr Leo.'

'Task*mistress*, Kyle,' Rachael corrected. 'Or hadn't you noticed?' She felt her skin reddening at her own unexpected brazenness.

'Funnily enough,' Kyle said, 'I *had* noticed...'

He looked like he was about to say something else, but he never got the chance.

Rachael didn't know how long Tom's PA, Ruth, had been watching them, standing in the doorway with her arms crossed and one eyebrow raised. There was something about that woman that gave her the creeps. She was always there when you didn't expect her, with her disapproving stare. It was almost as though she was spying on them.

Kyle stood up straight, like a schoolboy who'd been caught out by his teacher.

'Ruth.' he acknowledged her politely.

Ruth said nothing. She looked from Kyle to Rachael, then back to Kyle again.

And then she was gone.

Rachael gave Kyle a guilty look. Had they said anything indiscreet? Anything about Elixir? They both understood the need for secrecy – absolute secrecy – even in front of other employees of the company. But as she replayed their little conversation in her head, she was satisfied it had been nothing but innocent flirting. Ruth Adams couldn't have learned anything from what they'd said.

'I'd better get back to work, Kyle,' Rachael told him. He nodded. Together they downed their coffees and went their separate ways.

2.30 p.m., Eastern Standard Time.

Brett Tyler stared at his reflection in the mirror. For the first time in four days he was clean shaven. There were bags under his eyes but there was nothing he could do about that. At least he had a fresh shirt and a clean suit. At least – as Windlass would have it – he didn't look like a sack of shit.

There was a car waiting for him: a black Mercedes with smoked windows. As Brett exited his apartment, a black-suited man with a prominent earpiece that instantly marked him out as Secret Service opened the rear door for him. He barely made eye contact as Brett climbed into the back and took his seat next to Admiral Windlass.

The door was shut and the Mercedes pulling out before Windlass said anything. A glass screen separated him and Brett from the two Secret Service in the front, but the Admiral still spoke quietly. 'OK, Tyler, here's the deal. You call him Mr President. Actually, scratch that. You don't call him anything at all. Not unless you're spoken to. Got it?'

'Got it, sir.'

'If anyone asks you anything, you keep it short and to the point. And Tyler?'

'Yes, sir?'

'You wouldn't be the first kid to think that half an hour in the Oval Office makes you the President's best buddy. It doesn't. He meets a lot of people and he'll have forgotten your face the minute you walk out of there. Just do your job and do it like a professional. This is a matter of national security, not a chance for Brett Tyler to kiss ass.'

'Will it be just us, sir?' All this was happening a bit quickly. Brett was finding it hard to keep his tired thoughts in order.

'Of course it won't. At the very least there'll be the National Security Adviser and the Chief Scientific Adviser. Plus a few hangers-on, no doubt.' Windlass gave Tyler a sideways glance that made it quite clear to which group he thought his aide belonged, and they sat in silence for the rest of the journey.

Brett Tyler had walked around the perimeter of the White House grounds any number of times before, along with the tourists with their rucksacks and Nikons, but he'd never stepped through its gates. It felt a bit unreal – like he was living someone else's life, not his – especially once they'd left the Mercedes and passed through the airport-style security gates into the West Wing. Windlass walked confidently – the stride of a man who knew where he was going. Brett stayed about a metre behind him, his eyes darting left and right as he tried to take in the bustling sights and sounds of the President's staff going about their daily – and clearly frantic – business. As he turned a corner he found, to his surprise, that the way was blocked by a small child – probably no more than five or six years old. She had adorable blonde ringlets, a hockey-stick-shaped piece of pink and white candy in one hand and a mischievous expression. She held up a free hand, like a traffic control cop stopping a car.

Windlass and Brett stopped. For a moment Brett was confused but then, as he took another look, he realized who the kid was: the President's little girl, unaware that she was in such an important place, and just doing what little girls do.

A change came over the Admiral. He broke out into a smile, then crouched down so that his face was at the same level as the girl's. 'Hey little lady,' he said, sounding for all the world like an indulgent grandfather. 'You going to let us get passed to see your daddy?'

The kid made a great show of thinking about this request, before cheekily stepping aside.

'Attagirl,' Windlass grinned, before standing up and marching onwards. He wasn't much more than a couple of yards beyond the President's daughter, however, before the mask slipped. Windlass's brow furrowed and he was once more his ordinary, unapproachable self.

It took no longer than a minute to reach the ante-room to the Oval Office. It was much quieter here, and a formidable-looking woman sitting behind a neat desk gazed at them over a pair of half-moon spectacles. 'You can go straight in,' she said. 'He's expecting you.'

'Have the others arrived?'

'Oh yes, Admiral Windlass,' she said rather coldly. 'You're the last.'

Windlass nodded and headed straight for the panelled wooden door of the Oval Office. Seconds later, Brett was walking inside.

The office was smaller than he imagined, but still instantly recognizable: the large wooden desk, behind which an American flag was draped; the Presidential seal on the carpet in the center of the room. There were three comfortable sofas, but the people sitting on them – two men, one woman – were straight-backed and stiff. Brett reckoned he could put a name to them all. Don Jackman, the President's hawk-nosed Chief of Staff. Clifford Hawkins, the middle-aged but prematurely bald National Security Adviser. Professor Alison Maitland, the Chief Scientific Adviser, who looked even more severe than the woman in the ante-room. Along the back wall were four much younger men, standing quietly, each of them holding a number of folders under their arms. It was immediately clear, as Windlass took a seat next to the NSA, that Brett should join the less significant party of attendees. He did so, but as he walked over to them, he couldn't take his eyes off the President himself.

Brett had heard it said that when you meet someone you recognize from the TV, they always appear smaller. The opposite was true of the President. He was a tall, lanky man with dark hair that was just beginning to go grey around the temples, and a boyish face – more Kennedy than Nixon. His youth and vigour had been the Democrats' selling point for their candidate in the Presidential elections; his naivety and inexperience had been the Republicans' counter-argument. It was true, Brett thought, that the President didn't look entirely at home as he sat in a separate leather chair in the company of advisers at least twenty years older than him. When he spoke, however, his voice was full of authority.

'OK Nat,' the President announced. There were no greetings or introductions or small talk. 'You called this meeting. You have the floor. Go ahead.'

'Thank you, Mr President.' Brett was struck by how friendly his boss could sound when he wanted to. Windlass paused for a moment, as though gathering his thoughts. 'Certain information has come into my possession regarding a small vitamin pill company located in Laguna Niguel, about 50 miles outside of LA.'

Brett saw the NSA roll his eyes, and Windlass clearly did too. 'Bear with me, Clifford,' he said. 'You'll see where this is going. The company is called Pure Industries. My sources tell me that they are on the brink of bringing to market a new product.'

'Admiral Windlass,' Professor Maitland interrupted. 'This hardly seems like a…'

But again, Windlass held up one hand and the Chief Scientific Adviser allowed him to continue.

'This product,' he said, 'has the ability to extend the life of the user by a multiple of five. And counting… They're calling it "Elixir".' The Admiral sat back and folded his arms. 'Just thought you'd like to know,' he said lightly.

The silence that followed was uncomfortable. Brett was aware of his fellow aides shuffling from one foot to another; and the look the NSA was giving his boss had gone beyond scepticism and into something approaching anger.

It was the President that spoke first.

'*Human* life?' he asked.

'According to our sources, Mr President, yes.'

'Alison?' the President addressed his Chief Scientific Adviser. 'Does this sound even remotely plausible to you?'

Professor Maitland gave a little shrug. 'Sure,' she said. 'Of course it does.'

'Mr President,' the NSA butted in. 'May I respectfully suggest that we file this one in the same cabinet as Roswell?'

But the President acted as if he hadn't heard. 'Go on, Alison,' he said quietly

Professor Maitland spoke with quiet precision. She sounded to Brett like she was choosing her words very carefully. 'Well,' she said, 'there's no shortage of labs attempting to achieve this kind of result. We keep fairly careful tabs on those in the US that we know about – and I think I'm safe in saying that we know about them all. I can't say with any certainty that we're aware of every instance of research outside of the US, but there's plenty of it. I've heard whispers that the North Koreans are carrying out some extremely dubious tests on human subjects, but there's no concrete proof. All I can say is that if this company – Pure Industries, did you say? – have been involved in this field, it should be pretty straightforward to confirm.'

'With respect, Professor Maitland, I doubt that. My sources tell me that this Elixir was discovered by accident.'

'Who *are* your sources, Nat?' the President asked. 'Who've you got working on this?'

Windlass hesitated and Brett knew why. He wasn't the kind of man to share the limelight if he could help it.

'Nat, who are your sources?'

Windlass looked over his shoulder. 'I've partially delegated some of the responsibility to my assistant, Brett Tyler.'

For the first time, the President's gaze fell upon Brett, who also felt the full force of a stony look from Windlass. 'I think you'd better join us, Mr Tyler,' the President said. He gave Brett a reassuring smile. 'Why don't you take a seat?'

Brett nodded. He stepped forward and sat next to Professor Maitland. 'OK, Brett,' said the President. 'Why don't you take us through this from the beginning.'

And so Brett did. Everything he'd explained to Windlass, he explained to the company assembled in the Oval Office. They listened in silence as he told them about Al Templeton, and about his subsequent investigations. When he finished, there was a another silence in the room. Once more it was broken by the President.

'Seems to me, Nat, you've got a good man in Brett Tyler. Important to hold on to good folk when you find them. Hope you're looking after this one.'

'Of course, Mr President,' Windlass murmured.

'Ladies and gentleman,' the President continued, 'it hardly needs saying that if this is true, it represents not only the most exciting moment of this administration, but of *any* administration.' He stood up. As he did so, Brett saw Professor Maitland exchange a look with the NSA. A worried look. A look that suggested they didn't agree with the President's assessment.

The President started pacing the room. 'I mean, this is great news, right Don?' His chief of staff didn't respond. 'Just *think* of the benefits to mankind. Think of how this is going to change … everything. Not to mention the fact we've got the mid-terms coming up. We could sure use a bump in the polls.'

He turned to look at the others, his eyes shining. It was only then that he saw that his enthusiasm was, quite clearly, not reciprocated. He frowned. 'What's wrong with you guys?'

'Mr President,' Don Jackman said tactfully. 'I wonder if we ought to discuss this in a... a little more *depth*.'

The President looked at each of his advisers in turn. Then he took his seat again. 'Fire away,' he said.

Jackman coughed uncomfortably. 'Alison,' he addressed the Chief Medical Officer. 'I think it's fair to say none of us understand the science of this drug, and obviously there's a lot of work for us to do. But I think we'd all be interested to know what your first reactions are.'

Professor Maitland removed her glasses and massaged the bridge of her nose for a moment before replying. 'Mr President, did you ever hear the story about the man who invented chess?'

'Alison, what's that got to do with...'

'Bear with me, Mr President.' She replaced her glasses. 'The story goes that the Emperor of India was so pleased with the game, he offered the inventor anything he wanted. The inventor asked for rice. He said he would like one grain of rice for the first square on the chess board; double that for the second square; double that for the third – and so on for all the squares on the chess board. The Emperor thought he'd got away lightly. He didn't realize that by the time he got to the sixty-fourth square, he had to give the inventor more rice than had ever been grown in the history of the world. He wasn't a mathematician. He didn't understand what happens when a quantity increases exponentially.'

There was silence in the Oval Office as everybody waited for the Chief Scientific Adviser to continue.

'The science of aging is complex,' she said. 'It's not just a matter of extending life, because I think we're all agreed that none of us want to live to 400 if our bodies deteriorate at the same rate that they do when we're, say, 80. The key is to slow down – or even stop – the rate of cell degeneration. If we can do that, then the human body will continue to function normally throughout the period of an increased lifespan.'

'But that's… that's great, isn't it?'

'Well, let's think about it. If we halt cellular degeneration in humans, there's nothing to stop them reproducing.'

'You talk about them like they're rabbits.'

'No, Mr President. Humans are a far more successful species than rabbits. We've populated every corner of the earth. We can withstand extremes of environment. The current human population is, what? 7 billion? The human female is fertile for a maximum of maybe thirty years. What happens when that becomes a hundred years? Two hundred years? Longer? And what happens when the population stops dying to make room for new offspring? Every child born would potentially become the start of a new sequence of exponential growth.'

The President frowned. 'You mean, every new child is like a new grain of rice.'

'No, Mr President. I mean that every new child is like a new chess board. It wouldn't take more than a handful of generations before there are more humans on the planet than have ever lived. And that will keep growing exponentially. Like bacteria in a test tube. Now, population growth can be self-limiting.'

'That's good, right?'

Professor Maitland shrugged. 'I'm a scientist, Mr President. I don't deal in good or bad. I deal in facts. All I can do is encourage you to think about *how* a human population might limit itself. I think we can make a safe prediction that there will be a struggle for resources. These things can be modelled very effectively using fairly basic statistical analysis. There's a limit, for example, to the amount of food a planet can provide. We're likely to see starvation on a massive scale. And that's just the beginning.' She removed her glasses again. 'There's a reason,' she said, 'why we're interested in those labs that we know are carrying out research in this field.'

'And if I may, Mr President,' the National Security Advisor interrupted.

The President nodded soberly. 'Go ahead, Clifford.' His voice was much quieter than before.

The NSA cleared his throat. 'Everything we know about civil unrest,' he said, 'tells us that conflict and violence are more likely in situations where a large number of people compete for a limited quantity of resources. That alone suggests to me that widespread availability of a drug such as this will lead directly to incidents that threaten not only our national security, but also the national security of any country where Elixir is available. But it seems to me that there is a more pressing issue even than that.' The NSA paused for a moment. 'Mr President, I know you're a student of history, and I don't wish to patronise you. But consider: Pure Industries, whoever they are, are not a charity. Elixir will be a commercial product, from which they will surely attempt to make as much money as possible. This means that, inevitably, there will be people who can afford the Elixir, and people who can't. When you have that kind of division in society, I'm afraid there's only one consequence. We've seen it enough times before, but until now the unit of dissent has simply been the dollar.' He raised a bushy eyebrow in the President's direction. 'Can you imagine, Mr President, how much sooner the French Revolution would have happened if the country had been divided not into haves and have-nots, but into lives and live-nots?'

The President was barely moving now as he sat surrounded by his advisors, clearly deep in thought. For a few seconds, Brett thought the meeting must be over. The only movement in the room was the nervous shuffling of the aides against the back wall. But then Don Jackman rose. His nose appeared more hawk-like than ever. 'Mr President,' he said. 'Let me tell you about a friend of mine. Name of Frank. He's a doctor. Mid-fifties. Done pretty well for himself. Don't get me wrong – he's no Bill Gates. But he's comfortable. Looking forward to retirement. Play a little golf. Spoil the grandchildren. He hopes he's got another thirty years in the bag, and that's what his pension company hopes too, because they've done the math. But here's the thing, Mr President. One day Frank wakes up and there's some chick on TV advertising a little bottle of pills and telling him that he doesn't just have thirty years left, but a hundred and thirty, *two* hundred and thirty, whatever the hell it is. All of a sudden he's thinking, do I *really* want to retire. Do I like golf so much I want to play if for a hundred years? Is my pension company *really* going to pay out for another couple of centuries? I'm guessing the answer to all those questions is no. So what does he do? He carries on working, right?'

'I guess,' the President conceded.

'But here's the problem. Maybe Brett Tyler here, he's got a friend too. Younger than him, but a bright kid. Just borrowed his way through med school. It's going to take him a few years to pay off his debts, but that's OK. He's studied hard, his grades are good. He's going to land himself a career, just like everyone's told him he would. Only now...' Jackman held up one finger to emphasise his point. '*Now*, there's a problem. The space on the bottom rung of the ladder that would have been freed up by Frank hacking up the turf at his local golf club and feeding candy to his grandkids, suddenly it's not there anymore. Our young doctor finds himself with a shoulder full of debt and no realistic prospect of getting that job he's just spent so many years training for. He's broke. Certainly too broke to pay for the Elixir for himself. And you know what, Mr President, I reckon he's kind of pissed. Clever too, remember. We're not talking about some college dropout. We're talking about the Franks of the future.'

Jackman inhaled deeply, then looked directly at the President. 'My friend Frank, he's one of a million. We can't even count the number of upcoming, intelligent young people who are going to be consigned to a life of poverty by just this kind of situation. There'll be an army of them, Mr President. An army of clever, resentful youngsters with – literally – nothing to lose. I'd say it's not just *you* that can't afford to make that kind of enemy. It's the whole backbone of the United States administration.'

He paused again. Then, bowing his head, he retook his seat. When he started speaking again, he sounded more statesmanlike. Less dramatic. 'I don't need to tell anybody here that pension provision for the elderly currently costs the United States untold billions a year. Most developed countries have a similar liability relative to GDP. One of our most pressing political issues is how to sustain these payments for an increasing and aging population – and that's even without the help of the Elixir. If the population stopped dying, pension funds would collapse and the only place the man in the street would be able to come to would be the government. And the kind of financial assistance we could provide would be, frankly, insignificant. All this, of course would just exacerbate the kinds of problems Alison and Clifford have outlined. We were elected, Mr President, on a ticket of welfare and equality for all. This product hits the market, we'll be powerless to supply either of these things.' He gave the President a direct look. 'We'll be powerless period.'

The President stood up again. He walked over to the windows of the Oval Office and looked out of them for a full minute. Brett could just see the silhouettes of two Secret Service personnel outside; he could almost feel the tension in the room.

'Professor Maitland,' he said. 'How many labs in the US did you say were working in this field?'

'About 130, Mr President.'

'Just a matter of time, wouldn't you say, before one of them cracks it?'

'Almost certainly.'

'And what happens then? Do we really believe we're sufficiently powerful to stifle this innovation every time it occurs? Do we really think that just because we stop this happening now, we'll stop it happening in the future?'

There was no reply from the company assembled in the Oval Office. The President continued to look out of the window.

'Haven't doctors been extending the life of their patients since the birth of science?' the President continued. 'Isn't that... isn't that what doctors *do*? What if we'd banned penicillin? Or chemotherapy? Are you really telling me that I should just let people die when I know I can let them live?'

Nobody replied. It took a brave man, Brett reckoned, to contradict the President when he was in full flow.

'Nat,' the President said. 'We're yet to hear your view of the situation.'

Brett watched his boss carefully. He knew Windlass well, but even he failed to see any meaningful expression on the Admiral's poker face. 'Mr President,' he said, his voice perfectly calm. 'This is not the first time we've sat together in the Oval Office discussing matters of national security. It's not the first time we've had a tough call to make. And you know what? Half of me wants to say, hell, leave them to it. There's none of us here who won't be able to afford this Elixir. Guys like us, this is the jackpot.'

The President had turned and was looking inquisitively at his security adviser.

'But Mr President, sir, all I can say is this: if there was ever a time for you to listen to your advisers, now is it. Listen hard, Mr President, and listen long. This is the most important decision you'll ever make. Don't let it be the wrong one. This drug is a time bomb, and represents a clear and present danger to the state of the Union. And not just the Union: the state of the world.'

If the President was annoyed at being contradicted, he didn't show it. 'Only this thing isn't a drug, right? If it was, I could legislate against it. But we know that doing that will only force it underground – we have legislation against marijuana, after all. If Elixir is a natural compound, there's nothing we can realistically do to stop people selling it.'

'You're the President,' Windlass told him – rather firmly, Brett thought. 'You could issue an executive order today. I could have Pure Industries closed down in a matter of hours. Put the fear of God into the executives involved. Believe me, sir, you just need to give the word and we'll shut this thing down immediately, and for good.'

All eyes were on the President now. He paced in front of his desk again, both hands behind his back and concentration etched on his face.

Suddenly he stopped.

'Brett,' he said.

Brett startled. 'Mr President?'

'What do *you* think?'

The glare Windlass gave him was burning hot. Brett tried not to look at his boss, but he couldn't help his eyes flickering in the Admiral's direction. He felt he could almost hear his silent instruction to repeat the line the older advisers had all taken. To remain uncontroversial.

He stuttered nervously as he spoke. 'I think, Mr President, that you're surrounded by good advice.' He sensed the sudden tension in the room ease. 'But I also think that if you withhold this product from the public and it becomes common knowledge, the American people won't understand. They'll accuse you of allowing them to die, Mr President. And who knows? Maybe they'd be right.'

Brett set his jaw and looked straight ahead.

The President continued to pace.

He turned and faced his team 'I have a riddle for you all. What is greater than God, more evil than Satan, rich men don't want it, poor men have it, and if you eat it, you die?'

No one spoke. They knew the question was rhetorical.

'Nothing,' he said finally. 'And that's what I intend to do.'

The advisers glanced at each other. 'Nothing... *what*, Mr President?' Windlass asked.

'Nothing, I will not issue an executive order.'

'Mr President...'

'This is America, Nat. For generations, we've been at the forefront of scientific enquiry. We put the first man on the Moon, for God's sake. You think I'm going to use the office of the President to put an end to all that?'

'But Mr President...'

The President raised one hand and Windlass fell silent.

'I hear what you all say. I note it. Nat, I want you to meet with the CEO of Pure Industries. I want you to explain to him our concerns. I want you to make him understand that he has a responsibility that goes beyond the desire of his company to make money.' Windlass looked like he was going to argue, but the President continued quickly. 'Nat, I understand your desire for quick and decisive action. You're a military man and I value you for that. But sometimes a velvet glove is more effective than an iron fist. If everything I've heard today is true, Pure Industries are already extremely powerful. I want them as a friend of the American government, not an enemy. Get them onside. Make them understand everything we've discussed today. Report back to me when you've done it.' He looked round and addressed the room at large. 'I hope it goes without saying that everything we've heard today stays within these four walls?'

A buzz of voices as everyone murmured, 'Yes, Mr President.'

The advisers stood up. Brett followed suit and followed Admiral Windlass as he headed towards to the door. But before he got there, he stopped.

'Mr Tyler.' The President had called him back. 'A word.'

Windlass looked over his shoulder and gave Brett a poisoned look. But he had his instructions. Moments later he was alone in the Oval Office with the President of the United States, who gave him a reassuring smile.

'This is good work,' the President said.

'Thank you, sir.'

'A lot of people would have been tempted to use this information for personal gain. I appreciate that you didn't. I won't forget it.' The President walked back behind his desk and took a seat. 'Takes a brave man to contradict his superiors, Brett. Especially if their superior used to kill bad guys for a living. I have a lot of trust in Admiral Windlass. He's a patriot. Remember that.'

'Yes, Mr President.'

'Alright then. You'd better go. The Admiral will be waiting to give you a good old-fashioned Navy Seal beasting.' He winked at Brett, who smiled broadly, then headed out of the Oval Office and into the ante-room beyond.

Windlass was indeed waiting for him, and even the severe secretary in the ante-room appeared slightly taken aback by the aura of fury that was surrounding him. He said nothing to Brett – just turned heel and marched through the corridors of the West Wing, his aide hurrying to keep up. By the time they were back in the Mercedes, Brett could feel his shirt sticking to his back with sweat, and he was out of breath.

Neither man spoke as the Mercedes swooped out of the White House grounds; and as the Mercedes continued through the streets of Washington DC and past Capitol Hill, the perspiration was not limited to Brett's back. Windlass was about to go nuclear. He was ready to explode. Brett Tyler was preparing to absorb the blast.

They were five minutes out of the White House and traveling north up 16th Street when Windlass suddenly leaned forward and rapped his knuckles sharply on the glass separating them from the secret service drivers. The glass lowered.

'Pull over,' Windlass instructed.

Immediately the Merc came to a halt at the side of the busy road, ignoring the furious sound of a several horns from the drivers of the cars they'd cut up. Windlass instructed the drivers to raise the glass again, then he turned to Brett.

'Get out,' he said.

Brett blinked. 'Sir?'

'Jesus, Tyler. What are you – stupid? I said, get out.'

'We're not at the office yet, sir.'

'No sir, we're not. And you won't be needing to turn up there again. You're fired, Tyler. Don't let me see your face again.'

Brett shook his head. 'Sir, I…'

'If you think –' Windlass was shouting now, and his face had gone an unpleasant shade of red '– that I employ little shits like you to disagree with me in front of the President of the United States, you're even more of an idiot than you look. You're fired, Tyler. Get out of my car and get out of my sight.'

Suddenly Brett was aware that one of the secret service had climbed out of the car and was opening the rear passenger door. He put his head in. 'Everything OK, Admiral Windlass.'

'Everything's just swell. Leastways, it will be when this kid gets the hell out of here. Give him a helping hand, will you?' Windlass turned purposefully and looked out of his own window.

There was no point resisting. Brett knew that. Without another word, he climbed out of the car. The secret service guy slammed the door shut and, with an apologetic look at Brett, retook his seat in the front. The car slipped away into the line of the traffic and soon disappeared from sight.

Brett stood quite still on the sidewalk, ignoring the pedestrians bustling past him. He was strangely numb, as if what had just happened wasn't entirely unexpected. As if it made a strange kind of sense. He found himself remembering the President's words. *I have a lot of trust in Admiral Windlass, Brett. He's a patriot.*

Was he? Or did Windlass have some other agenda, well hidden? Could the President of the United States really have been fooled? Could he really have got it so wrong?'

It was with these thoughts echoing in his head that Brett started walking home through the streets of DC. Subway tickets cost money, he figured, and he was out of a job now.

8

WEDNESDAY, 9.23 A.M., PACIFIC STANDARD TIME

It was impossible to make an omelette, Theodore Croft knew, without breaking some eggs. He also knew he'd broken more than his fair share. Sometimes it felt like the whole damn country was littered with shells – the broken remains of the pathetic individuals on whom he'd trampled on his way to the top. Men, and a fair few women, who bore him more than a grudge. The way he saw it, this was inevitable. He had created an empire, and like all emperors he had his enemies. But he also had an army.

It was a small army. Just ten men, hand-picked. Croft knew more about them than they knew themselves. Their personal details, of course. Their histories. He could monitor their calls, thanks to well-paid informants at the major phone networks. He could read their credit card statements, courtesy of a similar arrangement with a number of bank employees. He knew that they were saying, what they were spending their money on. He knew their opinions and their companions. He knew who they were sleeping with and where they spent their free time. He knew everything. They were his. Entirely.

They were handsomely recompensed for their loyalty, and appropriately punished if it came into question. From time to time, a member of this little army would disappear. His colleagues knew they would never see him again; indeed, some of them would have 'disappeared' him themselves. They also knew the reason for these sudden disappearances: that the individual in question had done something to make Theodore Croft question his allegiance. In truth, Croft had most likely selected him at random. The occasional sacrifice of a perfectly good soldier was a small price to pay for the continued loyalty of the others. And men, even reliable ones, were a sustainable resource, after all. There was always someone waiting in the wings. Even now, he had an Irish immigrant up and coming. Ex-IRA. By all accounts he'd done some nasty stuff back home in their messy little war against the British. They always started out killing and maiming for a cause, Croft reflected, but once you'd killed a few men for an ideal, it wasn't so tough killing a few more for a payday. Mickey Connor, the guy's name was. Even now he was carrying out a job for him. Small, but important. Let the guy show he was trustworthy. Competent. That he could do what he was told

It was not arduous work, being a member of Croft's team. But when you *were* called upon to do a job, he expected you to do it without question. Like any emperor worthy of the name, Croft's word was law. And like any army worth of the name, this one was skilled in carrying out acts of violence with a cold, clinical efficiency. There wasn't a man among them who entertained even the remotest qualms about breaking a target's limbs so severely that they would spend the rest of their days in a wheelchair, drinking liquidised food through a straw. And if the order came down that an individual needed killing, he or she was already as good as dead.

There were three of these men sitting with Theodore Croft today. They didn't look like killers. More like young professionals. Bankers, maybe. Or realtors. Croft looked at them each in turn. Tony Foreman, 32. Balding black hair, smart trousers and an open-necked shirt. Jose Mendoza, 29. On loan from one of the LA gangs he'd befriended recently, picked for being smart and ruthless. Charlton Parker, 28. Blonde hair, knee-length shorts and sailing shirt. Harvard chic. They all wore expensive sunglasses and looked perfectly comfortable in the affluent surroundings of Croft's Malibu pad, sitting by the pool in the pleasant warmth of the morning sun, with tall glasses of iced water by their sides.

'Thanks for joining me so early, fellas,' Croft said. He scratched behind the ears of Rex as he spoke: the Doberman was standing by his chair, as much a part of the meeting as any of them. None of them replied, but he hadn't expected them to. They all knew they were here out of obligation, not choice. He smiled at them. 'You're looking well. Hope you haven't been enjoying yourselves too much. I'd hate to think you were letting yourselves go to seed.'

'You mentioned that it was urgent, Mr Croft,' Tony said. His voice was emotionless.

Croft sipped at his glass of iced water and slowly nodded his head. 'You got it, Tony. Urgent's the word. That's why I need my best guys on it.'

If the trio were pleased with the compliment, they didn't show it.

'I've got these guys,' he said. 'Two guys and a girl, actually. Kind of thorns in my side. I guess you all know how much I hate thorns, right?'

'Just give us name, Mr Croft. We'll deal with it.'

'Tony, I don't know what I'd do without you. Really – I don't.' He paused. 'But here's the thing. I'd kind of like a word with them before they…' Croft shrugged meaningfully. 'Before they slip from our tender embrace.'

For the first time, the men displayed some kind of reaction. It was almost imperceptible: just the slight tightening of skin around the eyes. Tony chose his words carefully. 'Mr Croft, I'm not sure that's a great idea. If you want to stay out of the loop, you've got to stay out of the loop, if you get my meaning.'

Croft sipped his water again, fixing Tony with a stare over the brim of his glass. 'You know what, Tony? I'm lucky to have a guy like you on the team. Ordinarily I'd bow to your professionalism in matters of security. But on this occasion, I rather think I'm going to have to insist.' A pensive look crossed his face.

Tony inclined his head. 'Whatever you want, Mr Croft. We'll do everything we can to keep your fingerprints off this thing. I might bring in our Irish friend when he's finished his current engagement. Could be a good opportunity for him to get his hands properly dirty.'

'No,' Croft replied quickly. A bit *too* quickly. 'I need men I can rely on. You three. Nobody else.'

Tony shrugged, as if to say: *you're the boss*. 'How soon do you want to go ahead?'

'Now. As soon as possible.'

'You got names for us?'

'Oh, I've got more than names, Tony. I have addresses, photographs, family members – whatever you need. I'm sure guys of your capability will find it all very straightforward.' Croft stood up. 'The details are inside,' he said. 'Why don't you come with me. I see no reason to delay the proceedings. They say that procrastination is the thief of time. Frankly, I couldn't agree more, could you?'

'No, Mr Croft,' Tony replied dutifully, and Croft's three employees followed him from the pool area to the inside of the house, ready to receive the remainder of their brief.

Pat Dolan stood by a fountain outside a well-appointed condo near central Laguna Niguel. He could do with a cigarette, he thought to himself; but to loiter outside smoking in a neighborhood like this was akin to being a wino with can of Special Brew in one of the posher areas of Belfast. He'd stick out. People would stare at him. And that could cause problems.

He checked his watch. A quarter to ten. Anybody who was going to work should have left by now, which meant it was time for Pat to start his own little bit of employment. He stepped round the fountain and into the lobby of the condo. A concierge behind a small desk looked up from his book and gave him an enquiring but not entirely welcoming glance. Pat gave the man his most winning smile. 'Top of the morning to you.'

The concierge returned the greeting with an grudging nod.

'Wanting to pay a visit to a Mr Byng,' he said. 'Apartment 11.'

The concierge looked back at his book. 'It's Wednesday morning,' he said.

There was an uncomfortable silence. 'Do you not speak to visitors on Wednesday mornings?' Pat asked finally.

The concierge placed his book on the table in front of him with barely disguised impatience. 'It's Wednesday morning,' he repeated, 'so most everyone here's at work.'

'Ah, of course.' Pat Dolan was playing the idiot Irishman for all it was worth, because he knew it was a stereotype people were all too willing to believe. 'Well, I'm sorry to be disturbing you.'

He turned and walked back towards the entrance, but stopped halfway there.

'Apartment 11, did you say?'

The concierge grunted.

'Maybe I'll just go and knock in his door then. You never know, hey?'

But if the concierge had an opinion of that suggestion, he didn't show it. His nose was back in his book, and Pat was free to walk past him and step inside the elevator that was already open here on the first floor. Forty-five seconds later he was outside Apartment 11 and pulling on a pair of latex surgeon's gloves.

It took less than a minute for him to pick the lock, but despite his facility in such matters he was unable to do so without forcing it a little and damaging the mechanism. He stepped inside the apartment and closed the door behind him. It was a sparsely furnished place. Stylish, Pat supposed. Very male. But he wasn't here to appraise the interior décor. He had work to do. And he needed to do it quickly, before anyone else was alerted to his presence...

The summons, when it came, was short. A single piece of paper. At the top, surrounded by a blue circle, was the presidential seal. And underneath, the most famous address in the world: The White House, Washington.

Tom sat in his office, acutely aware of Ruth hovering by the doorway. She had watched him open the envelope in silence, and was clearly waiting for Tom to tell her what the missive contained.

'Who delivered this?' he asked his PA. There was no postage stamp on the envelope bearing his name and the Pure Industries address.

'A courier, Mr Shaw. Not the usual sort. Suit and tie. Rather full of himself, truth be told. Insisted I sign for it.'

Tom read the letter again. It was curt to the point of rudeness, requesting and requiring him to attend the White House the following day at 11.00 a.m., signed on behalf of a certain Admiral Nathanial Windlass. No indication of the reason for his summons, nor any suggestion that he had a choice whether to attend or not. It wasn't an invitation. It was an instruction.

'Ruth, ask Dr Leo to join me, if you would.'

His PA nodded slowly and left the office. Five minutes later, Rachael walked in and closed the door behind her. She only had to take one look at Tom to realize something was wrong. 'What is it?'

Tom handed her the note and watched her eyes scan the message twice. She laid it on Tom's desk again.

'You think they know?' she asked. 'About Elixir, I mean.'

'Put it this way,' Tom replied. 'I don't think Admiral–' He checked the name on the letter '–Admiral Windlass wants my opinion on the shipping forecast.'

'How did they find out?' Rachael helped herself to a seat opposite the desk. 'We've been discreet, we haven't made any kind of announcement…'

'I don't know,' Tom said thoughtfully. 'I just don't know…'

'Well they're not dragging you all the way to Washington to shake you by the hand, Tom.' There was a hint of panic in Rachael's voice.

Tom nodded. 'You said it.'

'Tom, listen carefully.' Rachael's eyes were suddenly intense. 'You *can't* go.'

Tom looked meaningfully at the letter. 'You read it, Rachael. What do you think they'll do if I fail to show? Forget all about it?'

Rachael stared at him. 'You can't go,' she whispered. 'Tom, I brought Elixir to you for a reason. It *mustn't* end up in the hands of government. They won't be able to help using it for political ends. They'll… I don't know… use it for military purposes. Or keep it under wraps. We've got a duty, Tom. A duty to make it as widely available as we can. It needs to be put out to market – all over the world – by someone responsible. Someone like *you*.' She looked desperate. She *sounded* desperate.

Tom closed his eyes. He needed a clear head, and that barely seemed possible these days. So much going on. So much to think about…

'I have to go,' he told her quietly. Rachael opened her mouth to protest, but he held up one hand. 'Hear me out. I *have* to go, but I'm bringing you with me. Kyle too. And whatever happens, we're not handing over the formula. You have my word.'

'But what if they… what if they *make* you?'

'How *can* they? I don't know it. You're the only person with the full formula, Rachael. You're the only one who can decide who we give it to.'

'What if they make *me*?'

Tom glanced at the photograph of himself, Jane and Jack that sat in a frame on his desk. 'We live in America, Rachael. Nobody's going to make you do anything. You have my word. I'll inform Peter and Sylvia about what's happening. They can run the ship while we're away. I don't know who this Admiral Windlass is, but I promise you, he's not going to bully us.' He smiled. 'At least, he can *try* to, but we're not going to give in.'

Rachael looked far from sure. 'Someone must have told them,' she said. 'They *must* have. How else would they know?' Her eyes widened. 'Peter,' she said. 'He's been acting… *weird*. Ever since we told him about Elixir. Maybe he's…'

'*Rachael*,' Tom said sharply. 'Enough.' He knew he sounded like a stern schoolmaster, but he didn't mind. 'We're a team,

OK? Don't forget that. Peter can be prickly, I know, and you haven't hit it off. But you will. He's a good man and he has the best interests of the company at heart. I won't have you saying anything about him to me that you wouldn't say to his face. Understood?'

Rachael nodded mutely. For the first time ever, there was awkwardness between them. Tom picked up the phone on his desk and pressed a button. Ruth answered immediately.

'I need you to book me some flights,' he said firmly. 'Myself, Rachael, Kyle. Tonight. Washington.'

It was midday.

Kyle Byng was heading home from the office. If he was going to go to Washington, to the White House of all places, he needed to change and get a few things together.

His apartment was part of a large condo in a fashionable area near the center of Laguna Niguel. There was a fountain just outside, and a smartly dressed concierge in the lobby. Normally Kyle would stop to chat of his own accord, but not today. Time was short, so he just gave the concierge a friendly nod. The concierge, however, had other ideas. 'Hey, Mr Byng, some guy came round looking for you this morning. Told him it was Wednesday morning, most proper folk are at work. He still went up to bang on your door, though.' He shook his head, as if lamenting the manners of some people.

'Thanks, Al,' Kyle said quietly. 'Maybe he left a message or something.'

He stepped into the waiting elevator.

Kyle could tell there was something wrong the moment he put his key to the lock of his apartment. The keyhole was damaged. Someone had forced it and the door wasn't even latched shut. It swung slowly open at the lightest touch, leaving Kyle to stare from the doorway at the devastation inside.

It was a minimalist apartment. There was art on the walls – including an original by the German painter Sepp Hilz, whom Kyle had always admired. The main room was open-plan, with a slick white kitchen area in one corner and expensive modern furniture sitting on a burnished floor of solid oak. Ordinarily this room was immaculate. Kyle lived alone, and he had a sense of pride in his own space. Nothing was ever out of place, and that was how he'd left it when he'd gone to work that morning.

Now, though, it couldn't have been more different.

The leather sofa had been upended. The same went for the glass coffee table that normally stood in front of it, but which was now smashed into tiny pieces. Whoever had done this couldn't have been quiet, but on a working morning like this there would have been nobody around to hear them. Every door in the kitchen was open, the contents spilled out over the floor. The books had been ripped from his bookcase. One particular volume caught his eye, spread-eagled on the floor. It was a history of the Second World War – an interest of his, and one of his favourite books on the subject. He could see that some of the pages had come loose from the spine. Kyle closed the door behind him, blinking at the chaos and straining his ears to check if the intruders were still here.

Silence.

He walked across the room. At the far side, the door to his bedroom was open. In there, it was the same story. But it wasn't the bedclothes on the floor or the turned-out drawers that grabbed Kyle's attention. It wasn't the open closet doors or the mirror hanging at an angle.

It was Kyle's safe. No longer bolted to the floor inside the closet, but ripped up and jemmied open, its contents sprawled on the floor.

Kyle's safe was only small. Enough to hold a few valuables – his late father's watch, a pair of diamond cufflinks he'd received as a christening present. More valuable than either of these, however, was a small slip of paper on which Kyle had written, in clear block capitals, the following words: UV CURING FREQUENCY 365 NANOMETERS.

Kyle was no scientist. The information Rachael Leo had given him had been meaningless, and he knew he would have forgotten it had he not written it down clearly and concisely for his reference. 'Don't let anyone see that,' Rachael had warned.

'For my eyes only,' Kyle had told her. He remembered the mysterious smile that had played across her lips as he'd said that.

Back to reality. Kyle knew, before he even checked, that this small slip of paper would be the only thing that had been stolen.

He was right.

He didn't pause to tidy up the flat. He didn't even pause to contact the police. The very second he realized what the intruders had taken, he was pulling out his phone and hitting a speed dial.

The call was answered after two rings.

'Tom, it's Kyle,' he said immediately. His voice was shaking. 'You need to come to my flat. I know we need to get to the airport, but it's important. Bring Rachael. We've got ourselves a problem.'

Tom stared in disbelief at the state of Kyle's apartment.

'I haven't touched anything,' Kyle said. He looked pale. Shaken. 'Don't know why.'

'Are you sure it's gone?' Leo was even more ashen-faced than Kyle, like the blood had drained from her veins. 'I mean, maybe they were just looking for valuables and…'

'It was in the safe. Now it's not. Nothing else missing. I'm sorry, Rachael. I just… I thought it would be secure here. I mean, nobody even *knew* about it.'

'Looks like you thought wrong.'

'Rachael, I…'

But Rachael had turned abruptly away. 'You think this is linked to the White House letter?'

Tom blinked. 'What do you mean?'

'Isn't it obvious? They know about the Elixir, right? We're not going to Washington for a pat on the back, you said so yourself. And just to remind us how serious they can be, they do this. I don't know… to *scare* us, I guess.'

A pause.

'We need to get to the airport,' Tom said decisively.

'Tom, we *can't*. *Please*… they're only going to…'

'I can't avoid the White House, Rachael. You *know* that. You think I'm going to stay away from the Feds and the CIA? If they've started this idiocy, the only thing to do is talk to them.

Rachael looked like she might cry. Kyle made to put a comforting arm around her, but she shrugged him away angrily.

'What do you think they'd have done,' she demanded, 'if you'd *been* here. They might have… I don't know, Kyle, they might have *killed* you.' It was immediately clear to Tom that this was a thought Rachael couldn't bear. She turned to her boss. 'And what about the rest of us? What about Peter and Sylvia and you and me?'

'And what if it *wasn't* the government, Rachael.' He said it a bit more sharply than he'd intended, and for a moment Rachael was quiet.

'Who else could it be?'

'I don't know. But look, we all understand that this isn't going to be an easy ride, and maybe we could use some help. Nobody's going to kill anybody, Rachael. This is America, remember? We're the good guys. Maybe we *need* the President on our side. At the very least we need to hear what his people have to say.'

Rachael and Kyle stood there in silence.

'Come on,' Tom told them. 'We need to go. Our flight is scheduled for three and I still need to explain to Pete and Sylvia what's going on.'

Tony Foreman was happy with his life. Croft was a creep, no doubt about it. Cold. Tony had seen a show on TV once. It was all about psychopaths and how they were often charming and high-achieving. Theodore Croft was more than a psycho, Tony reckoned. There probably wasn't even a word invented to describe his boss. But it made no difference to Tony.

Being on a retainer from Theodore Croft was a cushy number, and he knew it. Those monthly payments from an anonymous bank account were enough to keep him housed in a fancy apartment with plenty of cash to spare to live the kind of life he wanted. Hell of a sight better than the US army wage he'd been drawing right up until the point where he'd earned himself a dishonorable discharge for the enthusiastic – and unwarranted – killing of three Iraqi civilians in Basra. He'd avoided a stretch in a military prison simply because the US government was trying to keep a lid on the adverse publicity, and there was certainly no way he intended to screw things up now by being anything other than highly – ruthlessly – professional. If Theodore Croft wanted a couple of people softened up, then as far as Tony was concerned they were already butter.

He checked his watch. 21.35 hrs. Dark outside his car – a 1960s Chevy – and humid. His shirt was damp and crumpled. That annoyed Tony – he liked to stay smart. No matter, he told himself. He'd be able to vent his frustrations very soon.

21.40. He saw headlights approaching from the other end of this spacious residential street. The car in question pulled over on the other side of the road and stopped just opposite Tony. A tall, thin man climbed out. In the yellow light of the street lamp, Tony could see he had a slight stoop in his shoulders. He opened the door of his own car and stepped out into the street.

The man with the stoop walked along the sidewalk for about ten yards, then turned left up the pathway of a modest detached house with white wooden railings around the perimeter. He was walking into the correct house, which meant he was Tony's man. Tony picked up his pace, crossing the road quickly and reaching the opposite sidewalk when his target was half way up the garden path.

Suddenly the man with stoop halted. He looked over his shoulder and saw Tony striding towards his house. A look of panic flickered across his face. He hurried towards his front door, but by now Tony was running. He stormed through the front gate, almost knocking it from its hinges. His target was at the front door, fumbling for his keys, desperately trying to insert one of them into the keyhole but unable to on account of his shivering hands. He looked over his shoulder again, and when he saw Tony just five yards away, his efforts became twice as frenzied and half as effective.

And by the time he had managed to slide the key into the lock, Tony was right behind him.

He stretched out his left hand and grabbed his target's left shoulder. A solid yank, and the man with the stoop spun round, his back against the door now. His eyes widened as Tony pulled a small firearm from his jacket pocket and pressed it against the guy's large forehead.

'Know much about guns?' Tony breathed.

The man shook his head, his eyes wild.

'Well let's give you a little lesson, huh? This baby here is a Browning semi-automatic. You're probably wondering what the long thing at the end is. Suppressor. Silences the shot. That means that when I shoot you, and the 9mm round goes through your skull and out the back of your head, all anyone will hear is a sound a bit like someone knocking on the door. And you know what? I've got a little confession to make.' He leaned in closer and spoke in a loud whisper. 'I quite like shooting people. Don't ask me why. Just the way I am, I suppose.'

The man was shaking. Tony wasn't sure, but he thought he caught the smell of urine rising from below.

'Are you Peter Wright?'

The man nodded.

'Anyone else at home, Peter?'

'N… no,' he stuttered. 'I live alone.'

Tony nodded. 'Turn around,' he instructed. 'Open the door and walk in quietly. I'll be right behind you, and you know what will happen if you do anything that makes me nervous, right?'

Peter Wright did as he was told. Seconds later they were inside the house.

It was dark in here, with the musty smell of a bachelor's house. Tony told his captive to switch on the light, which he did with trembling hands. They were in a sparse hallway: wooden floors and walls that needed a coat of paint.

They were also not alone.

Two other men stood at the far end of the hallway. Tony's associates, Jamie and Charlton, were side by side and had grim looks on their faces.

'How did you get into my house?' Peter breathed. He turned to Tony. It was almost as if, in the unexplained presence of these two extra men, he was looking to Tony for security. Better the devil you know. 'How did *they* get into my house.'

Tony answered not with words, but with violence. It only took a single blow to the back of his neck to make Peter Wright crumple to his knees. There was *definitely* a smell of urine, he decided. They guy had wet himself. Good. It meant he was helpless with terror, and terrified people are easy to control.

Tony looked over at Jamie and Charlton. 'Secure him,' he said. 'I'll get on to the boss, tell him we're ready.'

Theodore Croft was not far away.

He seldom had a chance to drive his Bentley convertible – his driver was always on call to ferry him wherever he wanted to go – but when he did, he always found it relaxing. Cruising down Highway 5 from LA to Laguna Niguel that morning had been a pleasant experience. It had allowed him to gather his thoughts. And there were plenty of thoughts to gather.

Now it was a little before 10 p.m. and he was still cruising, circulating round the wide residential streets of this sleepy suburb like a John searching for a hooker. Earlier on, the car had drawn admiring stares from the kids, but they'd all gone to bed now and the streets were practically deserted. Dead. Christ, he thought to himself. He'd kill himself if he had to live in a place like this.

He glanced at the passenger seat. It was empty apart from a small slip of paper. He read through the symbols. They meant very little to him, but that didn't matter. He already had the first piece of information, and the second was within his grasp…

His cell rang, and Theodore Croft startled. He was clearly more anxious than he realized. He answered the call immediately and recognized the voice of Tony Foreman. Good man, Tony. Did what he was told. Seemed a shame that he would have to…

'We've got him, boss. You know our location.'

Croft nodded to himself but didn't reply before hanging up. He pressed a couple of buttons on the vehicle's built-in Sat-Nav. The computer's voice – female and soporific – told him to perform a U-turn. He did so, and moments later was on the way to Peter Wright's house.

He rapped gently on the door once he had arrived. It opened almost immediately and Tony Foreman was there.

'You look dishevelled, Tony,' he said as he stepped inside, noticing the patches of sweat under his armpits. 'He's not giving you any trouble, I hope?'

'No trouble, boss,' Tony replied. His face had flickered with annoyance at Croft's comment. Funny, Croft thought to himself, how even the most violent men could be vain. He allowed Tony to close the door behind him, before leading him down the hallway and into a room off to the left. He stood in the doorway for a few seconds while he took everything in.

It was a shabby room. The curtains – thick and beige – were drawn, and the only light came from a standard lamp just next to the windows. Along the left hand wall was an old record player with a bookcase full of vinyl records beside it. It looked extremely old-fashioned, but not as outmoded as the shapeless sofa and two matching armchairs, upholstered in a gaudy, but faded Paisley, and surrounding a low mahogany coffee table.

Peter Wright, who despite the surroundings was an avid collector of antique furniture, was sitting on an ornately carved wooden chair between the back of the sofa and the window. Two lengths of sturdy rope fastened him to the chair, and a long strip of packing tape had been wrapped several times round his mouth and head to keep him silent. His eyes, however, shrieked his horror more eloquently than any screams. Theodore Croft took a moment to examine his own feelings. Somewhere in the back of his mind he had worried that he might feel nauseous at the sight of what was to come. After all, he had never yet been present at any of the similar occasions he had orchestrated. But no. So far he felt very little; except, perhaps, for a vague sensation of anticipation.

He stepped further into the room. As he walked round the back of the sofa, he saw that Peter's chair was sitting not on the greying carpet that covered the floor, but on a bright blue plastic sheet, approximately three yards square.

Croft looked round at Tony. 'The others?' he asked.

'Watching the front and the back.'

Croft nodded. He stepped on to the tarpaulin and stared into Peter's terrified face for a few seconds.

'First things first, Mr Wright,' he said, his voice little more than a whisper. 'I think it's very important that we understand each other. You have some information I need. You're going to tell me what it is, otherwise things are going to get extremely unpleasant for you.'

Wright struggled. Pathetic, really, Croft thought to himself, the way he battled against the thick ropes with his thin body.

There was sweat over his balding head, and a dark patch on the groin of his light grey suit trousers.

Croft turned away. 'Tony,' he said. 'I think we need to show Mr Wright that we mean what we say. Don't you?'

He walked off the plastic sheet and allowed Tony to approach. His henchman, he saw, was holding a pair of garden secateurs. He could tell they were new because the blades were shining and free of dirt and rust.

And sharp, he thought to himself. Very sharp.

He didn't know what Tony was going to do. This was his field of expertise, not Croft's. So he stood by the standard lamp and watched carefully.

Wright's eyes were bulging as he saw Tony approach. He started to make a noise – a muffled squeaking from behind the layers of packing tape – which grew louder as Tony knelt down to one side and grabbed the pinkie on his left hand. Croft's henchman looked as calm as a Malibu morning as he unclasped the secateurs, put Wright's little finger between the blades, and squeezed.

The secateurs did not sever the digit easily. Croft stared in fascination as blood started to flow copiously and to drip on to the blue tarpaulin – it looked almost black against it – and over Tony's hand. Tony looked at it in annoyance, and then up at Wright, as if this was all somehow his fault. Wright himself was silent. He had thrown his head back in shock and had scrunched his eyes closed. Croft wondered casually when their victim would, actually, want to scream. He realized that Tony had let go of the secateurs, but they were embedded in the bone and remained attached to the finger. Tony wiped his hand on Wright's suit, before returning his hand to the secateurs and giving a second, brutal squeeze. This time he managed to sever the bone completely. And it was now, as the finger itself fell on to the tarpaulin and spattered in the puddle of blood that had formed on the plastic sheet, that Peter Wright started to give voice to his agony. The squealing sound returned – a series of short, high-pitched whimpers that sounded curiously to Croft like the squeaking of an animal in pain. Tony wiped his hands on his victim's clothes again, then stood back to survey his work.

Wright was shaking, so much so that the blood seeping from the stump of his severed finger was now spraying all over the tarpaulin. Croft stepped carefully around it to the other side of the room, where he spent a few seconds browsing the record collection before finally choosing an album.

'You're a man of taste, Mr Wright,' he announced, holding up his selection. 'I'm a fan of Wagner myself. So powerful.'

He slid the record from its sleeve onto the turntable and gently rested the needle on the spinning vinyl. A swell of violins filled the air. Not too loud, but certainly loud enough to mask the continuing sound of Peter Wright's panicked, agonized squeaks from anyone who happened to be passing the house. Croft looked over at Tony. 'Remove the tape,' he said. 'If he screams, kill him.'

Tony approached the chair. His very proximity made Peter Wright shake even more vigorously, like he was being approached by the Devil himself. Tony placed the bloody secateurs carefully down on the tarpaulin and, like a surgeon swapping his tools, removed a flick-knife from his pocket.

He flicked it open, then walked closer to his victim, who was shaking his head and squeaking more than ever.

He slashed the packing tape twice – once under each of Peter's cheeks – then ripped away the section covering his lips. Peter's face started to bleed immediately: the knife had scored his skin and when Tony had pulled away the tape it had opened up the wound on the right-hand side. The thin, brutalised man drew a sharp intake of breath and for a moment he looked like he was going to scream. One glance, however, at Croft's stony face and the breath dissolved into a series of racking sobs.

'Now then, Mr Wright,' Croft continued. His voice was deathly quiet. 'I imagine you know what I want, so shall we put an end to this foolishness and get down to business? Pure Industries' magic potion. Tell me all about it.'

Peter shook his head. His breathing was coming in short, sharp gasps, and his chin and shirt were smeared in the blood that was now dripping from his face. When he spoke, it was in a reedy, rasping voice. Croft had to listen very hard to understand him. 'I don't know anything,' the old man whispered. 'Please... I don't know *anything*...'

Croft inclined his head. 'Tony,' he said. 'Take the whole hand off.'

The expression that crossed Peter's face was one of such horror that even Croft was momentarily taken aback. He opened his mouth to speak – presumably to beg – but no words came. The bleeding man's distress had no effect on Tony. He grabbed the hand and made to slice his knife across the wrist.

'Wait,' Croft told him.

He looked, dead-eyed, at Peter.

'Shall we try again?' he asked. 'The Elixir, Mr Wright. If I'm satisfied you've told me everything you know, I'll let you live. If not…' He shrugged his shoulders, as if to say: *it's up to you*.

The Wagner swelled. Peter Wright looked as if he was one the point of passing out.

And then he started to mumble.

At first Croft was unable to make out what he was saying. Wright's head had drooped and his chin was resting on his chest. If his lips hadn't been moving, Croft might have been unaware that he was even speaking. He stepped back to the turntable and swiped the needle from the record. It scratched noisily and fell silent. But Wright's mumbling continued. Croft moved closer. He was standing on the tarpaulin, his feet just inches from the puddle of his blood. He leaned in to listen.

'One hundred and fifty,' Peter was saying. '*One hundred and fifty…*'

'A hundred and fifty what?' Croft hissed.

A pause. Peter drew several deep breaths.

'Celsius,' he whispered. 'A hundred and fifty Celsius. For one hour…'

His eyes started to roll.

Croft stood up straight. He had what he needed. He stepped back from the tarpaulin and looked over at Tony. His employee was looking askance at him. Croft nodded, and Tony clearly understood what that nod meant.

The room was silent apart from the Peter's heavy breathing and the regular dripping of the blood from his wounded hand onto the tarpaulin. Croft didn't look back as he walked out. The old man was no use to him now, and he had no particular desire to watch Tony kill him. He had more important things to do. Much more important.

If Peter Wright's final moments were accompanied by a scream, Theodore Croft wasn't there to hear it. He had left the house, slipped back into his car and had already started to leave this quiet suburb of Laguna Niguel. He drove slowly. This was the last place on God's earth he was likely to be, and he really didn't feel like explaining his presence here to anybody at all.

9

Thursday, 4.28 a.m., Eastern Standard Time

Dr Rachael Leo's room was comfortable enough, but she hadn't even bothered trying to sleep. Three a.m. Eastern Standard Time when they'd touched down in Washington, and four a.m. when they'd checked into this hotel. Rachael couldn't even remember its name. She was too distracted for that.

She paced. Up and down. Up and down. Her fingernails dug into her palms. She chewed her lower lip. She hadn't even turned off the welcome screen on the television. Its bland elevator music played in the background.

Rachael caught sight of herself in the mirror. Her pale blue eyes were bloodshot. Black bags around them. She looked terrible. It crossed her mind that she had nothing, really, to worry about. She had the Elixir. Which meant she had everything, surely.

Except it didn't.

She stopped pacing. She closed her eyes. Then she spun round and left her room. Ten seconds later she was knocking on the door opposite. One of the hotel maids trundled past her with a trolley full of fresh towels and an enquiring look. Rachael ignored her and rapped on the door again.

Kyle appeared in the doorway. His hair was tousled and he'd clearly been catching some shuteye. For a moment he looked confused. 'Did I oversleep?'

Rachael shook her head. 'Can I come in?' she asked in a small voice.

'Ah... sure,' Kyle said delicately. He stepped aside and Rachael marched into the room. Once he'd shut the door and turned towards her, he had the look of a guy who thought his luck was in; but that soon fell away when he saw the anxiety on Rachael's face.

'Hey, what's up?' he asked gently.

'I'm sorry,' Rachael said. 'Back in your apartment, I was... I was just scared. Not just about the Elixir, but about... about *you*. You could have been hurt, and it would have been my fault.'

'Forget about it,' Kyle told her, and he smiled. 'You know I'm not likely to stay angry with you for long, right? And I'm big enough and ugly enough to look after myself. But, hey, something else is bugging you. Tell me what it is.'

Rachael chewed once more on her lower lip. 'It's Tom,' she whispered.

'What about him?'

Rachael was almost on the verge of tears. Kyle helped her to sit on the edge of his bed and put one arm around her shoulders. 'What about Tom, Rachael? What is it?'

'I just... I don't know what's going to happen when we get to the White House. I'm worried that Tom is just too ... *nice* ... to stand up to them. He's a good man, Kyle, but sometimes I think perhaps I took the Elixir to the wrong guy. I just don't see how he can stand up to the President's men. But it's vital that Elixir doesn't get into the government's hands. You see that, don't you?'

Kyle nodded. 'Even if the current guy doesn't start abusing it, the next one will. We'll have the military guzzling Elixir to the exception of everyone else. I totally get it, Rachael.'

'Then what are we going to do?'

'What we're going to do – what *you're* going to do – is stop worrying.'

Rachael blinked at him.

'Tom's a mild guy. But don't mistake that for weakness. He's made of tough stuff. You only have to see him sitting by his wife's bedside to know that. He's come here to do a job and he's totally going to do it, Rachael.'

'But what if he *doesn't*?'

Kyle hugged her a bit more tightly, and she rested her head on his shoulder.

'He will,' Kyle said quietly, but Rachael could help thinking he sounded as though he was trying to convince himself as well as her. They stayed like that for perhaps a minute without speaking. Rachael didn't know what it was that made her do it, but suddenly she raised her head again and brushed her lips against Kyle's. Then, just as suddenly, she looked away.

'Sorry,' she whispered. 'I just…'

But she didn't finish. Kyle was kissing her again, more seriously this time. For the briefest of moments she forgot about the White House and about Tom, and about the Elixir, and allowed herself to get lost in Kyle's warm, comforting embrace.

Admiral Nathanial Windlass never opened the Bible that sat by his bedside. It was as much a piece of decoration as the expensive silk curtains and the crystal chandelier that hung from the ceiling, chosen by his wife whose tastes were nothing if not exclusive. As he climbed out of bed the following morning at 6 a.m., however, he found his eyes lingering on the red leather binding and, for the first time in years, he opened it up.

The wafer-thin paper on which the tiny text was printed was gilt-edged. It appeared very delicate between the coarse fingers of Windlass's army hands. And yet he flicked through it with ease. As a child growing up in South Dakota, the Bible had been more important than any schoolbook, and it had been unthinkable not to attend the little wooden church on a weekly basis. He had soon lost his faith after joining the military – you don't have to kill too many people to stop believing in the sanctity of human life – but the scriptures that had been drummed into him as a child were still imprinted on his mind, like words engraved in tablets of stone. And as he sat on the edge of his bed, he found himself searching for something in particular. It didn't take him long to find it. Matthew, chapter 7, verse 26. *And everyone that heareth these sayings of mine, and doeth them not shall be likened unto a foolish man, which built his house upon the sand…*

A house upon the sand, he thought to himself. He looked around the lavishly furnished bedroom, thinking about the money Lynda was haemorrhaging in Vegas, money that was on credit from people you really didn't want to be indebted to, and a familiar sensation – somewhere between fear and panic – oozed into his stomach. He slammed the Bible down with a curse, dressed quickly and pulled open the curtains.

The early-morning sky was a clear blue. The manicured lawn, which led down to a high perimeter fence, had a jewel-like sprinkling of dew. But Windlass wasn't looking at the weather, or the scenery. He was staring through the railings of the electronic entrance gate fifty yards from the house. And at the man who stood there, leaning nonchalantly on his car.

He felt his blood freeze.

Windlass didn't recognize the man, or the car, but he didn't need to. He knew why he was there. He knew that the people to whom he owed money were neither impressed by his position of influence, nor fearful of his military background. All they wanted was their money, and the thug posted outside his house, dragging on a cigarette, was there to remind him that he was being watched. Day and night. And if he failed to pay...

The thug stubbed his cigarette out on the ground and looked directly up at Windlass's bedroom window. He gave a cold smile, then climbed back into his car. Windlass watched him drive away. He was left with a sick feeling that he knew would be with him for the rest of the day.

Windlass whipped the curtain closed again and stormed out of the bedroom. Minutes later, the electronic gates were opening, and the Admiral was driving away from his home.

'The Roosevelt Room, Mr Shaw. Please make yourself comfortable. Admiral Windlass will be with you as soon as he can.'

The young White House intern had short black hair and a short black skirt. She had obviously been told that Tom was the significant visitor, and so she barely acknowledged the existence either of Kyle or Leo who had walked several paces behind them along the corridors of the West Wing.

'Is there anything I can get you, Mr Shaw? Iced water? Coffee?'

'Nothing. Thank you.' The intern promptly left the room, closing the door behind her.

Tom looked around. The Roosevelt Room was dominated by a long wooden table with upholstered leather seats. Oil paintings hung on the wall – former Presidents and landscapes – and a mahogany grandfather clock ticked noisily.

Kyle and Leo were watching him. Not overtly, but from the corners of their eyes. They'd been doing it all morning. And when they weren't watching him, they were exchanging long glances at each other. Tom wasn't stupid. He had noticed the attraction between Kyle and Leo. Hell, he approved of it, with the warm affection of some indulgent uncle. But this was different. Not *lovers'* glances. *Anxious* glances. He didn't blame them. Everyone knew they hadn't been summoned to the White House to admire the artwork.

There was no talking. The grandfather clock continued to tick. Tom took a seat, not at the head of the table, but in the middle along one edge. He was nervous. It made no difference that he was in one of the most famous rooms in the country. What was coming? What did the government know? What were they going to say?

Tick tock. Tick tock. The clock struck 11.00 with a tinny little chime.

Bang on time, the door opened and a broad-shouldered man with a military bearing strode in. He was alone, and carried a wallet folder which he held close to his chest. Once he had closed the door behind him, he looked at each of them in turn, before settling on Tom.

'Mr Shaw?'

Tom stood up. 'Admiral Windlass.'

'Good to meet you, sir.' Tom held out his hand and the Admiral shook it firmly. 'Thank you for coming at such short notice.'

'Thanks for the invitation,' Tom said lightly. 'Not every day you get to visit the White House.'

'Never gets old, Mr Shaw. Believe me, it never gets old. A lot of great people have sat where you're sitting now. Your staff?'

'Rachael Leo and Kyle Byng,' Tom replied. 'Maybe Kyle's name if familiar to you. Has a nice little apartment in Laguna Niguel. Could do with tidying up.'

Windlass gave him an odd look. 'Can't say it *is* familiar to me, Mr Shaw. Can't say it is.' He took a seat opposite Tom, while Kyle and Rachael sat on either side of their boss. Them and us, but it didn't seem to bother Windlass. He shuffled his papers around without really looking at them, then fixed Tom with a piercing glare. Like the intern, he too barely seemed even to register the existence of the others.

'First things first.' Admiral Windlass spoke briskly. 'You need to understand that I speak with the full authority of the President of the United States.'

Tom had done some research on this guy, of course. As they'd sat in the lounge of LAX, he'd Googled Windlass's name and read up on his history. A divisive character, it seemed. Close to the President yet decried by some in Capitol Hill as a warmonger, too keen to solve problems with a military rather than a diplomatic response. Tom had found pictures of him as a younger man in a uniform with an impressive array of decorations. Although he could tell they were the same person, somehow he couldn't reconcile the fresh-faced soldier with the self-important looking man sitting opposite him now.

Tom inclined his head, but made sure his expression didn't give anything away.

'It has come to the attention of the President,' Windlass said, 'that you are about to take a product called Elixir to market. Correct?'

Tom didn't say anything. He didn't even let any sign of acknowledgement creep on to his face. All his life, Tom's default position was to defer to important characters like Windlass, he knew his place and these people were experts, in the employ of the President of the Unites States of America no less. Obviously, the crème de la crème. Who was he to argue? But something was stirring deep inside Tom, driven by a realization that the Elixir was important, not just for Pure, or, even the USA but the whole of mankind. He was the Elixir's Champion.

Windlass didn't look impressed. He cleared his throat and continued. 'The effects of this new drug…'

'It's not a drug,' Tom interrupted. 'Important to make that distinction now, I think, Admiral Windlass.'

Windlass scowled. 'The effects of this… He waved his hand as he searched for a word. 'This *thing* are well known to us. I suppose it doesn't need to be made clear why such a substance needs to be carefully monitored, why it's important that the administration has it firmly under its control…'

'No.' It wasn't Tom who interrupted the Admiral this time. It was Leo, and her eyes were flashing.

Windlass raised an eyebrow in Rachael's direction, but he didn't address her. Tom rather had the impression he wasn't used to treating women as his equal. Come to think of it, he didn't appear to treat *anybody* as his equal. 'Perhaps,' he said, his voice dangerously quiet, 'you mistake this conversation for a dialogue. It's not. This is me telling you how it's going to be.'

Rachael was about to speak again, but Tom laid one hand gently on her arm to stop her.

A silence in the room. Just the gentle tick-tocking of the grandfather clock.

'Admiral Windlass,' Tom said finally. He tried to sound as reasonable as possible, but couldn't help a note of steel entering his voice. 'I'm not aware how much you know about our new product, and I don't expect you tell me how you've found out about it. I imagine there are certain questions to be asked about the government performing unauthorized and illegal surveillance on private companies and confidential conversations. But as CEO of Pure Industries, I think it's important that I make certain facts perfectly plain. It seems clear to me that there will, in the future, be a need for dialogue between Pure Industries and the White House.' He paused. 'Not only as it stands under this administration, but under every administration that follows. Because make no mistake, Admiral, the Elixir will last a good deal longer than a couple of presidential terms.'

Windlass visibly bristled. He hadn't liked that one bit.

'It's our desire that this dialogue occurs in as open and honest a manner as possible. I trust that the President agrees with that.'

'It's not your position, Mr Shaw, to second-guess what the President thinks.'

'Well then, I shall leave that to you, Admiral Windlass. But let us be clear about one thing. Elixir is the property of Pure Industries and nobody else. We won't be bullied by government, we won't be threatened and we won't allow you to suppress or misuse it. Some things are too important to be left to politicians. This is one of them.'

If Windlass had been displeased before, he was fuming now. You could see it in his face, in the way it had reddened a couple of shades, in the way the skin around his eyes had tightened noticeably. He stood up suddenly and started pacing the room. Tom, Kyle and Rachael watched him closely.

When he finally spoke, he was so quiet that Tom had to strain to listen to him. 'Mr Shaw,' he said. 'We've done our research on you. I can only assume that your naïve response is down to your woeful lack of experience.' Windlass sneered. 'You really think that a tiny corporation nobody has heard of is a match for the office of the President of the United States. You really think we don't deal with bigger problems than you before breakfast?' His eyes were burning now. 'You think we can deal with rogue states and international terrorism and yet somehow you – *you* – can pose some sort of threat to us?'

Tom stayed outwardly calm, despite the anger that was flaring up inside him. 'If I didn't know better, Admiral Windlass, I'd say you were threatening me.'

'I *am* threatening you, you idiot!' Windlass roared. '*This* is what's going to happen. You will willingly disclose to the US government the formula of your new product. If you fail to do that, I will personally see to it that the President issues an executive order compelling you to do so. And if you still decline, we will seize it by whatever means necessary.'

Tom stood up; Kyle and Rachael followed suit. 'I think, Admiral Windlass, that our conversation is at an end. If the President wishes to discuss this any further, I'll be happy to do so in person.'

'I told you,' Windlass snapped. 'I speak with the President's full authority.'

Tom shook his head. 'No, Admiral,' he said. 'Nobody speaks with the President's *full* authority except the President himself. We'll be leaving now. Thank you for alerting us to your interest in our company. We'll double our security measures immediately. And I really wouldn't recommend raiding any more houses. It's really not going to get you very far.'

'You'll regret this, Shaw.'

'Time will tell, Admiral Windlass. I advise you to inform the President that we won't be bullied. Perhaps your intern could show us out.'

Windlass's anger was written all over his face. But he seemed to have exhausted his menaces. He strode out of the Roosevelt Room, slamming the door so forcibly that the oil painting over the fireplace trembled, and Rachael and Kyle's faces paled visibly.

'I think that went about as well as could be expected, don't you?' Tom said. He looked at his watch. 'With a bit of luck, we should make the midday flight. I bet Peter's counting down the hours till we get back. He doesn't like being left in charge much, even though I told him it wouldn't kill him…'

Brett Tyler sat on the edge of his bed, staring at his cell phone which lay on the bedside table.

'How did it come to this?' he wondered 'Not just jobless but my career totally ruined'.

He lay back and stared at the ceiling whilst he mulled over what had happened since Windlass went nuclear and dumped him unceremoniously on the street.

His 'situation' soon became clear to him when he started calling colleagues from the Department. Nobody, really, *nobody,* wanted to speak to him.

He was PNG - Persona Non Grata - not welcome, no longer a member of the 'club'. Windlass had done a good hatchet job on him and people who he'd previously considered friends now treated him like a pariah.

News spread fast in Washington and the collateral damage caused by Windlass's whisperings went way beyond his department and infected the whole of the Secret Service community.

He was not to be trusted. So, career over, period,

In desperation, he'd called Al Templeton and they met at the same bar as before.

At first, it was obvious Al was more disappointed with the fact that his one route into the corridors of power in Washington was no longer open to him but, he soon reconciled himself and listened to Brett in respectful silence.

'Windlass has ruined me, Al.' Brett said 'My whole career has gone up in smoke. The man is vicious, a total thug...'

Brett stopped and looked out of the window but with unseeing eyes as he contemplated a bleak future.

'Well, when you sup with the Devil...' Al started but then stopped for fear of upsetting Brett further.

'Look, I know I was trying to get out but, have you thought of joining the Bureau? You've got a good degree, you're fit and, I guess, you already have Top Secret clearance?'

'Higher actually.' Brett answered, Windlass insisted that all his staff were cleared to TS/SCI level - 'Top Secret/Sensitive Compartmented Information' .

'The FBI? No, it never crossed my mind....

'You'd have to go to the Academy at Quantico for nearly six months but, my guess is that you'd enjoy it.' Al added with a smile. 'Give it a go, knowing you as I do, you'll probably fly up the promotion ladder. Anyway, what other options have you got?'

Brett spend a few days mulling over Al's advice and then decided that he had no other options.

'Al could be right.' Brett thought as he fixed his stare on a small spider making its way across the ceiling, 'I would probably sail through the selection process.' Not arrogance, just a fact.

If questioned about why he was fired by Windlass, he'd tell them the truth, that they'd disagreed over policy but, the disagreement had taken place in front of the President and there was only one winner in those situations. As there was no love lost between the FBI and a few of the Government security agencies that operated out of Washington, particularly over policy matters, Brett suspected that he might even score some Brownie points.

Al had given him the number of the FBI Recruitment section and all he needed to do now was request an application form.

'A glorified cop, that's all I'll be.' Brett thought to himself. 'Not really what I had in mind when I graduated from Harvard but, desperate times call for desperate measures.'

He mulled it over a few minutes longer and then, with a sudden surge of excitement, which surprised him, sat upright on the edge of the bed, picked up the cell phone and carefully punched the numbers.

10

6 A.M., PACIFIC STANDARD TIME

Sylvia Lucas arose with the sun on the West Coast. Her husband Mac was sleeping soundly – he'd been up late preparing the kids' things for school – and she took a moment to watch him. He looked so different when he was asleep. So like a boy. She found herself wanting to reach out and stroke his cheek, but she stopped herself because she knew what a light sleeper he was, and she didn't want to wake him.

Silently she padded from the bedroom in her silk nightgown and went to check on the children. It was the last thing she did every night, and the first thing she did every morning. It was so difficult to find time to spend with them, and they of course knew nothing of their mother's habit of gazing over them when the house was quiet. Miguel and Cara looked so precious, wrapped snug in their bedclothes, like little china dolls that might break if you touched them without care. She drank in the sight of them for a full five minutes before creeping out and back to her dressing room, where she prepared herself for the day ahead.

It was not yet half past six when she quietly closed the front door behind her. Her car, a silver 5 Series BMW, was parked on the street right outside the Lucas family townhouse. It was rather busy outside, which always surprised Sylvia at this hour. But then, she told herself, she wasn't the only person with a busy day ahead. She approached her car and removed the keys from her bag.

Sylvia saw his reflection in the car window a fraction of a second before she felt the barrel of the gun pressed against the small of her back. She felt the blood draining from her veins just at the sight of him, so close. Even without turning round she could smell his aftershave – the same one her husband wore only much stronger, almost as though it was masking rather than enhancing. When she felt the weapon, her limbs refused to move.

'Get in to the car,' a Latino voice said very softly. 'And drive.'

'What… what are you…'

'I'm not going to say it again, bitch. You don't get straight into that car, little Miguel and Cara are going to wake up to see their mom dead on the sidewalk. Now move.'

Sylvia fumbled for the door handle and climbed behind the wheel. With a terrified look in the rear-view mirror, she saw her assailant climb into the back. He was smartly dressed in a freshly ironed shirt, and his black hair was thinning on top. There was a deadness in his expression. It wasn't so much that he didn't care about Sylvia's apparent horror; it was more that he hadn't even noticed.

'Drive,' he told her.

'Wh… where to?' Sylvia stuttered.

'Just drive, bitch. I'll give you instructions when you need them. And a word of advice: don't do anything to surprise me. The safety's off and my finger's on the trigger. It won't take a whole lot for me to paint the inside of this car a pleasant shade of scarlet.'

'Oh God…' she whispered. 'Oh my God…'

But the gunman said nothing more, and Sylvia Lucas had no option but to start the car, pull away from her house and drive to the outskirts of Laguna Niguel and beyond.

Theodore Croft was drinking hot coffee on the deck of his yacht *Delilah*. It was a sleek, expensive vessel, not the first he had owned but his favourite by some distance. Sixty feet of luxury. Ordinarily there would be a crew of six: a skipper, a mate, a chef and three others whose role was undefined but who spent their working days ensuring that Croft's needs were attended to. None of these six, however, were on board this morning. Croft could sail the boat himself, and the sort of assistance he would be requiring was of a rather more specialized sort.

Which was why he was accompanied, not by chefs and servants, but by Charlton Parker and his Doberman Rex, who was lying at his feet, well accustomed to life on board ship. Croft looked at his watch. Ten to eight. Jose should be here any minute. Along with the woman. Once they were here, they could leave their mooring and find a nice open patch of sea.

Hidden from land. Hidden from *everything*. Which was just where they needed to be.

He sipped his coffee and waited. And as he waited he ran through what he knew. His source inside Pure Industries had informed him that the Elixir was based on an herbal compound they were calling Legum, the recipe for which Pure had filed and was, therefore, public knowledge. But there were other processes involved. Three of them. The first he had learned yesterday morning, having been found by the Irish punk in Kyle Byng's safe. The second he had learned last night with the pathetic dying words of a pathetic man. The compound needed to be baked at a temperature of 150 Celsius for one hour. It wouldn't be long now before the final piece fitted into place.

Looking out to shore, he saw a vehicle approaching. He narrowed his eyes. It was a silver BMW, driving steadily down to the marina where *Delilah* was moored. It stopped at the end of the jetty and two figures emerged. One of them was clearly Jose. The second was a woman.

Croft gave a bleak smile. His guest had arrived.

She was crying, of course – Croft could see that the moment she arrived on deck – and she'd clearly been doing so for some time because the make-up around her eyes was smudged and running. It crossed his mind that she was an attractive woman. Older than the chicks he was used to, but maybe that wasn't such a bad thing. He quickly put those thoughts from his head, however. This was business, not pleasure, and he had to treat it as such.

He gave Jose a curt nod. 'Down below,' he said. 'I'll let you know when to bring her back up again.' He turned to the woman – Sylvia, he believed her name to be – and pinched her cheeks hard between his thumb and forefingers. 'Make a sound,' he hissed, 'and your children die. Understood?'

She nodded, terror in her eyes. Jose pushed her forcibly along the deck, into the main cabin and down below. The others would be waiting for her there.

Ten minutes later, Croft was at the bridge, navigating *Delilah* out of the marina by means of a burnished wooden steering wheel almost as tall as him. He could have used the on-board navigation system, of course, but he preferred to sail the boat himself. Especially today. It was not just because the morning sun was dancing prettily on the water. It was not just because today was a fantastic day to be at sea. There were other reasons why he wanted to feel his hands on the wheel.

To navigate *Delilah* one last time.

The marina slipped away. An hour later, there was no longer any sign of land, nor of any other craft. A quick glance at the radar screen told him they were unlikely to be disturbed any time soon. Croft turned off *Delilah*'s engines. He stepped out on to the deck and allowed himself a moment to enjoy the sound of the water lapping on the side of the hull. It was so peaceful here. The water was so blue. It almost seemed like an annoyance that he had to do what he had to do.

He stepped back into the main cabin and opened the door that led down below. 'Bring her out!' he called to his men. 'Now!'

Croft heard Sylvia Lucas before he saw her. The sobbing hadn't eased off – if anything, it had grown louder and more desperate. As soon as she emerged into the cabin, Lucas started begging him to let her go, but Croft barely even heard her. He realized, with a certain amount of surprise, that he was looking forward to this. 'Get her on to deck,' he told his men. 'tie her to the railings.'

The men did as they were told, while Croft remained in the cabin a little longer. There was a metal box in here, full of tools. He opened it up, selected a sharp knife intended to cut rope, then went outside to join the others.

They had done his bidding. As Rex sat just a few yards away, watching impassively, Sylvia Lucas had been tied to the railings of the boat: one length of rope around her waist, another around her ankles and a third tying her wrists. She was hyperventilating with fear, and her cheeks were streamed with tears. When she tried to speak, all that came from her mouth was a series of truncated gasps. She was too terrified even to beg.

Croft approached her. He held up the knife and for a moment examined the blade, acting as if Sylvia wasn't even there. He angled it so that sunlight reflected off metal, and even brushed the skin of his forefinger against it, to check that it was sharp. It was.

And then, he turned his attention to his petrified captive.

His experience the previous night with Peter Wright had taught him something: if they know you're serious, they're more likely to tell you what you want. He didn't mess around. With a single, slow swipe of the knife, he sliced into the flesh of Sylvia's left cheek, starting just below the eye and cutting a vertical line of two inches down. She gasped. Croft repeated the process for her right cheek, then took a step backwards to admire his work. Sylvia was shaking violently. Her wrists were straining against the ropes – she clearly wanted to press her hands against the cuts – but they were tied fast. The blood and the tears mingled. Croft idly wondered if the salt water made the wounds sting more, and he was distracted by the way it looked as if this woman was weeping blood.

And then she shrieked. It was a loud, piercing sound. Two seagulls that had been resting on the water flapped skywards in surprise, and the sea itself seemed to resonate the scream like a loudspeaker.

The blood was dripping off her face and on to her clothes now. Croft stepped forward again and waited for the screaming to degenerate into more sobs. Only then did he speak.

'We can continue this for a very, very long time,' he whispered. 'Or we can finish it now. Do you understand?'

'Please…' Sylvia managed to whimper. 'I… have two little children…'

'You think I don't know that?' Croft replied. 'Just think of their faces when the cops go round to tell them their mother is dead. Think of the tears rolling down their eyes. Think.'

Sylvia shook her head violently and some of the blood spattered not only on to the deck but onto Croft himself. It was warm and viscous. He touched his own face, then examined his fingertips. They were smeared red. He wiped them on Sylvia's clothes, feeling the soft impression of her breasts as he did so. He was vaguely aware that Rex had approached, and the he was licking the spots of blood from the deck. But Croft kept his eyes on his victim.

'You need to tell me one thing,' he continued. 'That's all. One little thing. You know what it is, don't you?'

The woman shook her head again, but this time it was less determined. She was not so sure of herself. It was amazing, Croft thought to himself, how easy it was to read people sometimes.

He smiled at Sylvia. 'There's no hurry,' he said. 'We can wait here for just as long as it takes.' He bent down and scratched the Doberman behind its ears. It made a snuffling sound. 'I think Rex might be hungry,' he said brightly. He turned towards his men. 'Perhaps you'd be so good as to bring his food up.'

It was Charlton who left the deck to carry out his politely framed instruction. When he returned, however, he was carrying two large buckets. He placed them on the deck just next to where Sylvia was tied. They were filled to the brim with dog food – the smell was unpleasant, as though it had been sitting around for a few days, and even Rex didn't appear keen to get too close. One of the buckets had a small, hand-held shovel stuck into it.

Croft tutted. 'Putrid,' he said. 'No good to man or beast.' He stopped and held up one finger, as if he had just had a very good idea. 'It seems a shame, doesn't it, to waste such good food? I can't help thinking there must be creatures out there that would be glad of a little meat.'

Sylvia was staring at him. The blood was still weeping from her face, and her body was still trembling with shock. But she appeared somehow transfixed by Croft's words. Transfixed and aghast, like she knew what was coming.

Croft approached the buckets and pulled out a shovelful of meat. He flung it out to sea like a tennis player performing an easy lob. A splashing sound as it hit the water, but by then Croft was already digging out another shovelful of the dog food and throwing it in.

'You know, when I was a kid, I used to love it when my mom took me to feed the ducks.' He spoke conversationally, like they were just chatting over a cup of coffee. 'It was great, the way they all crowded around you, wanting a piece of the action. Your kids like feeding the ducks, Sylvia? Little Miguel and Cara? They like it when their mom takes them to the pond, huh?'

He stopped for a moment, and waved a shovelful of the putrid meat under Sylvia's nose. She looked as though she might gag, but at the last minute he moved it away and flicked it over the side. He took a moment to stare out to sea. A couple of seagulls – perhaps the same ones who had been disturbed by Sylvia's scream – were diving at the water where the meat had landed, scavenging for this unexpected and unusual breakfast. But Theodore Croft wasn't looking for seagulls. He was looking for scavengers of an altogether more impressive kind.

And it only took a few minutes for him to see them.

Croft had emptied the first bucket and was halfway through the second when he noticed the first fin. It was circling about 30 yards from *Delilah*, its silvery color well camouflaged against the water. He looked over at his men. 'Untie her,' he instructed.

Sylvia was whimpering again. Croft barely heard it. By the time the men had loosened her cords he had counted another three fins. He grabbed Sylvia by the arm and forced her to look out to sea. 'Hey,' he said. 'Would you look at that? What would Miguel and Cara give to be feeding sharks instead of ducks, huh? You think they'd be excited, Sylvia? Or do you think they'd just be scared?'

Sylvia looked like she had forgotten all about the blood on her face. One moment she was staring at the circling sharks; the next she was staring at Croft, like he was a monster. Croft sneered. She just didn't understand.

'Tell me what you know,' he whispered. 'About the Elixir. It's the only way you can possible hope to stay alive.'

'Por favor,' Sylvia breathed. '*Por favor…*'

Croft looked meaningfully out to sea. 'You can't stop me finding out,' he said. 'Tell me now and maybe the sharks will go hungry.'

Slowly, and with an expression burning in her eyes that he vaguely recognized as hate, Sylvia shook her head.

Croft felt his lips thinning. He closed his eyes, telling himself that he really should try to keep control of his emotions. But he couldn't. With a sudden explosion of anger, he raised the shovel and smacked it against the side of Sylvia's bleeding face. She gasped in pain, but when she had regained what composure she was left with, her mangled expression was even more defiant, and that only made the anger run more hotly in Croft's veins.

He moved in closer to Sylvia and started to whisper in her ear. 'I have three men outside your house,' he hissed. 'One word from me and they kill Miguel and Cara. They'll make the kiddies beg for their lives, and they'll do it in front of your husband just before they kill him too.'

Sylvia said something under her breath. '*No… no… por favor…*' Suddenly her eyes were rolling, as if this final threat was too much for her to bear. Croft realized in a flash that it was not the threat of pain, nor even the threat of death, that would earn him the information he needed, but the promise that Sylvia Lucas's children would not survive her ongoing stubbornness.

'It'll hurt them, Sylvia. Before they die, they'll know what pain really is. I'll make sure of it.'

Her head nodded listlessly on to her chest. Croft experienced a moment of panic that she might pass out before she had the chance to give him the information he needed. He grabbed her face, squeezing his fingers against the wounded, bleeding cheeks, and lifted her head up so she was looking at him. 'The Elixir,' he said from behind gritted teeth. 'Tell me what you know.'

Her lips were moving. Croft pulled his hand away. Sylvia was whispering something. It was indistinct. He had to strain to hear it. In her confusion, she had reverted to her native Spanish, a language Croft did not speak.

'*Sangre de grado…*' she rasped. '*Sangre de grado… one milligram in a hundred…*'

Croft spun round and looked at his men. 'You,' he pointed at Jose Mendoza. 'Come here. Translate. *Now!*'

Jose approached. He frowned as he listened.

'*Sangre de grado… Sangre de grado…*'

'What is it? What is she saying?'

'It makes no sense,' Jose replied.

'*Sangre de grado…*'

Croft grabbed his henchman's collar. His eyes were aflame. 'What… is… she… *saying?*'

Jose Mendoza, clearly unused to being treated like this, knocked Croft's hands away. They locked gazes, but it was Jose whose resolve weakened first. He looked down. 'The blood of a dragon, boss,' he said. 'She's saying, *the blood of a dragon…*'

Sylvia Lucas had collapsed to the deck, her face a bloodied mess, her body perfectly still. Theodore Croft didn't know if she was dead or not. It didn't much matter either way. Nor was he repelled when his Doberman padded over to her body and started licking at her face. Croft was already marching away from the scene, off the deck and into the main cabin.

Delilah's onboard PC was situated on the bridge, alongside the bank of navigation computers. It connected to the internet via a satellite dish on the top of the vessel. Not fast, but reliable enough. Croft sat down at the screen and typed in the mysterious words Tony had just uttered.

The blood of a dragon…

It only took him a few seconds to scan down the Google page ranking before he realized what he was looking for. One click and he was directed to an unattractively designed site detailing the indigenous plant life of the Amazon.

And there he saw it.

Croton lechleri. Also known as *Sangre de Grado*. Also known as Dragon's Blood. A plant native to north-eastern South America. Renowned for its medicinal properties. How appropriate, Croft thought to himself, that sap of this plant resembled blood. Like the blood of Sylvia Lucas that was smeared over his hands.

Movement behind him. He turned to see Jose standing there. He looked shaken. For the first time ever, he did not have the air of the unquestioningly loyal employee. He looked like he doubted Croft. Like he was shocked by him.

'She's still alive,' Jose said. 'You want me to…'

He left the question hanging.

Croft shook his head. 'Lend me your gun,' he said.

Jose Mendoza didn't look happy about it and he handed the weapon over with obvious reluctance.

Croft didn't know a great deal about guns. He didn't need to. There was always someone else to take care of that side of things for him. But he knew enough. Enough to know that this was an automatic pistol, and that as such it would hold twelve or thirteen rounds. He knew that the two-inch-long suppressor would deaden the noise so there would be little, or no, retort out here where there was nobody to hear it anyway. He knew where to locate the safety catch, which slipped easily from the safe position to the live. And he knew how to cock the firearm in preparation for the first shot, by simply pulling back the slide so that it was loaded and ready to fire.

'The new boy from the Emerald Isle, Mickey Connor. You sure he's clean?' As he spoke, he examined the firearm like a curious child.

'As a whistle, boss … according to Tony.'

'Good. Well, I guess we'd better get to work.'

'You don't have to do it yourself, boss,' Jose said. 'That's what you pay us for.'

Croft inclined his head. 'True, Jose,' he said quietly. 'But you know, the way I see, you're not going to be all that keen to shoot yourself, are you?'

A puzzled look crossed Jose's face. 'Boss?'

And then he realized what Theodore Croft was telling him.

Jose dived at him immediately, but it was too late. Croft squeezed the trigger and a single round flew from the barrel, hitting him squarely in the chest. Jose dropped like a stone. He landed just inches from where Croft was sitting. He was still breathing – Croft could hear him struggling to get breath down his injured windpipe and into his lungs. For a moment he considered putting him out of his misery, but it only took a second for him to decide against it. It would be unwise to waste the rounds that remained in his gun.

He stepped over Jose's dying body and headed towards the deck.

It was silent out here. If Sylvia Lucas was still alive, she showed no signs of it. Charlton was looking out to sea, where the sharks were still circling. He didn't even know what hit him. Theodore Croft had no skill with a gun, but at this range – no more than five yards – it was impossible to miss him. The suppressed weapon made two near-silent thuds, and they were twitching and bleeding on the ground.

The Doberman looked on impassively. Croft enjoyed the silence. How quickly it had happened. Just forty-eight hours ago he had never even heard of the Elixir. Now he knew its principal components – Legum and Dragon's Blood. He knew the temperature at which it had to be baked, and he knew the UV frequency at which it had to be cured. He knew it all.

He found himself stroking the side of *Delilah*. He loved this boat and it seemed a shame to lose it. But boats could be replaced, and *Delilah* had a secret to take with her to the bottom of the ocean. At her stern, there was a rigid inflatable with a 50 horse-power outboard. Croft didn't go there immediately. First he slipped down below. It was the work of a couple of minutes to open the sea cocks so that the brine started to bubble into *Delilah*'s hull. Only then did he head up to the stern.

Rex was waiting for him there, sitting patiently by the inflatable. *Delilah* was sinking fast, but that didn't seem to perturb the Doberman. The inflatable was launched by means of a mechanical arm. Croft climbed into it, and the dog made to do the same. At the last minute though, Croft activated the launcher. It lifted him and the inflatable up into the air, leaving Rex whimpering on the deck.

'Sorry, bud,' Croft said. As the launcher deposited the inflatable in the water, he looked out towards the sharks. They were no closer, and Croft knew that if he wanted them to take care of the evidence they would need something to alert them to the presence of the bodies. Rex, splashing noisily in the water, would serve that function well.

He started the outboard motor and moved twenty yards from the sinking *Delilah*, before stopping again and turning to look at what was happening. The boat was almost fully submerged. Rex was in the water, swimming strongly towards Croft but unaware of the fins that were gliding towards him. The Doberman only yelped once as the sharks attacked. Croft caught a glimmer of silver as one of the beasts dragged the dog under. There was a moment of silence.

And then... screaming.

Croft narrowed his eyes. Clutching to what remained of *Delilah* was a figure. It was Sylvia Lucas, he realized. The shock of the water had clearly caused her to regain consciousness, and now she was clinging on to a sinking ship, trying to gain somebody's attention.

But there was no-one and nothing to hear her, except Croft and the sharks.

Sylvia screamed a little louder before she died. Was it pain or panic? Croft didn't know. But there was something curiously satisfying, he thought to himself, about watching her life being ripped away by these creatures of the deep. It made him, Theodore Croft, feel more alive, somehow.

And to be alive? Well, that was all that mattered.

Delilah had completely sunk now. The sharks were feeding furiously, removing all hint of his crime. He started the outboard again, turned away from the scene of carnage, and headed back towards the shore.

11

11.00 A.M., PACIFIC STANDARD TIME

'What do you mean you can't get hold of them? Try again.'

'Mr Shaw.' Ruth looked unimpressed at the way Tom had spoken to her. 'I have been trying to raise both Mr Wright and Mrs Lucas all morning. There is no answer from Mr Wright's house, and Mrs Lucas's husband insists she left before he even woke up this morning.'

'And you haven't seen them all day?'

'No, Mr Shaw. I haven't seen them all day.'

'Tom,' Rachael interrupted. 'I've got a bad feeling about this.'

Tom did too. The only time Peter had ever been late into work had been after heart-bypass surgery three years ago. Even then he'd been at his desk in less than two weeks, in direct contradiction of his doctor's orders. Tom couldn't help wondering if he was so devoted to his work because he had little hope now of ever finding a partner. Pure Industries was his life. If he wasn't here something was wrong.

As for Sylvia, Tom knew what her work meant to her. She was always available. Day or night. And while it was hardly significant that her cell had been ringing out for a few hours, Tom still had a cold, uneasy feeling. He'd had it ever since he'd seen Kyle's upturned flat, all the way to Washington and back to LAX. Now it was 3 p.m. Pacific Standard Time, and the uneasy feeling had just doubled.

'Call the police,' he said.

Ruth looked startled. 'Mr Shaw, I hardly think that a few hours of absence is…'

'Call the police, Ruth. Now. Inform them that Peter and Sylvia are missing.'

Ruth's characteristic pinched look returned and she walked primly from Tom's office without another word.

'You think something's happened?' Kyle said in a hushed voice once the three of them were alone.

'I know something's happened. Look at your apartment, for a start.'

'But *I*'m still here…'

Tom shook his head. 'You're lucky. You weren't around when the intruders caught up with you. And they found what they wanted in any case. They didn't *need* you.'

Rachael's eyes had widened. 'You think the White House's people are targeting us all?'

Tom sniffed. Truth was, he didn't know *what* to think.

'How long till we've stockpiled enough of the Elixir to launch?' he asked.

'Launch? We haven't finished the trials yet.'

Tom gave her a serious look. 'Rachael, the first time you told me about Elixir, you said you were a hundred per cent sure about it. Are you still?'

Rachael nodded.

'And these trials, they're just belt and braces, right?'

'Right.'

'So how long till we can launch?'

'Days,' Rachael whispered.

Tom walked over to his desk and sat down in his comfortable leather chair. He pressed his fingertips together and thought for a minute before speaking. 'With any luck,' he said finally, 'Peter and Sylvia are taking a well-deserved bit of time out. I'm sure they're fine. But I'm also sure about something else. We crossed swords with the government this morning. From everything I've researched about that Admiral, he's not going down without a fight. They want to put a lid on the Elixir and I'm not going to let them.' He drew a deep breath. 'We announce the product in two weeks.'

The other two stared at him. 'Two *weeks*?' Kyle breathed. 'But we're not ready. We're nowhere near…'

'We haven't got a choice,' Tom overruled him. 'It's the only way we can stop the government suppressing it. If everybody in the whole world knows about the Elixir – and believe me, they will – there's no way anybody can cover it up. I want to spread production all around the World, as quickly as possible. And if we *are* being targeted – personally, I mean – it's the only way to bring an end to that, too. The President's people will have bigger things to worry about than us.' He stood up again. 'In the meantime, I'm instigating security measures.'

'What sort?' Kyle asked.

'Rachael, I need to know the components of the Elixir.'

Rachael looked startled. 'But Tom, we agreed…'

'I know what we agreed, but the situation's changed. I'd like to think Peter and Sylvia are going to walk through that door any moment, but we've got to prepare for the worst. If our people are being targeted, there has to be more than one person who knows how to make the Elixir. Kyle, if anything happens to Rachael or myself, the remaining person needs to tell you what they know. Are we agreed?'

Both Rachael and Kyle nodded.

'Next up, I want close protection for the three of us, and for Peter and Sylvia as soon as they surface.' He frowned. '*If* they surface. I don't want any of us going anywhere without an armed guard. If you have any family members you're worried might be targeted, Pure Industries will pay for them to be protected too.'

'Come on, Tom. Don't you think you're overreacting?' Kyle asked.

The door opened. Ruth walked back in. She hadn't even knocked. She was pale and Tom could immediately see that something was wrong. 'What is it,' he demanded tersely. 'Ruth, what is it?'

The PA didn't reply, because at that moment someone else walked into the room: a black police officer with a neat uniform and a serious frown. 'Mr Tom Shaw?'

Tom stepped forward.

'You are CEO of Pure Industries?'

'That's right.'

'You're acquainted with a Mr Peter Wright?'

'Yes,' Tom breathed. Time seemed to have slowed down, and somehow he knew what was coming.

'I'm sorry to have to tell you that Mr Wright's body was found at 11.30 this morning. We're treating it as a homicide. I'd like you to come to the mortuary with me to formally identify the body.'

Tom heard Rachael sob, and was vaguely aware of Kyle putting his arm round her to comfort her. A million thoughts rebounded in his brain. Thoughts of Peter. Thoughts of Sylvia. And thoughts of his own family. Were they safe? He needed to get to them. *Now*…

'Mr Shaw?'

Tom blinked. The police officer was staring at him. 'Is it really necessary for me to go?' Tom asked. 'I mean, there must be someone else.'

'I'm afraid not, sir. Mr Wright has no immediate family that we know of.'

Tom swallowed hard. It didn't sound like he had a choice. He walked over to Kyle. 'Security,' he said under his breath. 'For all of us. Sort it now.'

Kyle nodded, and Tom returned to the officer. 'Let's go,' he said.

It only took fifteen minutes to reach the mortuary downtown, but another fifteen for the police officer to arrange the necessary paperwork before he led Tom into the basement. It was icy cold down here, but Tom didn't ask why. That much was obvious. He walked as if in a dream, following the officer and strict-looking female coroner. And moments later, he was staring down at Peter's body.

Tom had only ever seen one dead body: his father's. The memory of it still haunted him. But now, he knew, he would have another image to replace the memory of that corpse. More chilling. More gruesome.

Peter Wright's skin was as grey as his hair. There were gashes on his face, which was sallow and smeared red-brown with dried blood. He didn't look peaceful in death. He looked terrified.

Tom nodded. 'It's him.' He spoke in a hushed voice, like he was in a church.

'Can you think of any reason, Mr Shaw, why anybody would have wanted to harm him?'

Tom didn't take his eyes from Peter's still body. What could he really tell the police? That this was government work? That it went higher up than this LAPD officer could even imagine? That in all probability, someone in the White House itself had sanctioned Peter's assassination? And that for all Tom knew, his own life was in danger, as well as that of his family and the other members of his Board?

'I can't think of anything, officer,' he said as the coroner covered the body. 'I really can't think of anything at all.'

'Well, we may need to ask you some more questions at some stage.'

'Of course,' Tom replied mildly. 'I'll do whatever I can...'

And then they were walking back up from the basement. Tom did everything he could to keep his pace steady, not to give this police officer any hint of anything. They sat silently in the squad car that returned him to Pure Industries, and it was only when the officer had driven away again that he moved.

And when that happened, he was like a racing hound, suddenly released from his starting box. Tom was driving away from Pure Industries within seconds, with only one thought in his mind.

Jack's school was a small establishment. Intimate, Tom and Jane had thought when they first went to see it. It was situated in their neighborhood and there was no doubt that Jack had thrived there, at least up until the moment when Jane's doctors had confirmed her diagnosis and they'd had to sit down and explain to the boy that his mom might not be around much longer. It wasn't just at school that he'd lost his spark. It was in every aspect of his young life.

Tom was seldom to be seen here. When she was well, it had always been Jane who took Jack to school in the morning and picked him up in the afternoon. Since she had been bedbound, a succession of carers and babysitters had taken on that role. Small wonder, then, that as he rushed through the gates and across the school yard, an elderly janitor in a check shirt and baseball cap called out to him, challenging Tom to explain who he was.

'I'm getting my son,' Tom stated, refusing even to stop.

'Ain't home time yet, sir,' the janitor called, but Tom was already storming into the entrance.

He found himself in an empty reception area. It smelled of kids and sport and took him back to his own schooldays. No time for nostalgia, though. He vaguely remembered the way to the principal's office and ran along the corridors, attracting glances from the occasional students who happened not to be in class. When he reached the principal's office he barged in without knocking. A rather severe-looking PA gave him a frosty glare.

'I'm Jack Shaw's father. I'm here to take him out of school.' The PA started to say something. Tom didn't even register what it was. '*I'm here to take my son out of school!*'

Thirty seconds later he was being led towards Jack's classroom.

There was much intrigued chatter as Tom led Jack out of class, and his son looked as perplexed as all his buddies. 'What's wrong, Dad?' he asked as Tom practically dragged him along the corridors towards the exit. 'What's the matter? Is it Mom? Is she…'

'She's fine,' Tom replied curtly. He knew he sounded abrupt, that he was probably scaring his son, but that wasn't the most important thing right now. Getting Jack and Jane to safety was.

They drove in silence to the hospice. Tom was aware of his boy staring at him from the passenger seat where he was never normally allowed to sit. When they reached their destination, they stopped in the car park and Tom inhaled deeply. 'Listen, champ,' he said. 'What's about to happen is going to seem kind of weird. But you and your mom, you're going to have to trust me, okay?'

Jack nodded. 'Okay,' he said, but he sounded uncertain.

'Then let's go and get her. I think it's time she came home for a while, don't you?'

The boy nodded again, but this time he didn't say anything. Father and son climbed out of the car and walked towards the entrance of the hospice.

It was such a sad place, this building where people waited to die. Its bleak, utilitarian structure gave no sign of the melancholy and the suffering that existed within. Tom was far better known here than he was at Jack's school, and the receptionist at the desk – Tom knew her name to be Suzie – gave him a friendly smile as he approached. 'Mr Shaw,' Suzie greeted him. 'She'll be very pleased to see you both.'

Normally he was as cheerful with the receptionists and nurses as this place allowed him to be. Not today.

'My wife will be discharging herself this afternoon,' he told her.

Suzie blinked. 'Mr Shaw, I don't think that's a very good idea. She's very sick. We can keep her comfortable...'

'This afternoon, Suzie.' Tom turned and started marching away, pulling Jack along with him.

'I'll need to speak to the nurses...' Suzie called after him.

'Do whatever you have to do,' Tom shouted back, and he trod the familiar route to Jane's room, and opened the door.

He stopped. His blood froze.

Jane's eyes were closed. Her face was deathly white. The room was still.

He looked down at Jack, standing next to him in the doorway. 'Stay here, champ,' he breathed, and he stepped into the room, shrouded by a terrible premonition.

Tom was a metre away from Jane's bed when she coughed. It was a horrible, weak sound, but it sent a rush of elation through him. She was alive. He leant over her bed and put one hand on her cheek. Her eyes opened, but she didn't give him the usual frail smile.

'What's wrong?' she whispered.

'I have to get you out of here.'

Jane's eyes closed. 'Tom, I can't. You know that. Anywhere other than here is too… too difficult for me.'

He took hold of her hand. 'Jane, you trust me, don't you?'

'You know I do.'

'This is going to be hard for you. I know it is, and I wouldn't ask you to do it if it wasn't absolutely necessary. But you have to get out of bed now, and you have to come with me and Jack.'

Jane moved her head slightly and appeared to notice Jack for the first time. Neither the illness nor the surprise of Tom's request could stop the pleasure from showing in her face.

'Jack,' Tom said. 'Go find your mom a wheelchair. We need to get her to the car.'

Jack – sensible, serious Jack – did as he was asked.

'What's going on, Tom?' Jane said the moment he disappeared.

'I'll explain when we're home. I promise.'

Tom's promise had always been good enough for Jane, and it was good enough now.

He had forgotten how thin her body had become as he helped her onto the edge of the bed. She had a moment of giddiness as she sat up, and it took both Jack and Tom to help her into the wheelchair the boy had found. She sat in it slightly slumped, and it was only then that Tom noticed a nurse – Jane's principal carer, an overweight, matronly lady called Hilary – standing over them.

'Mr Shaw, what's going on?'

Tom didn't answer. He was too distracted by Jane, who was clearly having difficulty breathing.

'Mr Shaw, your wife can't go anywhere, she's too unwell.'

'I'm discharging her.' Tom manoeuvred the wheelchair so that it was facing the door, but the nurse stood in her way. She was a considerable barrier.

'It's not up to you to discharge her, Mr Shaw. It's up to the medical staff, or to your wife herself.' Hilary stepped forward and bent down so she was at Jane's level. 'You don't have to go, dearie,' she said in a soothing voice. 'Not if you don't feel up to it.' She laid a calming hand on Jane's bony knee. 'Would you like me to help you back into bed?'

Tom held his breath. There was no doubt that Jane looked terrible. Weak. Pale. Trembling. She gave her husband a worried glance. 'I do feel very tired,' she murmured.

'Jane... you *have* to trust me...'

She gave a weak little nod. 'I want to go.' It sounded like a great effort to say it.

Hilary stood up straight. 'Then I'm coming with you,' she said. 'She needs nursing care, Mr Shaw. You can't do it by yourself. Not with your son to look after too.'

But Tom shook his head. It was true that Jane needed care. But he had to choose someone himself. That was the only way he could be sure of trusting them...

He hesitated. Since when had he been so paranoid? But paranoia wasn't always a bad thing. 'I'm sorry, Hilary. You'll... you'll understand soon. Thank you for everything you've done.'

He wheeled Jane out of the room, closely followed by little Jack. None of them spoke, and five minutes later Tom Shaw was driving his listless, barely conscious wife and young son back home. He needed them together. Somewhere they could be protected.

It was not in Tom's nature to drive recklessly, but he did so now, carving up the traffic and running red lights. Panic was surging through him. Panic and horror. He couldn't get the image of Peter's damaged corpse out of his mind. And he couldn't shake the dread feeling that Sylvia had met a similar fate. It all added up. The intruders in Kyle's apartment. The summons to the White House and Admiral Windlass's brash and bullying behaviour. Peter and Sylvia, gone. Did the government have all the elements of Elixir's formula? Was that even on the agenda, or were they simply trying to eliminate everyone who knew about it? And how did they have this information anyway? There had to be a leak inside Pure Industries, but who could it be? Nobody other than the Board members had access to the information. Nobody other than them even *knew* about the Elixir...

These problems rebounded in his head. Cars skidded to a halt around him. Furious drivers screamed out of their windows. He barely noticed.

'What's happening, Tom?' Jane's voice was listless. Barely there. She looked sicker than ever.

'I have to get you home,' Tom said.

'And what then?'

What then? It was a good question. The truth was, Tom didn't know how to answer it.

12

Friday, 9.00 a.m., Pacific Standard Time

Back in the Province, Pat Dolan thought to himself, it had never been like this.

The kind of undercover work he was used to had involved dingy pubs where the urinals and the bar had the same smell, where pasty-white barmaids with nicotine-stained fingers served cheap drinks to the paramilitaries' foot-soldiers, with very little between their ears. And now here he was, standing in the sunshine beside the glittering pool of a West Coast mansion. Jesus, he reckoned it would cost him a week's pay to buy just one of the marble flagstones that surrounded the pool. Whoever said that crime didn't pay had never been to Theodore Croft's gaff, to be sure.

'It's a swell view, huh?' A voice rang out from the entrance to the house. Pat turned to see a bronzed, well-dressed man of about forty walking towards him with a toothpaste-commercial smile and an outstretched hand. 'Heard a lot about you, Mickey Connor. You did a good job turning over that apartment. Tony told me you're a useful man to have around.'

Pat nodded curtly. 'Where are the others, then?' he asked, exaggerating his Ulster accent just a little. 'They said they'd be here.'

Croft, Pat noted, refused to catch his eye. 'Tony will be here soon,' he said. 'The others have business out East. Don't suppose we'll be seeing them for a little whiles. It's why I'm glad to meet you, Mickey. I need good men around me.' He waved an arm expansively around him. 'Lot of jealous folk out there, Mickey. Always wanting what someone else has got. Means I can't be too careful. You understand what I'm saying?'

'Sure, I understand. Not their style, though, to disappear like that. You sure they're…'

'I'm sure.' Croft pulled a wad of notes from the back pocket of his shorts. 'May be that I'm calling on you, sometime in the next few days or weeks,' he said as he counted out what looked to Pat like at least two thousand bucks. 'Make sure I can always contact you, right?'

He handed over the money. Pat pocketed it. 'Right,' he said. 'But about the others…'

'You don't need to worry about them. You and Tony are my boys now. Just make sure you're there when I need you.' Croft looked at his watch. 'I'm going to have to ask you to leave now, Mickey. I have a few things to attend to. I hope you understand?'

Pat shrugged, but didn't say anything. A piece of work like Mickey Connor wasn't going to be polite, even to someone who'd just handed him a couple of gees. He shuffled away from the pool, and back through the glamorous surroundings of Theodore Croft's house. Another person was waiting in just by the main entrance. He was a thin, nervous-looking man who watched Pat anxiously as he passed; Pat just scowled, but his scowl hid that he was clocking every detail of the man's appearance: a high forehead; skin that looked as if it had been pockmarked by acne in the past; long thin fingers that he clenched and unclenched absent-mindedly; a slight stoop. And as he walked out of the house, Pat looked back over his shoulder. Theodore Croft was watching him leave. For some reason, Pat was in no doubt that he was waiting for Mickey Connor to be gone before speaking to this new arrival, whoever he was.

'How long do you need?'

Theodore Croft's guest was everything he imagined a scientist should be. Socially awkward and bad-breathed, he clutched his hands together and stuttered his way through their conversation. Croft found himself breathing deeply just to calm his temper and maintain his patience.

'It's... it's very difficult to predict these things.'

'Dr Jacobs, I'm paying you a great deal of money to predict these things. How long?'

Dr Jacobs swallowed hard, and a few beads of sweat appeared on his unnaturally large forehead. 'To create the compound, baked and irradiated to the levels you've specified... a couple of days? And to check it has the... the *effect* you're expecting...'

'Yes?'

The scientist's cheek twitched. 'My lab has very sensitive equipment. We can measure the decay rate of fast-degenerating cells very quickly … a couple of hours … of course they won't be human cells, but it would give an indication…'

'You have forty-eight hours.'

Dr Jacobs blinked. 'Mr Croft, it's really not as straightforward as…'

Croft felt his temper rising again. This man was like a fly buzzing around his head. An irritation. 'Mountfield Estate Nursing Home,' he interrupted.

The scientist blinked again. 'I… I'm sorry?'

'Mountfield Estate Nursing Home.' He handed Jacobs the wallet file he was holding. Jacobs opened it up and stared at the three black and white photographs inside. Croft knew what they showed, of course: Jacobs' elderly mother, walking in the gardens of the residential care home where she was weathering the winter of her life. 'Old people,' Croft breathed, 'are the easiest to kill, but then I'm sure I don't have to tell *you* that. There are so many ways to do it. A "mistake" with the medicine. An unfortunate fall. You know, Dr Jacobs, it would be a terrible shame if anything like that happens to your mom. But don't make a mistake about this. It will, unless you've told me within 48 hours whether this formula does what it's supposed to do. Understood?'

Dr Jacobs's eyes bulged. 'You wouldn't…' he whispered.

'Oh Dr Jacobs. You'd be surprised at just what I'd do.' He looked meaningfully at his watch. 'Time's getting on,' he said brightly. 'I'd say you should get back to that laboratory of yours before mom has a nasty little tumble down the stairs, wouldn't you?'

Jacobs stared at Croft. Then he stared at the photographs. Then he stood up and half walked, half ran to the exit of the house. Croft, however, stayed where he was, sitting on his leather sofa and staring into space. Forty-eight hours wasn't long, he knew, but it seemed like a lifetime and he was impatient for it to pass.

'I'll tell you one thing: the guy's a psycho. I should know, I've met a few.'

On leaving the Croft residence, Pat Dolan had climbed into his old Ford, then driven around the outskirts of LA for an hour. He'd used every technique he knew to ensure he wasn't being followed: pulling over in quiet streets and checking in his rear-view mirror to see that nobody else was doing the same; performing sudden U-turns; quickly turning into quiet industrial lots to see if anyone followed. . It was impossible to be totally sure that he didn't have a tail, but if he did, and they were still following, they almost deserved their success. Now he was sitting on a park bench, three yards from a very still pond which had clouds of bugs hovering just above the surface, and a slightly unpleasant smell of algae. People avoided this place, which made it perfect for his purposes. It meant anybody conducting surveillance on them would stick out.

Another man sat next to him. He was dressed in an anonymous grey suit and had an anonymous grey face. Pat didn't know his name. The identity of Agent 2 was as much a mystery to him now as it had been when the CIA operative had walked into the briefing room the night they'd first learned about Operation Jaguar.

'You've made contact.' It was a statement, not a question. Pat briefly wondered whether he'd had men watching him all the time, but he knew better than to ask.

'I've done more than that. I'm on the payroll. One job down already.'

'Which was?'

'Turning over a flat near the city center. There was a slip of paper in a safe that he wanted. Don't ask me what it said – some sort of scientific gobbledegook. To be honest, I think maybe he was just testing me out. Seeing if I got what it takes, you know.'

'You've taken money from him?'

'And some. Your man's got a bob or two, I'll give him that. Gave me a couple of grand in greenbacks like he was dishing out sweeties.'

Agent 2 didn't seem at all interested in that.

'What was the money for? Why did he want to see you?'

Pat scratched his nose thoughtfully. 'I think he just wanted to make sure I was on board, and to have a bit of face time. He said that some of the other guys had gone away and he needed somebody else he can call on to... you know... do his dirty work. My guess is they suddenly became surplus to requirements. Wouldn't surprise me if their bodies ended up scaring the kiddies out for a nice day on the beach. I'll be honest with you, pal – they weren't lookers even when they were alive...'

Pat liked to tease Agent 2. To treat him like he was just some fella sharing the craic over a pint of plain. He knew it drove his CIA handler mad.

'What else did Croft say to you? I want chapter and verse.'

Pat shrugged. 'Said me and Tony were his boys now – you know, Tony Foreman who was my way in in the first place. He used those exact words. Course, Tony's still king of the hill, but I reckon I'm his number two. Croft said I should make sure I'm always on call. I had the feeling he'd be making contact soon, but he didn't say what for.'

Agent 2 stretched down and picked up a briefcase he had by his feet. He laid it on his lap and opened it up. Pat glanced into it. The briefcase was empty except for a black and white photograph, which Agent 2 handed to him.

'Looks like he's seen better days.' Pat said. The photograph showed a corpse – a thin, balding man with vertical cuts on either side of his mouth, and a look of stricken horror on his face.

'LAPD found him yesterday. Body wrapped in a tarpaulin and dumped outside a church.'

'Hallelujah,' Pat murmured.

'We also found a vehicle registered to your friend Tony Foreman.'

'No friend of mine, pal,' Pat replied, though secretly he was wondering how much of the information he'd just reported was already known to his handler. 'You're about to tell me there's a link with John Doe here, right?'

'Right. The deceased's name is Peter Wright. When he was found, his wrists were bound behind his back using a length of rope. We haven't had time yet to identify any DNA samples from the rope itself, but actually that's not such a big problem.'

'How come?'

'Seems Peter Wright was a meticulous kind of guy. He marked his antiques with a forensic-coding anti-theft system. We found traces of it on him which helped identify him. We also found traces of the same chemical in Tony Foreman's car. Our working theory is that Foreman was responsible for the homicide of Peter Wright.'

Pat was quiet for a moment while he processed that information. Finally he said: 'So what's the link? What did Peter Wright have to do with Operation Jaguar. Was he a threat to Croft's dealings with the Black Hawks?'

Agent 2 shook his head. 'Peter Wright has never even come up on our radar. Of course, that doesn't mean he's necessarily clean, but as far as we can tell he's nothing to do with the narcotics industry whatsoever. He's the financial officer for a small pharmaceutical company in Laguna Niguel.'

'So why is Croft…'

'I don't know,' Agent 2 interrupted. 'Frankly I don't care. We've got nothing concrete to link Croft to this homicide, but we know he's actively committing felonies. I don't much care if I put him away for homicide, or narcotics trafficking. Hell, I'll do an Al Capone on the son of a bitch and do him for tax evasion if it stops him from financing the Black Hawks. I get the feeling he's going to call on you to get your hands dirty kind of soon.'

'Yeah,' Pat replied. 'I get that feeling too.'

'So the minute – no, the *second* – you get anything on him, you need to call us in.'

'Sure, you'd better keep your cell phone on.' Pat knew he sounded facetious, but he didn't much care. When you were deep undercover, calling in the cavalry wasn't quite the same as dialling out for pizza.

Agent 2 put one hand into his inside jacket. He pulled out a BlackBerry and handed it to Pat. 'Press 5 twice on that phone – no, not now. You do that, we'll be able to locate your position using its enhanced GPS chip. As soon as we get that contact, we'll send the troops in.'

Pat examined the phone. Things had come a long way, he thought to himself, since the days when he had to keep a pocket full of change to feed into a phone box whenever he wanted to contact his handler.

'How quick?' he asked.

'Depends when we get the signal, where you are and how well defended your position is. You should work on it being a couple of hours to play safe. When we come, we'll come in hard – like, special forces hard – so keep your head down and be prepared for things to go noisy.'

Pat Dolan twisted the BlackBerry around in his hands. When he spoke again, he had lost all hint of the facetiousness that had marked the conversation up till then. 'If Croft tells me to do away with someone and you don't get there in time, do I…'

'You do whatever your conscience allows you to do,' Agent 2 said firmly, 'and you keep your cover. You get it?'

Yeah. Pat got it. The buck stopped with him as everything he did was deniable. If he made the wrong call, he was on his own. He stood up and looked out over the insect-infested pond. Then he nodded once at his handler and walked slowly away.

When he glanced back over his shoulder a couple of minutes later, the bench by the pond was empty. Agent 2 was nowhere to be seen.

'Why are those soldiers standing outside our house, Daddy?'

Jack's face was so close to his bedroom window that his breath misted up the glass. The lawn below was neatly trimmed. At the end of the lawn was the wall that surrounded Tom and Jane's house. The electronic gates at the end of the driveway were closed and standing by them were two armed men. Jack called them soldiers, and they certainly looked like that. They wore body armour and camouflage trousers. Tom was not sufficiently well-versed in weaponry to know what the small but efficient-looking weapons were that they had hung around their necks and which they held lightly but with obvious skill. These soldiers, however, were not patriots. At least, not any more. Their loyalty was only to the money they were paid. And Pure Industries, as of twelve hours ago, was paying them a lot. Private security, Tom had discovered, didn't come cheap.

'Don't worry about it, champ,' Tom replied.

But Jack clearly *was* worrying about it. He wasn't stupid, after all. 'Is it to do with why you brought Mom back home?'

'Really, Jack, you…'

'The nurse didn't want her to come, did she?' Jack turned away from the window to look at him, and Tom saw that his eyes were full of tears. 'What if she gets too ill to...' He looked down at the immaculate floor of the bedroom. 'What if she dies? She needs to be in the hospital. She told me.'

Tom stepped forward and put one hand on his son's shoulder. 'Do you trust me, Jack?'

Jack nodded, but his eyes told a different story. 'Can I go outside?' he asked. 'To play?'

'No, champ. I'm sorry. We have to stay indoors for a while.'

'Because of the soldiers?'

'Because of the soldiers.'

'How long will they be there?'

'I don't know, champ. I just don't know.' Tom looked around the room. It was immaculately neat. Jack's books were all on their bookcase; the wires to his Playstation were out of view; his loft bed was neatly made. It didn't look like a ten-year-old's room, and somehow Jack didn't look like a ten-year-old. Made sense. He was having to deal with adult stuff, after all. 'You'll be OK for a bit?' Tom asked. 'I'm going to go check on your mom.'

Jack nodded. As Tom left the room he was still breathing on the window, staring out at the armed guards.

Tom chewed on the nail of his right thumb as he walked downstairs. There was so much going on in his head. Peter dead. Sylvia still missing. He kept remembering Admiral Windlass's words: '*You really think that a tiny corporation nobody has heard of is a match for the office of the President of the United States. You really think we don't deal with bigger problems than you before breakfast?*' Maybe that was true. But now that he, Rachael and Kyle had close-protection units assigned to them, now that Pure Industries was surrounded by the kind of personnel you'd expect to see around the residence of the corrupt leader of some banana republic, even the President's men were going to find it difficult getting close. The security meant Pure was haemorrhaging money it didn't have, but that didn't matter: once Elixir was on the market, it would be insignificant.

He'd installed Jane in a room on the ground floor – the space Tom ordinarily used as a home office – so that she wouldn't have to negotiate the stairs. The room itself looked out on to the back lawn, but with the blinds drawn and the windows closed it was dusky dark and smelled of sickness. Jane lay in a single bed, her head propped up on three pillows, her eyes closed. Next to her, in an armchair, was a young redhead in her mid-twenties. Her name was Monica, and the moment this private nurse had arrived yesterday evening, she had told Tom that Jane needed to be in hospital. When Tom had curtly replied that this was out of the question, she had pursed her lips and gone about her business of making Jane as comfortable as possible. Now she was sitting quietly, listening to her slow, heavy breathing, quiet like a tomb.

'Could you give us a minute, Monica?'

'She doesn't need disturbing,' the nurse replied.

'I only need a minute. And you need a break.'

The young woman stood up reluctantly, placed a concerned hand on Jane's forehead, and left the room. He was nervous and to be nervous in front of his wife, the woman from whom, until now, he had held no secrets – it was almost as unpalatable a sensation as the one he got when he thought about Peter's body, cold and grey in that awful mortuary. It wasn't right that he was keeping her in the dark, especially now that he'd ripped her from the place where she was as comfortable as was possible in her state. The secrecy had to end. Now.

And yet, what if she didn't say what he prayed she would?

He stared at her pallid face for thirty seconds before reaching out and brushing her left cheek with the back of his hand. Jane's eyes flickered open. Normally, when she awoke to see Tom there, she would smile. Not today. Smiling was obviously too much of an effort.

'I need to tell you something,' Tom whispered.

Jane managed to nod her head in acknowledgement, but she didn't speak. She just lay perfectly still as Tom started to talk. He told her everything: about Rachael Leo's discovery in the lab, about the President's man and about Peter and Sylvia. He explained why he'd removed her from the hospice, and why their house was now surrounded by enough men to start a small war. As he spoke, Jane listened without expression, or reaction. And when he finished, she just continued to breathe steadily and made no response.

'Jane…' he said quietly, afraid that she had fallen asleep again and that his moment of bravery had passed. '*Jane…*'

'I can't take it, Tom. You know that, don't you?'

Silence. Tom could hear a bird trilling outside the window.

'I just thought…'

Jane's eyes flickered open. There was something in them. An expression Tom didn't recognize. Anger? Could it *really* be anger?

'Do you really think this is a life that I'm living, Tom? Would you really force this on me for any…' She burst into a fit of weak coughing before she could finish her sentence. It appeared to leave her even weaker than before, and her head lolled against her pillow at an angle.

It was exactly what Tom hadn't wanted to hear. He noticed that his hand was trembling.

'I just thought…' His voice trailed off as he lost the courage to say what was on his mind.

'What did you think, Tom?' Jane breathed.

Tom inhaled deeply, steadying himself. 'I just left Jack,' he said. 'He's in tears. It's not the first time. It happens every day. He's a brave kid. He keeps a lid on it when he's with you, but Jane, he's crumbling inside. He can't cope. So I just thought…' Now it was Tom's turn to close his eyes. 'I just thought that for him… I know it would be hard for you, Jane, but it would give us the one thing we don't have. Time. Time together. Time as a family. Time… time to find a *cure* for this goddamned illness of yours. When the Elixir goes to market, we'll have all the money we'll ever need. We can put it into research, have the best doctors in the World trying to work out a way to make you better.' He opened his eyes again. 'People have already died because of Elixir,' he said. 'How about we start using it to make people live. People like you. And Jack.'

He said all this quickly. Somewhere deep down, he wondered to himself how honest he was being. Was he *really* trying to persuade Jane to take one of the five little pills he had stolen from the lab just for Jack's sake? Or was it for *his* sake as well? Was he being a diligent and loving husband? Or was he just selfish? Selfish beyond measure?

Jane was looking at him. Even in the state she was in, Tom felt as though his wife could see right through him. She'd always been able to. He could keep no secrets from her.

'How long?' she asked.

'How long what?'

'How long have you been planning to say that to me?'

A pause.

'I'm sorry,' he whispered.

'You don't know what it's like, waiting to die.' She started to cough again and then, when it had subsided, spoke so quietly that Tom had to strain to hear her. 'You think that to live forever would be a blessing? Nothing could be worse than an eternity of this.'

'I'm sorry,' Tom repeated. He couldn't think of anything else to say. He felt foolish. Embarrassed. He wished he'd kept his mouth shut.

'Give it to me,' Jane breathed.

He blinked. 'I thought you said...'

Jane had closed her eyes again. 'For Jack,' was all she managed to say. 'I'll endure it for Jack.'

Tom walked over to the study door. There was a key in the lock which he turned to shut them both inside. As he returned to Jane's bed, he pulled from his pocket a small, enamel pill box. Perching on the edge of the bed again, he opened it up and removed one of the tiny white pills. He held it up to the light and examined it curiously for a moment. It was so small. So insignificant. It just looked like any other medicine – an aspirin, perhaps. He realized his hands were shaking as he stretched out and pushed the tablet through Jane's dry lips and on to the rough moistness of her tongue. She put up no resistance. Even if she'd wanted to, she wouldn't have been able. Tom took a glass of water from her bedside table and put it up to her lips. A little liquid spilled over her chin and on to her bedclothes, but most of it went into her mouth. She swallowed with difficulty, and when Tom put his hands into his wife's mouth again, the tablet had gone.

Tom didn't know what to expect. Perhaps he had been imagining something magical. A sudden change. A glow of health. There was nothing of the sort. Jane just lay there, looking and sounding like she was asleep. For someone whose life had just been saved, she appeared remarkably close to death.

He stood up and dropped the enamel pill box back in his pocket. He stared at Jane's sleeping body for a couple of minutes. Half of him felt guilty at having forced her into this. Half of him felt elation that her passing was not something he, or Jack would have to deal with – at least, not yet.

With a final glance back at his wife, he walked back to the door, unlocked it and stepped outside. The nurse was waiting there, two arms folded disapprovingly as she gave Tom a baleful stare.

'She's fine,' he said.

'I think *I* should be the judge of that, Mr Shaw. I hope you didn't do anything to get her too excited.'

Tom had no reply. He just nodded curtly to the nurse and went to find Jack. Funny, he thought to himself, how when you know you have all the time in the World, the need to fill each moment with something worthwhile becomes all the greater. And what could be more worthwhile than spending time with your child?

'Jack!' he called. '*Jack!*'

Tom found him in his den, slouched out on a beanbag watching cartoons with a blank look on his face. Jack grunted monosyllabically as Tom walked in, but he didn't complain when his dad plonked himself right down beside him started watching in silence too.

Jack's anger had gone. He rested his head against his dad's shoulders.

Everything's going to be alright, Tom told himself.

It has to be.

It has to be.

The cartoons continued to play. Jack didn't laugh. He didn't respond at all. And nor did Tom. He was too busy thinking. About Peter. About Sylvia. And about the government.

Whoever was targeting his people, they had information. How had they got it? Were the offices of Pure Industries secure? Was the place being bugged? Or, was it something more sinister than that? Everyone who knew about the Elixir had been targeted. Everyone except him, and Rachael Leo. But Rachael, surely, wasn't leaking this information. Elixir was her invention. She could have taken it to anyone...

But if Rachael wasn't the leak, who was? The problem gnawed at his brain until the sun went down. And it continued to gnaw for many hours after that.

13

SATURDAY, 09.00 A.M., PACIFIC STANDARD TIME

Dr Rachael Leo had already been in the lab for three hours. When she'd arrived at 6 a.m., escorted by the two-man close protection team that, rather than make her feel safe just increased her anxiety, she was surprised to see that the security men – four at the entrance to the perimeter, two at the main building entrance and several more dotted around – were already there. When Tom had said security, he'd *meant* security.

She'd put in three hours' work with her guards standing sentinel outside the lab. Working on a Saturday had never bothered her much; today she positively welcomed it. It was only when she was immersed in her science that she could forget everything else that was worrying her, not least the horrible, growing realization that her discovery had led directly to the gruesome, premature death – no, murder – of Peter Wright. And what about Sylvia? Where was she? Nobody had heard from her, and that couldn't be good.

Now she needed a break. Her two close-protection men were still standing outside the lab. As Rachael walked along the corridor, they followed several paces behind. Rachael stopped and looked back at them. 'Hey guys, you probably don't need to accompany me to the restroom, right?' The men looked a bit awkward and returned to their positions outside the lab door.

Ten minutes later she was in the common room,. She smiled as Kyle appeared in the doorway. She hadn't forgotten the kiss they'd shared in Washington. Even in the midst of everything else that was going on, the slightly nervous, slightly excited sensation in her stomach remained.

'I see you've managed to shake off Tweedledum and Tweedledee,' Kyle observed.

Rachael nodded. 'How about you?'

Kyle looked up and down the corridor and winked. 'Reckon we might have a couple of minutes to ourselves.' He stepped inside and shut the door behind him.

Rachael felt a little thrill, but as Kyle stepped towards her, it was suddenly clear he didn't have romance on his mind. 'I need to talk to you,' he breathed.

'What is it?'

'Someone knows about the Elixir, right? Someone inside the company. If the President's men are targeting us, someone has to have told them. Someone who knows about it.'

'I guess...' Rachael said. 'But who? There's only the five of us, and Peter and Sylvia are...' The sentence dissolved in her mouth.

Kyle looked over his shoulder, clearly checking that the door was locked. 'Ruth's here this morning,' he said. 'I just walked past Tom's office. She was rooting around in a filing cabinet. It seemed like she was looking for something.'

Rachael felt her brow furrowing. 'She's his PA,' she said. 'There's nothing unusual about…'

'About being here on a Saturday morning? When she thinks nobody's going to be around to see her? Come on, Rachael, it all makes sense. She was in the office the morning you told us about Elixir. What if she overheard? What if *she's* the leak?'

'I… I don't know, Kyle…' Rachael knew that Ruth Adams had no great fondness for her, and the feeling was mutual. But if what Kyle was suggesting was true…

'We need to find out,' he said. 'You think you can get to Tom's office with me without the goons following?'

Rachael nodded mutely.

'Come on, then. If you can distract her, I'll have a root through her things, see if I can come up with anything.'

'And if you can't?

'Then we'll just have to keep looking.'

Kyle opened the door of the common room very gently. Standing at the opening, Rachael could hear her two guards talking in low voices along the corridor to her left, but as the lab was round the corner, she knew that she could sneak in the direction of Tom's office without them seeing her. It was only if they came to check she was alright that they'd know she wasn't there.

The corridors were deserted, but Rachael found herself holding her breath in any case. When Kyle gently took her hand in his, she didn't resist, and together they crept past the Board Room and towards Tom's office.

The office door was slightly ajar. Kyle motioned at Rachael to look inside. She did so. Sure enough, Tom's PA was in there, flicking through the top drawer of a filing cabinet. Rachael nodded at Kyle, who mouthed the word 'Go!' to her, and she stepped inside.

'Morning, Ruth,' she said.

Ruth slammed the drawer shut so quickly, Rachael was briefly concerned that she might have hurt her fingers in it. The PA spun round to look at her, and was unable to stop a look of guilt appearing on her pinched, unfriendly face. 'Dr Leo,' she said tersely. 'I'm sure there's a reason for your entering Mr Shaw's office without being invited.'

Rachael could sense Kyle disappearing down the corridor in the direction of Ruth's own little cubby hole. Distract her, he'd said. But Rachael was terrible at things like this. She heard her voice shaking as she spoke.

'Ruth, I, er…'

'I'm extremely busy, Dr Leo. If you'll excuse me.' Ruth walked towards the door.

'This is silly,' Rachael blurted out.

Ruth stopped. 'I beg your pardon?'

'This. You and me, behaving like this. It's silly. I… I'm sure that if we got to know each other, Ruth, we could… I don't know… be friends?'

Ruth Adams blinked. Rachael rather had the impression that she thought she was talking to a lunatic.

'Friends, Dr Leo?'

'Er, yeah… friends.'

'I'm afraid I don't quite understand.'

A noise from along the corridor. What was Kyle doing? Where was he?

'Well... we work together, and it just seems to me that it would be better all round if...'

'Please excuse me, Dr Leo,' Ruth interrupted crisply. 'I understand that the weekend might be the time when most of Pure Industries relaxes, but I really do have a great deal of work to be getting on with.'

Rachael couldn't help her eyes flickering towards the filing cabinet in which Ruth had been rooting around. The PA's skin visibly reddened.

'*Excuse me*, Dr Leo.'

Rachael didn't see that she had much choice. She stepped aside, and let Ruth pass through the doorway.

'I think it would be a good idea if I locked Mr Shaw's office, Dr Leo. Wouldn't you?'

'Yes,' Rachael replied, her voice very soft. 'I think it would.' She stepped out into the corridor. As Ruth locked the door she saw her two close-protection guys striding towards them. They were scowling, clearly annoyed that Rachael had given them the slip.

'Dr Leo,' one of them said. 'We didn't know where you'd gone.'

'Sorry...' Rachael muttered. 'I just... let's get back to the lab.'

'That's sounds like a very good idea, Dr Leo,' Ruth said. She walked rather primly away from them, in the direction of her office.

Rachael felt almost like a prisoner as the two guards led her back past the common room towards her laboratory. But her mind was too active to let it bother her. What if Ruth had found Kyle in her office? What if he'd been going through her things and…

They turned a corner. Kyle was there, outside the lab, waiting for them. He was clutching his cell phone.

'Kyle…' Rachael breathed.

'Thanks guys,' he said to the two guards. 'You'll give me and Dr Leo a bit of space, I hope?' He held the lab door open and followed Rachael inside.

'I thought she'd find you,' Rachael exhaled with relief once the door was shut. 'I couldn't hold her for…'

But she stopped talking as Kyle handed her his cell phone. The screen had a photograph on it. It looked like a scrap of paper with thin, spidery writing on it. 'I found this,' he said. 'In one of her drawers.'

Rachael held the screen closer to her eyes. The picture was small, but it was sufficiently large for her to make out the words scrawled on the paper. She read them twice, just to make sure she hadn't made a mistake. 'Four elements or processes … Legum … one process known by each Board member…'

She blinked. Then she looked up at Kyle. His face was grim. 'I think we've found our leak,' he said. 'Do you want to call Tom, or shall I?'

'I don't believe it. Jack, I told you not to *touch* anything.'

Tom stood at the far end of the lab with Kyle and Rachael. Jack, loitering somewhere near the middle of the room, had picked up a Perspex petri dish and was staring through it.

'It's alright,' Rachael said calmly. 'He can't do any harm.'

But Tom was already striding towards Jack. He grabbed the petri dish from his hands and slammed it back down on the worktop. Father and son exchanged a glare, and Tom instantly regretted his loss of temper. All this was getting to him, but it wasn't fair to take it out on Jack. The boy's wide eyes only compounded this feeling. 'Sorry, champ,' he whispered, but Jack was clearly embarrassed. He avoided his father's eye.

Tom walked back to the two other adults who had watched this little exchange with frowns of concern. 'I don't believe it,' he repeated. 'Look, I know Ruth can be prickly, but she's been here forever. She's loyal and Pure Industries is her life.'

'Alright then, Tom,' Rachael breathed – Jack was looking over in their direction now. 'Analyze it. You tell me who *you* think the mole is, and why Ruth has details of the Elixir written down in her office…'

'She's not a murderer, Rachael.'

'Nobody's saying she's a murderer, Tom,' Kyle interjected. 'Can't you see she's just a tiny cog in a bigger machine?'

Tom closed his eyes. His head was buzzing. Try as he might, he couldn't think of any explanation other than the one Rachael and Kyle had suggested. 'I need to get rid of her,' he said finally.

'No.' Kyle sounded definite.

'But the police…'

'I know,' the younger man said. 'But listen, Tom. We don't know exactly who we're up against, but whoever it is, they're not playing by the rules. That means they win, unless we do the same.'

'What are you suggesting?'

'We keep Ruth where she is. Feed her misinformation.'

'Like what?'

Kyle shrugged. 'We can pretend we're pulling the Elixir. Get the government off our backs. Then, when we're ready to launch…'

Tom looked at his two employees. Rachael was biting her lower lip, but she still looked determined. She was standing very close to Kyle. Closer than a colleague normally would.

'Okay,' Tom said. 'We'll do it your way. But Rachael, we need to get this thing to market…'

'I'm working as quickly as I can, Tom.'

'I know.' He glanced over at Jack. 'This is a strain on him,' he murmured, more to himself than to the others. 'His mother, she's…' Tom caught a sharp glance from Rachael, which he avoided. 'She's not good. It's difficult for him to be stuck at home all day.'

'Bring him in here,' Rachael suggested. 'I can watch him while I work.'

Tom raised an eyebrow.

'It's a change of scene,' Rachael continued, 'and he's a bright kid. Maybe he'll find it stimulating.' She gave a small smile. 'I could do with the company sometimes, too.'

'I don't know,' Tom replied. 'He needs to be safe.'

Rachael gave him a slightly withering look. 'Tom, Pure Industries has more security around it than some heads of state. Are you honestly telling me Jack's any safer at home than he is here?'

'I guess not.' He looked over at Jack again, who seemed to know they were talking about him. The boy's ears went red – though whether this was because he was a topic of conversation, or because the attractive young scientist was smiling at him, Tom wasn't sure. 'You want to hang out with Rachael for a bit, champ?' he called across the lab. Jack gave a noncommittal gesture, the closest Tom would get, he knew, to a yes. 'Looks like you've got yourself a companion,' he told Rachael. 'Make sure he doesn't leave your sight, got it?'

'Got it.' Rachael turned to Jack and smiled. 'Jack, you can stay here with me as much as want. I'd love your company.'

The smile Jack returned was tinged with delight. For the first time in weeks, Tom felt a weight lift from him. He turned to Kyle.

'Come with me,' he said softly. 'If we're going to deal with Ruth, we need to talk it through.'

'Somewhere she can't hear us,' Kyle pointed out.

'Yeah,' said Tom. He felt as though there was something solid in his stomach. 'Somewhere she can't hear us…'

Theodore Croft stared at Dr Jacobs, whose Adam's apple slid around under his skin as he swallowed nervously.

'You're sure?' he demanded.

'Quite sure, Mr Croft.' Jacobs was digging his fingernails into the palm of his hands. 'I've treated a number of cells with the compound. It makes no difference to their rate of decay … Mr Croft … *Mr Croft?*'

Croft barely heard him. He had turned to look out over the ocean, where the sun was setting and had colored the water a deep blood red. He felt an anger like he had never known rising up inside him. He knew he would burst any minute, and when that happened, he wouldn't be responsible for his actions.

'Get out,' he whispered.

'Mr Croft, I…'

'*Get out!*'

Croft spun round and the scientist, with one look at the expression on his face, edged backwards towards the door. As soon as he had exited the room, Croft heard Jacobs start to run, and it was only then it struck him he was making a mistake. The man fleeing the house knew about the Elixir, and about Croft's interest in it. That made him a danger, of course. A danger he couldn't risk singing.

Croft didn't even look at the alabaster lamp that he pulled from its occasional table as he passed it, yanking the power cord from the wall and dragging it along behind him. He knew Jacobs would still be fumbling at the front door and that as it was locked he'd still be there when Croft arrived in a few seconds. Sure enough, the tall, nervous man was desperately pulling the mechanism, trying to get outside, and didn't even realize Croft was upon him until he was two yards away.

Jacobs turned. His glasses slipped down the sweat that covered the bridge of his nose. When he opened his mouth to scream at the sight of Croft raising the heavy alabaster over his head, no noise came.

The thud of marble meeting skin was dull and wet. Jacobs crumpled immediately as a red welt spread immediately over the right-hand side of his face where the lamp had made contact, and the redness of the scientist's blood was matched only by his attacker's vivid fury. Croft got down to his knees and started pounding the alabaster against the scientist's head. He could both feel and hear the skull crunching with each blow, and it was obvious that Jacobs was dead long before he had finished venting his fury upon his silent corpse, his body moving only with the impact of Croft's fury.

And then everything was silent. Theodore Croft looked with distaste at the blood all over his visitor's face, and the lamp, and his own hands and clothes. How much easier it is to kill someone second time round, he thought to himself, as he stood up again and spat on Jacobs' body.

Tony could deal with the body, he decided. Tony and that goddamn Irishman who no doubt had plenty of experience disappearing stiffs. Croft had other things to worry about. He showered and put on fresh, unbloodied clothes, before returning to his office and removing a thin file from the safe he kept beneath his desk. He opened it up and looked through it.

Theodore Croft was a careful man, and now that his anger was subsiding, he was able to think clearly again. He had failed to find the formula. Maybe one of the components was wrong. Maybe he had been lied to. No matter. The time had come to stop tiptoeing around the subject. His contact in Pure Industries needed to up their game. To earn their keep.

He pressed his fingers together, closed his eyes, and thought.

And then he picked up his cell phone and rang a number.

'It's me,' he said.

No reply, but then Croft wasn't expecting one.

'You need to get here immediately. We have to talk.'

'It's not convenient.'

'*Make* it convenient.'

A pause.

'The usual place?'

'One hour.'

Croft hung up. Then he stood and, taking the file with him, descended to the basement car port where his Bentley convertible was waiting.

His destination was not the kind of place where Bentley convertibles would go unnoticed. A dirty, low-rent suburb of the city that was a short distance from the beachside luxury of Malibu only in geographical terms. In every other respect, it was a million miles away. Every store front was shuttered; the corner of every block was manned by a black-skinned dealer who spoke to the thin, filthy, desperate junkies handing over their pathetic, crumpled dollar bills as if they were the lowest form of scum, but pocketing the money anyway before sending them on to their equally surly associates down the road to pick up the merchandize. Croft found himself sneering. Everybody had their drug of choice, whether it was crack or Krug. But there was only one drug he was interested in, and his need for it was even greater than the helpless addicts he passed now.

His destination was a subterranean parking lot. It was an oasis of wealth amidst the filth and the squalor of this part of town, full of expensive cars – enormous black Land Cruisers, for the most part, the status symbols of the dealers. Croft handed a hundred-dollar bill to the sour-faced attendant – the fee every visitor to this parking lot paid to be sure of an alibi from the old guy who'd seen a market opportunity and grabbed it – then parked up in a far, empty corner of the lot. He saw nobody among the other parked cars. It was too early yet. The insects had not yet crawled out from under their stones. He pressed a button on his key fob and centrally locked the vehicle anyway. You couldn't be too careful in places like this. Then he sat in the dark and waited.

Theodore Croft was not accustomed to waiting for anybody, but on this occasion he knew he had to be patient. His contact would be here in the fullness of time. And sure enough, fifteen minutes later, a second car entered the parking lot. It stood out, not because it was flash, but because it wasn't. A simple Ford saloon. The gentle screech of this vehicle's tyres against the smooth concrete floor echoed around the lot, and the Ford drew up exactly alongside Croft's Bentley.

The two vehicles sat silently next to each other. Engines off. No lights on.

And then Croft saw the passenger window of the Ford slide down. He lowered his own window and looked left into the other car.

The driver didn't look at him. He still had his hands on the steering wheel and was staring straight ahead, as though he was still driving. He was a young man in his late twenties. Good looking. Smart. He slowly turned his head to the right so that he was looking across his passenger seat and into Croft's own car.

Croft smiled.

'Good evening, Kyle,' he said. 'Good of you to come at such short notice. Why don't you join me in the Bentley? We've got a lot to talk about, so really I think we should make ourselves as comfortable as possible, don't you?'

'Nobody suspects you, I hope?'

'If somebody suspected me, I'd have told you. They found Peter Wright's body. It was clumsy of you to leave it lying around.'

Croft waved his hand, swatting away Kyle's objection like it was an irritating bug. 'The information I have is wrong.'

Kyle narrowed his eyes. 'What do you mean, wrong?'

'Tell me which bit you didn't understand. It's wrong. I had someone try to make up the compound. It doesn't work.'

'Maybe they *did* it wrong.'

Croft turned to look at Kyle. He knew nobody could hold that gaze for long, and soon the younger man's left cheek twitched and he looked away.

'So what do we do?' Kyle asked quietly.

'The first thing *you* do, Kyle, is answer my questions. Does anybody suspect you?'

'Nobody. They realize there's a leak, but they think it's Tom Shaw's PA. I've encouraged them to take that particular suspicion to heart.' He inclined his head. 'It was a good idea of yours,' he added, 'to make it look as though my flat had been raided.'

But Croft, impervious to compliments, spoke over him. 'Putting together the formula piecemeal isn't working,' he said. 'We need to go straight to the horse's mouth.'

Croft sensed his companion tensing up. Kyle continued to avoid his gaze.

'Well you'd better hurry up,' he said. 'We're almost ready to launch. Once that happens we won't stand a chance.' He thought for a moment. 'Tom Shaw knows everything,' he said finally. 'When Peter and Sylvia went missing, it was decided that he should...'

'Tom Shaw is no good to me, Kyle,' Croft purred. 'He's not a scientist. I can't be sure he knows everything *I* need to know.' His hand crept into the inside pocket of his jacket. Kyle visibly flinched, but relaxed as Croft brought out nothing more than a little plastic box. 'Peppermint?' he offered.

Kyle shook his head curtly as Croft popped one of the tiny mints into his mouth and sucked thoughtfully. 'If I were a betting man, which, to be honest with you Kyle, I *am*, I'd say that there was something *between* you and the fragrant Dr Leo. Would that be an accurate analysis of the situation?'

'She's just a chick.'

'Just a chick,' Croft repeated. '*Just a chick*. And yet, you seem very keen that I should focus my attention on Tom Shaw, when it's quite clear to you and me that Rachael Leo is the one who can construct the Elixir. The one that can give us what we want. Perhaps you are thinking to the future. Perhaps you have decided who you want to spend forever with. But it's a long time, forever. Surely men like you and me, Kyle, do not expect to share it with just one person.'

A pause. Then Kyle looked Croft straight in the eye.

'I just thought that security around Rachael would be tighter. Tom would be an easier target. Do what you want,

Theodore…' Kyle said firmly. 'She's nothing to me. She's just a chick'.

There was a silence – a full thirty seconds – while Croft considered this. Did he mean it? Croft was angry he hadn't taken this approach before. He had only done so because Byng had insisted. But it hadn't worked. This would.

'We are united, I hope, Kyle, in our common purpose?'

Their 'common purpose', the very mention of it was enough to make some of Kyle's arrogance fall away.

'You know we are,' Kyle replied.

'You saw the scum we passed on our way here,' Croft continued relentlessly. 'The junkies and the dealers. You think just *anybody* should be allowed the Elixir?'

'Of course not,' Kyle replied, but Croft barely heard him.

'Pure blood,' he breathed. 'Only the right people must be permitted to survive…' He shook his head, reviving himself from his reverie. 'If I have any sense that young Dr Leo has been tipped off about our intentions, I'll be in no doubt who the guilty party is, of course.'

Byng looked at him finally. 'Are you threatening me, Theodore?'

'Certainly.' Croft smiled blandly. His voice expressed his genuine surprise that Kyle might imagine he was doing anything else. When he continued to speak, however, it was with more than a hint of menace. 'I regard it as extremely fortuitous to have found you working at Pure Industries, but unless you do exactly as I say, I will destroy you.'

Kyle visibly flinched, and Croft had a sudden vision of the first time they had met, when Kyle had joined his hedge fund straight from college. The young man had soon found himself embroiled in – and actively enjoying – the black arts of insider trading. But he decided to leave after a brush with the Security and Exchange Commission. Croft even remembered what he'd said to him the day he resigned. *You're a coward, Byng. But I've seen the enthusiasm with which you embraced the darker side of our business. It's well documented. You'll never escape from it.*

'You want me to kill her?' Kyle asked quietly.

'Perhaps,' Croft said. 'We shall see. But for now I think our time is best spent discussing your friend in the White House.' He removed the file from where it was lying on the dashboard, opened it up and read out a name. 'Admiral Windlass?'

'What's he got to do with anything?'

'I went to the trouble of running a few checks on the Admiral. It's amazing what you can find out about a man, if you just ask the right people the right questions. It seems Windlass has got himself into a bit of... *difficulty*.'

'What sort of difficulty, Theodore? For God's sake just say what you mean, can't you?'

'Debt, Kyle. Massive debt. Catastrophic debt. The sort of debt that could quite ruin a man's life, if he let it.'

He could tell he had Kyle's interest, so he continued.

'Of course, debts can be bought and sold, as we both know. The markets are just like real life. Windlass's debtors weren't exactly Chase Manhattan, of course, but they were happy enough for me to take over the Admiral's debt. Which gives us a certain amount of leverage, wouldn't you say?'

'I still don't see what the hell Windlass has to do with this.'

A shadow crossed Croft's face. He didn't like Kyle's tone. But then, he reminded himself, he didn't *have* to like it. Kyle Byng was necessary. He would have to swallow his annoyance.

'We'll only have one shot at putting our hands on Rachael Leo,' Croft said. 'If we mess it up, her security will become impregnable. We need the best. That's what Windlass can give us. He has the authority to mobilize a government Special Forces unit. Extracting Leo from some two-bit security firm, that's their bread and butter.'

'He'll never do it,' Kyle objected. 'Not without the President's say-so. Trust me, Theodore, I've met the guy and he's…'

But Croft had started to shake his head and tut like a disappointed schoolteacher. 'Kyle,' he breathed. 'Kyle, Kyle, Kyle… don't you see? I *own* Windlass. I can ruin him with a click of my fingers. The money is insignificant to me. But he'll know what it means for him if the press get hold of the contents of that folder: the debt, the helpless gambling addiction, the wife that's screwing anything in a pair of trousers that *isn't* her husband. The guy does what we ask, or he won't be able to show his face on Capitol Hill again. Are things becoming clearer to you now, Kyle? Do you understand where I'm coming from.'

If Kyle Byng was impressed with Croft's strategy, he didn't let it show in his face.

'What do you want me to do?' he asked.

'Contact Windlass. Tell him you need to see him urgently, without Shaw or Leo and somewhere other than the White House. That'll be enough to raise his interest. Do it tonight. I want to be on the first available flight out of LA.'

'I can't come with you. I've got too much security around me. It was difficult enough slipping away to meet you tonight. If I try to make a flight to DC, Tom and Rachael will know about it.'

'All you need to do is set up the meeting. I'll take care of everything else. And Kyle?'

'What?'

Croft smiled at him. 'If you still want to see some action between the sheets with Rachael Leo – and hell, I wouldn't blame you if you did, my friend – now's the time to do it. Sorry to say, but I guess she's not going to feel in the mood by the time we've extracted out of her everything we need.' He glanced up at the rear-view mirror to see a Land Cruiser driving into the parking lot. It had blacked-out windows and shook to the beats of ear-splitting gangster rap. 'Time for me to take my leave, Kyle. I'm heading straight for the airport. Don't let me down, now.'

Kyle didn't reply. He didn't even look at Croft. He just climbed out of the Bentley and strode quickly to his own car. The tyres of the Ford screeched more loudly this time, as he quickly reversed and drove out of sight, leaving Theodore Croft to leave at a more leisurely pace, a mysterious smile on his face and the thrill of excitement burning once more in his blood.

14

Sunday, 9.00 a.m., Eastern Standard Time

Nathanial Windlass didn't know whether to be intrigued or disturbed. The call had come through just before midnight. His first thought was that it was just some goddamn joker. His second, less comforting, thought was that it was the guys he owed money to, trying to scare the living crap out of him.

'You need to pay attention,' the voice had said.

'Who is this, I said, *who the hell is this?*'

'My name's Kyle Byng. We met about the Elixir. I work with Tom Shaw.'

Windlass had sat up in his bed. He furrowed his brow and thought back. There *had* been someone else in that meeting. A man and a woman, though Windlass was damned if he could remember either of their names. 'Listen, young man…' he'd started to say.

'No. *You* listen. There isn't much time. You want to earn yourself some Brownie points with the President, you be at this location tomorrow at 9.00 a.m. You listening?'

Windlass was. And that was why he sat here now, in an otherwise deserted diner in a Western suburb of Washington, a skinny latte on the table in front of him and an uneasy feeling nestling in his stomach. The waitress kept staring at him from behind the counter. She clearly recognized him, but was unable to place him exactly. Windlass was used to that kind of look. He stonewalled it, and took a sip of his coffee.

The door to the diner opened. A man walked in. He was tall and tanned. Expensive clothes. Looked more like he should be walking into the Four Seasons than this crummy place. Windlass looked away when he realized he didn't recognize the guy – this wasn't who he was waiting for – but couldn't help a look of mild outrage when the man sat down at his table anyway.

He smiled. A slow, oily kind of smile that Windlass didn't take to at all. 'Eggs,' he said brightly. 'I don't know, after a long flight I always get kind of a craving for them.'

Windlass started to tell him, in no uncertain terms, that the seat was taken, but the arrival of the waitress at the table silenced him and he listened as the stranger ordered omelette and coffee. Only when the woman had disappeared into the kitchen did he continue talking. The stranger just held up one finger.

'Quiet,' he said.

'Do you know who the *hell* you're talking to?'

'Of course,' said the stranger. 'Admiral Nathanial Windlass. Special Adviser to the President, war hero and…' – he gave a regretful smile – '…a man living sadly beyond his means. Are you sure you can afford that coffee, Admiral? If my bank balance looked anything like yours, I think I'd consider making one, or two small economies.'

Windlass fell silent. He felt his skin redden and the anxiety in his stomach increased tenfold. 'I don't know what you're talking about,' he whispered, but he knew that he sounded very unconvincing.

'Admiral, *you're* a busy man and *I'm* a busy man. Neither of us want to spend any more time on this unhappy conversation than we need to. So let's cut to the chase. Those guys who've had you looking over your shoulder every hour of the day? You won't be seeing them anymore. I've bought them out. You don't owe them, you owe me. You look relieved, Admiral. So you should. I'm not much of a one for all this cloak and dagger nonsense.'

The stranger's coffee arrived, and he directed the full force of his smile at the waitress, who blushed as she set it down in front of him.

'Who *are* you?' Windlass hissed when they were alone again.

'Forgive me,' the stranger smiled at him. 'I seem to have forgotten my manners. Theodore Croft, a pleasure to make your acquaintance.' He took a sip of his coffee, keeping his eyes fixed on Windlass over the brim of the cup. 'And it ought to be a pleasure for you too, Admiral. I could be about to make you a very rich man. Shall we discuss the Elixir?'

This confident, arrogant stranger had Windlass's full attention now. He liked the word 'rich'.

'The kid who called me…' he started to say.

'Kyle Byng. An old associate of mine. He and I agree that a discovery of such magnitude should be in control of the more...' He smiled again. 'The more *enlightened* members of our society.'

'Enlightened *how*?'

Croft simply sipped at his coffee again.

'You said you were going to cut to the chase,' Windlass said after a moment of uncomfortable silence. 'I suggest you do that, before I stand up and walk out.'

Croft inclined his head. 'There are two people who know the full formula for the Elixir,' he said. 'I believe you've met both of them. Tom Shaw, the CEO of Pure Industries, and Dr Rachael Leo, his chief scientist. Shaw is a nobody. He's stumbled across this thing by accident and he's groping in the dark. Leaving the Elixir to him is idiocy, and you and I are not idiots. Agreed?'

Windlass shrugged noncommittally; underneath, however, he couldn't help but concur with Croft on that point, at least.

'Rachael Leo, however,' Croft continued. 'She's a different matter. She's the brains behind it. She's the one we need to get our hands on, Admiral.'

'You do realize, Mr Croft, that my first loyalty is to the President.'

Croft shook his head in a maddeningly complacent way. 'Your first loyalty,' he replied, 'is to yourself. Your second loyalty is to me.' He raised a finger to halt Windlass's sudden interruption. 'You're either with me, or against me, Admiral Windlass. If you're with me – my man at the heart of government – then believe me when I say you will become one of the wealthiest, most powerful men in the World.'

'And if I'm against you?'

'Then I will destroy you. I'll humiliate and break you. You'll be lower than the bums on the street, and your life will be so wretched you won't *want* to take the Elixir. Ah! My omelette!'

The waitress placed the food in front of him, and he tucked in eagerly. 'You know?' he announced, having swallowed several mouthfuls. 'This is delicious!'

Windlass watched him eat, his face calm but his mind a riot. The man in front of him was mad, quite clearly, but he had him by the *cojones* and was offering to cut him a deal. A deal that could change his life very much for the better.

His omelette finished, Croft drained his coffee cup and the two men waited while the waitress cleared the table.

'So?' Croft asked.

'What do you want me to do?' Windlass replied stiffly.

'You're a military man, Admiral.'

'Obviously.'

'A former US Navy Seal. So not, how can I put it, *squeamish* in any way?'

'What do you want me to do, Mr Croft?' Windlass repeated.

'I'd like to talk with Dr Leo. Unfortunately, Tom Shaw has taken the precaution of surrounding everybody who knows about the Elixir with a high level of security. I have certain people who I could lean upon to try to breach that security, but we'll only get one shot at this. It's a specialist operation and one for which I need professionals. Unfortunately, one doesn't just pick up the Yellow Pages and put in a call to Delta Force. That's where you come in.'

Windlass didn't allow any expression into his face. 'Go on,' he said.

'You must have contacts, Admiral. Properly trained men for whom this sort of thing is a walk in the park. Put together a team. Extract Rachael Leo alive. Anybody else, with the exception of Kyle Byng, is expendable. Bring her to me, and I will arrange for her to be persuaded to share her secrets with us.'

Windlass nodded slowly. 'Mr Croft,' he began.

'Call me Theodore.'

'*Mr Croft*. Perhaps you think I look like an idiot?'

Croft raised an inquisitive eyebrow. 'I'm afraid I don't quite follow you, Admiral.'

'I can deliver Rachael Leo to you. No problem. But what security do I have? How do I know you're going to keep your side of the deal once my work is done?'

'A good question, Admiral. A very good question.' Croft took a paper napkin from the holder on the table and dabbed the corner of his mouth. 'When the Elixir is in my possession, I'll need a man close to the President. That will be you. In return, not only will your debt to me be cancelled, but I'll cut you into the profits the Elixir makes. And I guess I don't need to tell you what kind of profits they will be.'

No, Windlass thought to himself. You don't need to tell me that.

Croft had leaned forward, his elbows on the table and his eyes intense. 'You do realize, Admiral, that the Elixir is the only thing that matters, don't you? Whoever owns it will be the most powerful man on earth. Keep your loyalty to the President if you like, but remember: you'll be backing a losing horse. Not to mention the small matter of your livelihood and reputation.'

Windlass could feel himself sweating. Was it anxiety, he wondered, or anticipation?

'It seems like you leave me no choice,' he said quietly.

'You know?' said Croft. 'Somehow I was sure you'd come round to my way of thinking, sooner, or later. Time is of the essence, Admiral Windlass. We haven't any to lose. How long will it be before you can get a team together.'

The Admiral gave it a moment's thought, then sniffed.

'I can't mobilize a special operation without the President's authorization,' he said. 'But I have contacts. Freelancers. Ex-DEVGRU and Delta Force. Guns for hire, basically. If they take a commission from me, they'll probably assume it's a deniable government operation anyway. They won't ask any questions and they'll do what's necessary.' As he spoke, Windlass experienced a sensation he thought he'd forgotten. The thrill of planning an op. Of doing what he was trained to do. 'Especially,' he added, 'if I lead the team myself.'

'I leave the details to you, Admiral Windlass. Just answer my question. How long?'

'They need paying, of course. Services like this don't come cheap.'

'Money no object. Can you do it?'

Windlass surveyed him coolly across the table. 'Of course I can do it. Leave it to me Mr Croft. You want Rachael Leo? She's all yours.'

Windlass left the diner ten minutes after Croft. After all, he thought to himself, when you're getting into bed with the Devil, the fewer people know about it, the better. But by that time, he'd already made a call, keeping his voice low so the waitress, whose eyes he had noticed lingering after Croft, could not hear what he was saying.

His name was Khan. Third generation Pakistani, though you wouldn't know it to look at him. Short, squat, slicked-back black hair and tougher than a Sherman tank, he was as American as a Big Mac, and to Windlass's mind about as wholesome. Khan and Windlass had nailed untold numbers of Vietcong side by side back in the day, but while Windlass's career had meandered toward Capitol Hill, Khan's had stayed firmly in the arena of the military. He had a profitable business matching ex-SF personnel to jobs ranging from low-level security to no-questions-asked numbers. The Feds and the CIA knew what he did, of course, but they turned a blind eye because it was an open secret in the intelligence community that Khan's men had been involved more than once in operations that the American government had sanctioned and paid for – not that you'd ever find a signature confirming it, or a money trail linking the two. No, Khan's set-up was useful enough that he was allowed to deploy his men worldwide without anyone paying him too much attention. Even so, he made his base in San Diego. Windlass knew perfectly well that this wasn't because he liked the beach. It was because he could get the hell over the Mexican border if anything went pear-shaped.

And it was Khan's voice at the other end of the phone line.

'Yeah?'

'It's Nat. Nat Windlass.'

A pause. Just long enough for it to be clear that this wasn't a call Khan was expecting.

'Is this line secure?'

'Damn well should be,' replied Windlass. 'Been a long time, Khan. I hear word of you, of course, on the grapevine.'

'I bet you do. And you know what else I bet? That you haven't just called me up to chat about the good old days.' Khan never had been much of a one of small talk. 'What do you want, Nat. Make it quick. I'm a busy man.'

Windlass's eyes narrowed. This was the second time that morning someone had spoken to him in such a way that he wouldn't normally put up with. No matter. He kept his cool.

'Four men,' he said. 'Your best.'

'What's the job.'

'Can't tell you, Khan.'

Another pause.

'Then I guess,' Khan said, 'that's the end of our conversation. Lovely to hear from you again, Nat. We must do this again in another twenty years.'

'You can name your price, Khan. Make it enough to help you swallow the fact that I'm not going to tell you what the job is, and that the men you're going to send me will be in the dark too.'

Silence. Windlass could almost hear Khan contemplating the offer over the phone line.

'Of course,' Windlass continued smoothly, 'there's the added complication that the President doesn't know about your little operation. Just one of the secrets that we need to keep from him from time to time. He's got a thing about private military contractors, though. Be a shame, wouldn't it, if someone accidentally let slip all the unpleasant things your guys are supposed to have done...'

'Listen, you piece of...'

'Four men, Khan. Can you do it?'

Heavy breathing. Had he made him nervous? Khan was *never* nervous. Windlass liked the idea.

'Weapons?'

'Suitable for close-quarters combat. Silent. The last thing I want is anything going bang.'

'Insertion?'

'Vehicle and foot. Outskirts of LA. And I mean it, Khan. Your best. Don't even think of sending me some kid who'll wet himself at the first sign of blood.'

'I'll treat that comment with the contempt it deserves, Windlass. When's the job?'

'You'll get 24 hours' notice. Make sure you're ready.'

'It'll cost you two hundred G.' Khan spoke quickly, as though even he was embarrassed to quote such a price.

'Make it four,' Windlass replied. 'I'll be in touch.'

Windlass hung up. He left a twenty-dollar bill on the table and walked out of the diner with a sudden sense of purpose. For the first time that morning he noticed that the sun was shining. It was going to be a beautiful day, and he had work to do.

PART THREE

FOUR WEEKS LATER

15

Dr Rachael Leo had been living, she realized, with a sense of suppressed anxiety for some weeks now. In the months running up to her announcement of her discovery to the Board, she had daydreamed about the excitement of it all, but as the announcement date grew closer, she worried that her nerves were going to get the better of her. Whereas before her dreams had been populated by writhing nematode worms and bright-eyed lab mice, now another image dominated the scant few hours of sleep she managed to catch each night. It was a warehouse, huge, cavernous. And in the middle of a warehouse were pallets piled high with unmarked boxes. They were quite unremarkable in every way, but in her dreams and when she was awake, Rachael Leo knew that those boxes were more valuable than gold or even diamonds. And they weren't just figments of her imagination. They existed.

The Elixir was ready.

She rubbed her eyes tiredly, looked across the lab and then smiled. Little Jack was a good kid. He was only ten, but Rachael liked having him around. He was now a frequent visitor to the lab and she'd set him up with a microscope and a few slides, and he appeared happy to spend, well, hours examining the simple cells and sketching them on a notepad that he kept on the bench next to him. He reminded Rachael of herself as a child. Quiet. Serious. But sad too. He had an indescribable aura of melancholy about him. Hardly surprising, really. Jack hadn't mentioned his mother to Rachael, but that didn't mean she wasn't in his every waking thought. Rachael remembered how she had felt when she knew her own mother was terminally ill. The memory chilled her even now, so many years later. And she thought of Tom, who never gave any sign of the strain he was under, but who had appeared grateful when he'd brought Jack in that morning that the kid had somewhere to be other than at his mother's bedside, leaving him to return home to be with Jane. Things were busy at Pure, but she respected him for knowing where his true priorities lay.

Rachael walked over towards Jack. Almost directly behind him was the main entrance to the lab, and through the Perspex panes on the door she could see the ever-present figures of her two close-protection guys standing guard outside.

'What you looking at, Jack?' she asked, more breezily than she felt.

Jack started, as though he had been lost in his own little world from which Rachael had suddenly removed him. He stepped back from the microscope and allowed her to take a look. But Rachael didn't lean over the apparatus. Instead she gave Jack a sad little smile. 'Things *are* going to be OK, you know?'

Jack frowned, and looked like he might cry.

'I know they seem difficult at the moment, but…'

She stopped.

Something had caught her attention.

Something was wrong.

She looked around the lab. Everything was normal. And then, from the corner of her eye, she realized what was missing.

The close-protection guys. She could no longer see the back of their heads through the pane in the door. What she could see was a faint spatter of red over the Perspex.

Her heart stopped. And it was only then that she heard the scream.

Admiral Nathanial Windlass looked at each of the four men in turn. They were dressed in casual clothes – jeans, T-shirts, Nikes – but their abdomens bulged unnaturally from the body armour they were wearing, and each of them carried the same weapon in their hands: a Heckler and Koch MP7. Short. Stubby. Manoeuvrable. Lethal. Capable of firing its 30mm rounds at a rate of 900 a minute, though it was unlikely any of them would need to fire more than a single round at a time. They held them with the light touch of professionals who were unaccustomed to wasting ammunition. Windlass knew, because he was a professional too.

They were sitting in the back of an unmarked van, two along the bench on one side, three opposite them. On the floor between the two groups of men was a battered flight case from which they had each taken their weapons and a stash of

40-round magazines. All that remained inside it now were the black woollen balaclavas they would don when the op was go.

Windlass knew none of their names, and they respectfully pretended not to know his. For the purposes of the next few hours, he was Control and they were call sign Delta Sierra One, Two, Three and Four. Each of them was clean-shaven, had short hair and a collection of scars on their faces and forearms. Windlass knew their type. He knew them well.

'You've all examined the aerial imagery of the target.'

'Roger that,' replied Delta Sierra One. Of all of them, he was the most battle scarred, with a nose that had clearly been broken more than once and a patch on the right-hand side of his head where the hair had been burned away to leave a mottled pink blotch.

'Your target is Dr Rachael Leo. This was taken three days ago.' Windlass handed round a photograph, which the men studied intently. He knew what they were doing: cataloguing her physical details as a kind of mental inventory that they would be able to recall in an instant. The color of the eyes. The exact length and shade of her blonde hair. He doubted they were often tasked to target women, but he also knew that they wouldn't hesitate to do whatever needed to be done. Their training had systematically removed from them anything that resembled qualms. 'We can expect to find her in the main lab on the western side of the Pure Industries compound. You have that location memorized?'

The men nodded.

'Keep collateral damage to a minimum,' he said. There was no point telling them to avoid fatalities altogether. These weren't the kind of professionals you called in if you wanted a bloodless operation. Armed men would be going up against armed men. The unit in the back of this van all knew that the only way they could be sure of seeing the sun rise the following day was to take down any threats to their own wellbeing the moment they saw them.

'When the target has been acquired, she's to be taken to this location.' He handed round a slip of paper with grid reference written on it. 'Memorize and destroy it,' Windlass instructed.

He caught Delta Sierra Two and Three glance at each other, which instantly raised his heckles.

'Listen to me, all of you. I don't know how much, or how little that slimy little creature Khan has told you about me, but be sure of this: I've seen more action than you kids can even imagine. I know what I'm talking about, and we're going to do this *my* way. Any of you got a problem with that–' he pointed towards the rear door of the '–*that*'s the way out.'

He looked at each of them in turn.

'No problems, Control,' said Delta Sierra One.

'I'm delighted to hear it.' He pointed at the grid reference again. 'Now memorize it.'

Three minutes later, Delta Sierra Four was setting fire to the slip of paper with a cigarette lighter. Windlass checked his watch. '07.36 hrs,' he said. 'Target is five minutes away. Expect two armed security at the main gates. They need to be taken out noiselessly so we don't alert anyone else inside the compound. I suggest we bind and gag them and hold them in the back of this van until we're done. Agreed?'

'Agreed, Control.'

'We advance by vehicle to the main building. Delta Sierra Three and Four, you're to cover the parking lot. Anyone who leaves the compound will have to do it by that route. You see anyone trying to raise an alarm, you know what to do.'

The two men nodded grimly.

'One and Two, you accompany me and we advance to target.'

An awkward silence. Delta Sierra One gave Windlass a wary look. 'Accompany *you*, Control?'

'You're not deaf. Glad to hear it. Lot of guys like you are. Guess it's all the bangs.'

'Control, we work as a four-man unit.'

'Good for you. Today you work as a five-man unit, under my orders.' At Windlass's feet there was a bag. He bent down and pulled out of it a weapon of his own. His was also standard Marine Corp issue but unlike the others his firearm of choice was the Beretta M9 semi-automatic pistol. More his era. 'Delta Sierra One, drive. We move in at 08.00 precisely.'

Oscar Aston was tired, and he was bored. He'd been on duty since midnight, his cigarettes had run out and the firearm strapped to his waist was digging uncomfortably into his skin. He checked his watch. 07.55. Changeover at nine. It couldn't come soon enough.

There was a pecking order to security work like this, and Oscar – as a former officer in the police department whose career was brought to a premature halt thanks to a desperate junkie with a blade – was at the bottom of it. It was always the ex-military guys who were assigned the role of point men to individual high-value targets. Perimeter work like this – less specialised, less dangerous – was always doled out to the bacon.

He glanced across the entrance booth that manned the perimeter of the Pure Industries compound. His colleague, Mal, was exactly the kind of guy you didn't want to get stuck with on a job like this. Also ex-LAPD – he never talked about why he left, and Oscar assumed it was under less than glorious circumstances – he always turned up for his shift with a bag of junk food which he chewed his way through constantly, barely ever directing a single word at Oscar. Oscar had been in the security business for five years now. He knew the deal: he'd never even taken his weapon out of its holster, let alone fired a shot in anger. The people who hired security firms like his were normally paranoid and this lot, Pure Industries, were more paranoid than most – like they were guarding the goddamn nuclear codes or something. But in truth, the job involved a whole load of sitting around, and it was nice to have someone to talk to.

07.59. Oscar happened to glance up in the direction of the orange and yellow barrier they were manning. A white van was approaching slowly. He glanced at the computer screen in front of him and tapped a button on the keyboard. A list appeared: all today's expected deliveries. There was nothing for 8.00a.m.

He looked over at Mal again. His colleague showed no sign of getting up so, with a sigh, Oscar hauled himself out of his seat and stepped out of the booth.

The van came to a halt. Oscar clocked a single driver, who stepped down from the driver's seat and walked round between the front of the van and the barrier, brandishing a clipboard.

'Hey, pal,' said the new arrival. 'Delivery for a Dr Leo...'

Oscar shook his head. 'You're not on the list. No deliveries without a...'

He stopped.

Something was wrong. He didn't know what. There was something about the way the van driver was looking at him. As if... as if he was *waiting* for something...

And then he saw it. Just a glimpse, peeping out from behind the zip of his jacket. Gun-metal grey. Military hardware.

Oscar spun round, desperately grabbing at the handgun strapped to his waist. But it was too late. Another man was just half a metre behind him and he wasn't even bothering to hide his weapon. He had it raised, and pointing at Oscar's chest. Beyond him, two more armed men were advancing into the booth, where Mal looked, quite literally, as though he might wet himself.

This is it, Oscar thought to himself. This is the moment I die.

He closed his eyes, but the sound of gunfire never came. Instead, a brutal thump on the side of the neck. Oscar felt himself slip into unconsciousness, and he knew nothing more.

'Jack,' Rachael breathed tensely. 'Jack, get away from the door.'

The little boy gave her a confused look.

'JACK!' she shouted. 'Move!' She grabbed him by his collar and tugged him towards the opposite end of the lab. Her mind was on fire. Something was happening. She could sense it. *They were coming for her...*

Her blood turned to ice as the doors to the lab swung open. Three men appeared. They had guns. Black balaclavas over their heads. Two of them had their weapons pressed into their shoulders and were advancing on them. The third man held back in the area of the door.

Suddenly everybody stopped. The guns were trained on Rachael, who had shoved Jack behind her, and who had started to tremble uncontrollably.

Slowly, the man by the door peeled off his balaclava. Rachael stared. She knew him. That face, she *knew* it...

'Good morning, Dr Leo,' said the man. 'We've met before, of course.'

Rachael swallowed hard. What was his name? *What the hell was his name?*

'You're probably aware that these two gentlemen will do whatever I tell them to. One of the privileges of Office. Leave the kid, Dr Leo. We've no interest in him. Only you.'

'This is illegal,' Leo breathed. *What was his name? What was his name?*

The man smiled. 'How quaint,' he said. '*Now*, Dr...'

The door to the lab swung open again and Leo saw one of Kyle's bodyguards standing there. In a moment of brief irrationality, she found herself worrying about Kyle himself. Was he OK? Why had they left him? Then she remembered that it was she and Jack who were at gunpoint...

It all happened so quickly. One of the balaclava'd gunmen spun round, the speed of his reactions so fast it was almost as if he'd had a premonition that the guard was about to appear. He fired a single shot.

Rachael screamed.

The precision with which the round hit the guard's forehead was astonishing. There was a sudden flash of red as the frontal lobe blew away, revealing not only blood, but flashes of skull and brain matter. The guard dropped heavily to the floor.

Panic coursed through Rachael's veins. She grabbed hold of Jack again, and pulled him to the ground. Together they scurried behind one of the lab benches. Rachael could feel her clothes sticking sweatily to her skin, but one look at Jack's face was enough to make her forget about her own discomfort. She didn't know what was worse: his obvious terror, or the look of bewildered confusion on his face. The kid didn't know what was going on. That made two of them.

More gunshots. To Rachael's untrained ear they sounded different to the one that had killed the guard. She sensed them flying above her head, felt the displacement of the air. A second guard must be fighting back, but she couldn't tell if that was a good thing or a bad thing.

'It's going to be alright,' she whispered to Jack. '*It's going to be alright*.' But she didn't know if she was trying to persuade the boy or herself.

She had to do something. To let somebody know what was happening. Tom. He knew the man who had removed the balaclava. What was his name? *What was his name?* Rachael's panicked mind wouldn't work. The damn name wouldn't come. She placed her trembling hands into her lab coat, and pulled out her mobile phone. There was more gunfire – two way this time – and Jack was trembling even more than Rachael was. She swiped past the home screen and desperately started to type a text message with her shaking thumbs.

THE G...

She had only typed four letters when a horrific screaming sound came from the direction of the doorway. '*He's down!*' shouted the government man. '*Get the woman!*'

Her heart in her throat, Rachael carried on typing.

...OVERNMENT AGENT...

Footsteps. Running in their direction. She didn't have time to finish. Her hands shaking worse than ever she brought up her contacts, ready to find Tom's number.

She didn't get the chance.

Suddenly, the two gunmen were standing over her. They were ignoring little Jack, and both had their weapons pointed directly at Rachael. She blindly pressed a contact at random to send the message, by which time one of the men had bent down and roughly pulled her to her feet.

The vision that met her eyes as she looked around the lab was one of utter devastation. Windows were smashed, scientific apparatus that had been sitting on workbenches had been shattered and blasted away. There were two bodies by the door, their limbs grotesquely contorted and a slick of dark red blood oozing from them.

Immediately, the top of her arm held in a crushing grip that would have brought tears to her eyes despite everything else, she was being hauled across the room. She put her head over her shoulders and called to Jack. 'Don't move, Jack! Stay down! Stay safe!'

But then, to her horror, she saw the boy's head raise above the parapet of one of the worktops. His young face was filled with a sudden, childish fury. He ran out from behind his hiding place in the direction of the two men who were abducting Rachael.

'No!' she screamed. '*NO!*'

Jack sprinted towards them. When he was just a metre away, he hurled himself against the man who was clutching Rachael. Jack's child's body barely made an impact. He tumbled immediately to the ground and, just as quickly, jumped to his feet again and started banging his tiny, clenched fists against her abductor's forearm.

'Jack!' Rachael screamed. 'Get back! *Get back!*'

But Jack was shouting too: 'Let her go! *Let my friend go!*' Hot tears were streaming down his face, and though he was obviously no match for the armed men, he was an annoyance: Rachael heard her abductor swear under his breath as he pushed Jack effortlessly away and continued to drag Rachael towards the door.

But the boy was persistent. He ran up towards them and hurled himself at the abductor once more.

What happened next was like a dream. Not a dream. A nightmare. Unreal. It seemed to happen in slow motion, as if some outside force was forcing Rachael to remember every detail of the horror.

The government man was there. There was a terrifying look on his face. He didn't appear angry, or violent. He was totally calm, as though what he was about to do failed to move him at all.

He raised his weapon, pointing it at the young boy.

There was movement by the door. Rachael saw Ruth storm into the room, and her eyes were ablaze. 'Leave that boy alone!' she shouted, like an angry mother as she pushed past the astonished guard and right up to the government man, who turned to look at her, a look of greedy insanity in his face.

Ruth grabbed Jack and, such was her fury, managed to shove the surprised man back a step and immediately placed her small body as a barrier between the boy and the muzzle of the gun. There was not a trace of fear on her face, just a look of total defiance.

Time stood still.

'Stupid woman'. the government man sighed with a slight shake of his head.

Rachael tried to scream, but the sound stuck in her throat.

He fired.

The sound echoed round the lab, and a single round entered Ruth's throat with a sick, squelching sound.

She dropped. Blood everywhere.

And immediately the government man turned his weapon back to Jack who was bearing down on him again. *'The boy's a witness, so there's no option…'* a cold calculation, an instantaneous and deadly conclusion.

He fired again.

The second round entered Jack's chest. The impact knocked the little boy backwards and he fell to a sitting position. Rachael screamed again. She tried to break free from her abductor's grasp, but it was much too firm. Jack looked at his chest in confusion, and as a small fountain of blood pumped weakly through his clothes, he touched it with his finger tips and stared at the sticky fluid that had reddened his skin.

He coughed. A thin, pathetic sound. More blood foamed from his mouth and when he tried to breathe again, there was nothing but a reedy gasping. He tumbled to one side, and the blood from both his chest and his mouth oozed on to the hard lab floor.

Rachael felt dizzy with shock. Sick. She wanted to run to him. To hold the boy in her arms. But it was never going to happen. The men were moving her again and no matter how she struggled, she couldn't break free of them. She almost slipped in the puddle surrounding the two dead guards; as she was dragged over their bodies and out of the lab. She glimpsed Clint who – terrified – was pressing himself against the wall at the back of a darkened storeroom, as yet undetected by the attackers. Her vision was clouded with tears, but she could just make out Jack's body, lying still on the floor, strangely peaceful amid the unspeakable carnage that surrounded him.

There was a sense of great peace in Jane's bedroom. A clock ticked metronomically; in the garden beyond the window, there was the cooing of a bird; and Jane's breathing was soft, her thin chest rising and falling gently.

Tom sat by her bed, a place he knew – with a sense of guilt – he had not spent enough time. The Elixir was in her blood, it was true; but her extended life was a burden, and he ought to be there to share it with her.

The door opened. Tom looked up sharply. One of the security guys was there. He was a squat, grizzled-looking guy with a couple of days' growth on his face. Tom couldn't remember his name. He looked like the bearer of bad news at the best of times, with his furrowed brow and dark eyes. Even more so now...

A twinge of irritation hit Tom. This was private time. He didn't want any interruptions. But when he saw the man just standing there, as though he had something to say but was unable to say it, his irritation turned to something else.

'What is it?' he breathed.

The man stared dumbly.

Tom stood up. '*What is it?*' he roared, loud enough to make the man flinch and for Jane to stir in her sleep. '*What the hell's happened?*'

The man stuttered as he told him. Tom felt his knees buckle. He had to support himself on the side of Jane's bed. He could sense his blood pumping fast through his veins, but it was glacier cold.

'Take me there,' he whispered.

The police cordon had already been established by the time Tom arrived at Pure Industries. Three squad cars were parked up at the entrance, their blue neon flashing silently. The security guy driving the car had to argue with the police officer standing watch and preventing entry; Tom neither heard nor cared what he said. He was numb.

The car entered the premises and pulled up. Tom didn't wait for his security man to open the door or even to accompany him – though he was aware of the man trotting behind him at a respectful distance as he strode towards the building. Kyle was waiting outside. He looked ashen-faced and was wringing his hands in a most uncharacteristic way.

'Where?' Tom demanded. His voice croaked.

'The lab,' said Kyle. 'But Tom, really, you don't want to...'

Tom had already walked on. Thirty seconds later he was striding down the corridor to the lab. There were more police officers here, and the sound of radios crackling. There was something on the ground. When he was about five yards away, he saw that it was a body. The face was grotesque and white, and the gun wound in his neck looked like pulverised liver. There were spatters of blood along the white walls and the floor.

Of the three officers surrounding the body, none looked especially horrified by the corpse. Somewhere in Tom's addled brain, it occurred to him that they were used to sights like this. The officer who was now approaching looked more concerned by Tom's presence. 'Sir,' he said flatly, 'this is a crime scene. I have to ask you to...'

'My son's in there,' Tom replied abruptly.

The police officer looked taken aback. 'Mr Shaw?' he asked.

Tom nodded.

'Mr Shaw, I'd advise you to wait...'

But Tom had no patience for this. He pushed past the police officer and, aware that the others had their eyes on him, headed for the entrance to the lab.

He had to step over another corpse lying in the doorway, and he felt his sole slap into a puddle of sticky blood, but he barely even noticed this. All his attention was on another figure, leaden and immobile on the other side of the lab.

Tom ran towards it, before stopping about a metre away. His skin prickled with horror as his eyes confirmed what his ears had refused to believe.

He had heard it said that people looked peaceful in death. Jack didn't. His pale face was a grotesque mask of suffering. His eyes were still open and staring. His chin was stained with blood. His pale blue T-shirt was stained red. His head lolled at an angle, and he looked for all the world like a puppet whose strings had been cut.

A sound escaped Tom's throat – a low moan, almost inhuman. He fell to his knees and shuffled through the blood to his son. He held Jack's desperately cold body tight towards him and started to shake.

He could never have said how long he remained like that, mired in Jack's gore, holding him close as if by so doing he could breathe the life back into him. A minute? An hour? It was impossible to say. Gradually, however, he became aware of something else. A figure, standing next to him.

He laid Jack gently back down on to the ground and brushed the palm of his right hand over the boy's eyes so that they fell closed. Ignoring the blood that had stained his own face, hands and clothes, he looked up.

Kyle was standing there. His head was bowed, like a mourner at a funeral.

'I'm sorry, Tom,' he whispered. 'I… I don't know what to say.'

Tom looked back at his son's corpse. No, he thought to himself. There *was* nothing to say.

'That's Ruth…' nodding towards a blood stained sheet that covered another body 'they shot her too and….they took Rachael,' Kyle said quietly.

Tom blinked. His mind was like treacle, and it took a moment for him to understand what he was saying.

'They *took* her, Tom,' Kyle repeated.

'Who?'

Kyle gave a helpless, hapless shrug. 'I don't know,' he said. 'But she sent me this, at exactly the time the raid happened.'

Kyle handed Tom his mobile phone. The screen displayed a text message. Short. Unfinished.

THE GOVERNMENT AGENT…

Tom stared at it. 'Windlass?' he breathed.

'Could be,' Kyle replied.

In his confused mind, Tom found himself back at the White House, in the Roosevelt Room, sitting opposite the brash, unpleasant Admiral who had summoned him there. *You need to understand*, he was saying, *that I speak with the full authority of the President of the United States*.

'You think we should tell the police?' Kyle asked.

Tom found himself shaking his head. 'There's no point,' he said. 'We're fighting the government now. He stood up. 'And believe me, Kyle, they'll wish they never started this.'

Tom Shaw's jaw and knuckles were clenched. He was unable to keep his eyes from his son. Which was why, as they stood there, he failed to see the flicker of a smile that played across Kyle Byng's lips, as Tom's mind – his whole body – filled with images of Admiral Windlass and the President himself, and became suffused with thoughts of nothing but the deepest revenge.

16

Dr Rachael Leo awoke.

The first thing she noticed was the darkness. Thick. Impenetrable. The sort of darkness that wasn't just an absence of light, but an entity of its own.

Then she noticed the pain. She tried to move her fingers to touch the swelling that pounded at the back of her head, but she realized that her hands were bound behind her back, and the rope that tied her was digging agonizingly into her skin.

And then she remembered.

She remembered Jack.

She remembered being dragged from the lab and bundled into the back of a white van. There her memory failed her. They must have hit her then – knocked her into unconsciousness. How long ago had it been? Rachael had no way of knowing.

Nausea. Panic. Horror. She felt all these things. Whoever it was that had abducted her wanted the Elixir. That much was clear. It was the least of Rachael's worries. She knew she would never give up the secret to the wrong person. It didn't matter what they threatened her with, nor what they did to her. She would *never* reveal it. Her thoughts were with Jack; with Tom and Jane; with – and this surprised her – Kyle. Was he OK? Had they targeted him too?

Time passed. She shivered and sweated. One moment she felt the need to vomit, the next to sleep. She did neither.

Light. It came from a single bulb hanging from the center of the room, and it split her head like an axe. She clenched her eyes shut, and opened them only very slowly as her vision became accustomed to the light. She saw that she was in a bare room. The walls and floor were concrete; the ceiling above her consisted of bare rafters with floorboards above them. She sensed that she was in a basement. The basement itself was large – ten yards by ten – and Rachael was strapped to a heavy wooden chair almost precisely in its center. She faced a door, but it was closed and the room was otherwise empty. Whoever had turned on the light had done so from outside.

And now they switched it off again, plunging Rachael into darkness once more.

She grew cold. The concrete seemed to leach all the warmth from this place. She tried to cry out, but her throat hurt so badly it was like swallowing a knife even to speak.

They would come to her, she knew. Sooner or later they would come to her. She understood what they were doing. Scaring her. Disorientating her. It was working. Rachael closed her eyes and, when the light came on again maybe an hour later, she kept them closed, even though tears threatened to erupt from them.

They were coming for her. They had killed Jack. They had killed Peter and Sylvia. They would do whatever was necessary to extract the information they needed.

It was this information that was keeping her alive.

She would never reveal it.

She would never reveal it…

In the room above the basement, Pat Dolan flicked a switch. Tony Foreman sipped on his cup of coffee and grinned at him. Pat, out of necessity, grinned back. He hoped it didn't show on his face how sickened he was.

He'd seen them bring the woman in. Seen the way they handled her, and the ugly things they'd said. It had been all Pat could do to keep focussed on gathering the detailed information he knew his handler would require. All he could do to observe the military parlance of the four men who had roughly carried the unconscious woman into this run-down farmhouse in the middle of nowhere, a good two miles from any other habitation; all he could do to observe the professional way they handled their weapons; all he could do to fix in his mind the strangely familiar features of the man who was clearly commanding them. He recognized the face, but couldn't quite place it.

Tony was clearly having the same problem. Once they'd installed the hostage in the basement room and returned upstairs, he brought it up immediately.

'The dude in charge,' he said. 'Reckon I seen him somewhere before.'

Pat had shrugged. 'It's a small world, our one. Back home, I was forever running into…'

'No. He's not a player, Mickey. He's bigger than that. Government, I reckon.'

Pat had scoffed. 'You're seeing things, my friend.' But inside, he'd noted what Tony had said. It alarmed him. His handler was working for the CIA. If they hadn't told him about a political figure being thick with Theodore Croft, it meant one of two things: the CIA had suffered a catastrophic intelligence failure, or they weren't being straight with him. Pat Dolan had dealt with intelligence agencies for long enough to know which of these options was most likely. He nervously fingered the BlackBerry in his pocket. He only had to press a button and a SWAT team would be despatched to his location within minutes. But something held him back. It wasn't just that he knew his handler would have his balls on a plate if he blew his hard-earned cover with nothing to show for it except a frightened woman in a basement. No, something else stayed his hand: an uncomfortable suspicion that if he wanted to do something to help this poor woman, calling in the cavalry wasn't it.

Their instructions were clear. Mess with her head. Mess with her body if they wanted. Just make sure she was scared. Properly scared. The lights had been Pat's idea. 'We used to do it back in the Province,' he'd told Tony. 'Y'know, to scare the living daylights out of any British Army boys we captured, before we slotted them.' Total fantasy, of course, but he knew

Tony would have more elaborate tortures in mind, and he wanted to buy himself a bit of time before he had free rein. And so they had sat there, among the dusty furniture of this deserted room, watched only by the dark oil paintings on the wall, switching the light on for two minutes every hour.

Only now, four hours later, Tony was clearly growing impatient. He'd been sitting there, toying with their hostage's cell phone, which he hadn't let go of since the SWAT team had handed it over.

Suddenly he stood up and stuck the phone in his pocket.

'I'm going down there. Soften her up some for when Croft gets here,' he said.

Pat made a half-hearted attempt to stop him. 'You don't think he'll be wanting her more, you know… untouched?'

Tony snorted derisively. 'You don't know the guy like I do,' he replied. He looked around the room. It was a shabby, dusty place. Pat had been surprised that the old kettle sitting on the floor, plugged into a yellowing socket, hadn't tripped the electrics in the whole house; and when Tony had made instant coffee in the chipped and stained mugs that he'd found in an old mahogany cabinet, Pat had had to force himself to drink it. His stomach was churning and his mouth tasted of bile. He wasn't sure he'd be able to hold anything down. Under one of the old oil paintings was a brass candlestick. Tony grabbed it, slammed it into the palm of his left hand a couple of times to check its weight and, with a curt nod at Pat, disappeared from the room.

Pat knew the basement was directly beneath them, and when Tony had been gone for thirty seconds he crouched down and pressed one ear to the carpet. At first he heard nothing;

then just a murmur of voices – too indistinct to make out anything they were saying.

The screams, though, were clear enough.

The woman's throat was hoarse and raw, but the sound that came from it was sufficiently loud to force Pat to lift his ear momentarily from the floor. It was the first of five screams, each more pathetic than the last, each making Pat wince at his inability – or rather his decision – not to stop them.

The screaming stopped, and Tony Foreman returned, looking as relaxed as if he'd just taken a walk around the block. 'Give it an hour,' he said, 'and you can have a go.'

Pat nodded, and they sat in silence.

'She got a name?' Pat asked after a few minutes.

Tony shrugged. 'Who cares?'

'I just wondered,' Pat said quietly, 'you know, who she was.'

'Christ, Mickey, what's wrong with you? You got the hots for her or something? Because if you have, feel free to just go down there and...'

'I don't have the hots for her,' Pat interrupted. 'I'm just wondering what's going on. Don't tell me you're not curious why Croft has got some bit of fluff tied to a chair in the basement, courtesy of a government figure with a team of pros, now.'

Tony gave him a sharp look – a look that told him more clearly than any words that he knew more than he was letting on. 'Take it from me, Mickey. Croft doesn't like his guys asking too many questions. Do what he says, take the money and keep your goddamn mouth shut. You got any cigarettes?'

Pat nodded silently, pulled a pouch of baccy and a packet of skins out of his pocket, and threw them over to Tony.

They sat, and smoked, and waited.

An hour passed. Pat was careful not to look too eager to go. He rolled himself another cigarette, glanced at his watch, and said: 'I guess it's time to pay our friend another visit.'

'You want me to go?' Tony asked.

'Ah, you're OK. I'm getting kind of bored anyway.'

'Well, leave your tobacco, and make sure she's in a fit state for Croft to question her.'

Pat gave what he hoped was a menacing grin, chucked the baccy at his accomplice once more, switched the basement light on and headed down there.

He entered the basement room quietly to find the poor girl still sitting there with her eyes screwed up tight. The place was totally empty apart from her and the chair on which she was sitting. On the far wall, butting up to the ceiling, was a ventilation grate through which a little daylight was visible. Otherwise the walls were plain and grey. Pat glanced up, and pictured Tony kneeling at the carpet in the same way he had done an hour or so previously. And if Tony was listening, it meant Pat had to give him something to listen to.

He stepped up to the chair just as the woman opened her eyes a little. She gasped in surprise – clearly she hadn't heard him enter – and shook her head at him. Pat put one finger to his lips and, just as a look of confusion was crossing the woman's face, he slapped her hard with the other hand.

She shouted out in pain and surprise, then started to whimper. 'Please don't hurt me… *please don't hurt me like he did … please …*'

Pat glanced over his shoulder. The door was firmly closed. He looked around the room. There was no sign of cameras or peepholes. Could he risk it? As he listened to the terrified noises coming from the woman in the chair, he knew he had to.

He took another step closer to her, and she startled as he raised his hand again. But this time he didn't slap her. Instead, he moved the loose hair from over her ear and whispered. 'You need to scream. Scream like I'm hurting you bad. Do you understand?'

She nodded desperately.

'Do it now.'

The woman's voice was hoarse, but her scream sounded even more pained on account of it.

'Good girl,' Pat whispered. 'Now listen carefully, I'm here to help you but you can't let anyone else know. Understood?'

More desperate nodding.

'Why have they kidnapped you?'

A pause. And then…

'Elixir,' she breathed.

It meant nothing to Pat. Nonsense talk. Perhaps she was hallucinating through fear. He'd seen it happen before.

'Scream again,' he said.

The woman gave him a drained, exhausted look, as if to say that even screaming was now too much effort.

'Don't make me hit you again, girl,' Pat whispered. 'If they think we're having this conversation, I'm a dead man.'

She screamed. It sounded half-hearted to Pat's ears, but it was better than nothing. He spoke quietly in her ear again. 'Do you know who abducted you?'

Her head lolled. 'Government...' was all she seemed able to say. '*Government...*'

Pat's heart sank as her words confirmed his worst suspicions.

'Listen carefully,' he said. 'I'm police, but I can't call for back-up if this is government business. They'll just stamp on it...'

'Tom Shaw,' the girl whispered. 'Call Tom Shaw... my cell... where is it?'

The door opened.

Pat felt a wave of nausea. He was still leaning over, whispering in the woman's ear. He looked over his shoulder to see Tony standing there, an expression of suspicion on his face.

'What's going on?' Tony breathed.

Pat stood up slowly.

'Just giving the bitch an idea of what's to come,' he said.

Tony didn't look convinced. 'That's enough talking, Micky,' he said dangerously, not taking his eyes from Pat. 'Let's see you sort her out.'

Pat gave what he hoped was a nonchalant shrug. He turned to look at the woman again, not even daring to mouth the word 'sorry'. Without hesitation, he yanked the heel of his hand against her chest. She exhaled sharply; the chair tottered on its back legs and fell backwards to the floor. The woman's head cracked against the hard concrete, and she cried out. Pat glanced back at Tony, who had his arms folded as if to say that he wasn't yet convinced of his accomplice's commitment to the cause, so Pat kicked the woman twice just below the rib cage. It was too dangerous for the blows to be anything but solid, and there was a dull thump as boot met flesh. A gasping, croaking sound escaped her throat.

Pat turned to Tony. 'Let's leave her like that,' he said, walking towards the door.

Tony inclined his head grudgingly. He seemed satisfied with Pat's violence. Together they left the bedroom and headed back upstairs, but before they entered the sitting room where they'd been waiting, Pat said: 'I need to splash my boots.'

'John's over there,' Tony told him, pointing to a painted wooden door at the end of the corridor.

It was a relief to be alone. As soon as the door was shut, Pat backed up against it and closed his eyes. When he opened them again a few seconds later, he caught his reflection in an old, clouded mirror. Jesus, Pat Dolan, he thought to himself. Roughing up innocent girls. Is this really what you signed up for? But then he reminded himself of his motives. He was going to help this woman. He just didn't know how yet.

'Elixir'. He was sure that was what she'd said. What did it mean? Why was she so precious to Croft; and what was Croft's link with the US administration? None of it made any sense. All he had was one thing to go on. A name. Tom Shaw. Christ, it wasn't much.

He flushed the unused toilet and returned to where Tony was waiting for him, slouched in an old armchair like a bored teenager. Pat saw that he was fiddling with the woman's cell phone again. If he was moved in any way by what he'd just witnessed in the basement, he didn't show it. He nodded at Pat. Was it a conciliatory gesture? Difficult to say, but Pat needed more information, and he sensed that now was the time to dig for it.

'So who is she, Tony?' he asked casually.

'Does it matter?'

Pat shrugged. 'I guess not.' Don't dig too hard, he told himself. Let it come naturally.

A pause. And then...

'She's a doctor, or a professor or something. There's a company called Pure Industries. Croft's got a thing about them. Bumped off half the goddamn Board as far as I can tell, now he's getting to work on this one. Don't ask me why – far as I can make out, they've got some kind of drug he wants to get his hands on.' And he gave Pat a look that said anyone who tried to work Croft out was wasting their time.

But alarm bells were ringing in Pat's head. *Pure Industries.* Agent 2 had mentioned that company; Peter Wright had worked for them. It all fitted with what Tony had said, and if it was true, it meant the woman in the basement was in mortal danger.

Unless...

Tony slung the cell phone onto a mahogany occasional table, stood up and wandered out of the room. 'Take a leak,' he muttered.

Pat didn't know how long he had. He couldn't rely on more than a couple of minutes. He strode over to where the phone was lying and – aware that he was holding his breath – flicked through the contacts. There were only a handful – maybe ten or fifteen – and SHAW, TOM was the last of them.

He memorized the number, and just in time, because a moment later Tony reappeared. He was pulling up his zipper and looking just a little flustered.

'Croft's here,' he said, in a brisk, business-like tone.

'He certainly is,' said a voice from the corridor. Five seconds later, Theodore Croft himself was walking into the room, a mysterious smile on his face. Outside in the corridor were a couple of broad-shouldered bodyguards, but Pat's attention wasn't focussed on them, because behind Croft was the government man he had recognized. 'Tony Foreman, Mickey Connor, this is Admiral Nathanial Windlass. I suggest you all get to know each other.' His smile grew broader. 'You've been taking care of our guest, I hope? Mickey, why don't you pop into town, bring us all something to eat. I have a feeling it could be a little while before she gives us what we want, and I'd really hate for us all to get hungry.'

17

Pat Dolan cursed the fates that had got him into this situation. But more than that, he cursed the speed limit.

There were no cars around. The farmstead where Croft and his men had their abductee, was twenty miles from the center of Laguna Niguel, and at least a mile from any other habitation. Even though there was nobody on the roads, however, he kept one eye on the speedometer. If one of his colleagues unknowingly pulled him over, a terrified woman in a concrete basement would pay for it with her life.

It took an excruciating half an hour before he entered the suburbs of the town. More than once he pulled a sudden U-turn, to shake off any potential tail that he hadn't clocked in the rear-view mirror. Only when he was as certain as it was possible to be that nobody was following him, did he pull over by a pay phone. He dug his hands in his pockets and pulled out some loose change as he walked towards the phone; seconds later he had filled the blue AT&T machine with dimes and was dialling the number he had memorized from the woman's phone.

A ringing tone. It clicked on to voicemail. 'This is Tom Shaw, leave a message.'

Pat slammed the receiver back on its cradle and dialled again. 'This is Tom Shaw, leave a message.'

Muttering a few choice expletives, Pat tried for a third time.

The phone rang twice, and then a voice answered. It sounded cracked. Broken. 'Who's this?'

Pat took a deep breath. A life depended on how he played this conversation. 'You don't know me,' he said, 'and I'm not going to tell you my name. Not yet. But there's a young woman needs your help. I got your number from her phone.'

A pause.

'I'm calling the police,' said the voice.

'I swear to you, Tom. If you call the police, you're signing her death warrant.'

More silence.

'Where are you?'

Pat looked around. Jesus, he hadn't even been paying attention. He saw a street marking – Alton Parkway – and his eyes hunted out a Chinese takeout joint on the other side. 'The Lotus Flower restaurant,' he said. 'Fifteen minutes. If you're longer than that, or I see anybody with you, there'll be nothing I can do for her.' *But even if he comes,* Pat thought to himself, *what can I do for her then?*

The question echoed in his head as he stood by the phone box, eyes on the restaurant, and waited.

Tom Shaw didn't know where his tears were. They should be flooding from his eyes, surely. A torrent. But his cheeks were dry. He felt drained of everything: emotion, sensation. A husk.

And now this. He looked at the cell phone in his hand, then round the office. Police were crawling over the place, and he knew that questions would come sooner or later. For now, though, they were leaving him alone to grieve. He stared at the picture on the desk: him, Jane and Jack in happier times. Once more he found himself clenching his face as he weathered the sudden sensation that his soul had been scooped away.

How would he tell Jane. *How the hell would he tell Jane?*

He stood up suddenly and walked out of the office. His two security men – clearly shaken by the death of their colleagues – shot him an enquiring glance.

'I'm going out,' Tom said, and, before they could complain: 'I've just lost my son. I want to be alone.'

Minutes later he was driving out of the Pure Industries campus.

A voice in his head told him he was being stupid. This was a trap. A set-up. Truth was, he didn't much care anymore. If it was true, and the man who had phoned him had information about Rachael's whereabouts, fine. If not, and all he wanted to do was slot a bullet between Tom's eyes, then that was fine too. Preferable, even. At least it would ease the pain.

He drove slowly, distractedly. Each time he caught his reflection in the mirror he was shocked by the way he looked. Like a corpse himself, had it not been for the pulsating vein in his temple, barely covered by his shaggy, greying hair. He barely listened as his SatNav directed him in the direction of Park

Road South, nor was he even aware of the other traffic on the road. When, just under 15 minutes later, he pulled up outside the Lotus Flower, he had nearly killed himself three times, and nearly killed other road users even more than that. He neither knew, nor cared whether he should be parked where he was; he just left the car, two of its wheels up on the sidewalk, outside the restaurant and looked around.

It was a run-down part of town. Tom had lived in Laguna Niguel all his adult life, but he'd never ventured into this neighborhood. There was trash on the sidewalk, and the passers-by had their heads down, as if they didn't want to catch anybody's eye. The Lotus Flower was empty, with the exception of a bored-looking Oriental woman behind the counter; Tom had a sudden, very bad feeling about all this, and he decided he needed to be gone. Fast.

He was just climbing back into his car when he noticed him. He was standing on the other side of the street, dressed in shabby clothes and with a shock of scruffy black hair that was greying at the sides. He looked rough, but even from this distance Tom could see his piercing blue eyes that were staring straight at him.

That was his man. Tom didn't know how he knew. He just did.

He crossed the street with barely a glance at the oncoming traffic, strode up to the man and spoke immediately.

'Where is she?' He suddenly grabbed the stranger by the scruff of the neck. '*Where's Rachael?*'

The man didn't struggle or fight back. His gaze remained steady. 'So that's her name,' he said. He had a soft Irish accent that Tom recognized from the phone. 'She wasn't in a state to tell me.'

'You son of a bitch,' Tom hissed.

'Listen to me, my friend. My name's Pat Dolan. I work for the Los Angeles Police Department and I've just put my life in danger telling you that, as I did when I told Rachael. She said I should contact you. She also said something about "Elixir". Now you need to listen to me carefully. The men who have your friend, or your lover, or whoever the hell she is – they're going to kill her soon. And if I'm not back there within the hour, chances are they'll have a pop at me too. So if you want to have even a whisper of a chance of saving her, you'd better tell me what this is all about. And you'd better tell me now.'

Tom was shaking. But slowly, he let go of this man who called himself Pat Dolan. He looked left and right, checking to see if anybody was watching them. Nobody was.

'*Now*, Tom,' Dolan said softly. 'If you want to save her, you have to tell me now.'

And so Tom Shaw started to speak.

It was the strangest five minutes of Pat Dolan's life, standing here in the run-down suburb of a West coast town, listening to the truth of this drug called Elixir. Under any other circumstances, he'd have thought the guy was a fantasist. But it wasn't just that Tom Shaw believed what he was saying; it was that so many other people did too. And they were willing to kill on account of it.

'You're telling me that Rachael Leo is the only person who knows how to make it?'

Tom Shaw looked at it his shoes. 'No,' he said. 'One other person knows.'

'Who? *Who*, for God's sake?'

'Me,' he said simply.

Pat blinked. His mind was reeling. He was no fool. If the Elixir truly existed, it meant this unassuming figure with a haunted face and dark rings under his swollen eyes was the most powerful man in the world.

But not for long.

'They'll do everything they can to make her talk. You know that, right?'

Tom's dark face grew darker. 'I don't think she'll *ever* tell them.'

'You don't know what they can do.'

'*You* don't know Rachael.'

Pat looked at his watch. Nearly an hour had passed since he'd left the farmstead. If he was too long, Croft and Tony would get suspicious. And he'd taken too many risks today already...

'You have to tell them,' he said.

Now it was Tom's turn to blink, in astonishment. 'What do you mean?'

'You *have* to tell them. If you want to save that poor girl's life. It's the only way.'

A sneer crossed his face. An ugly, aggressive, unpleasant expression. 'They killed my son,' he breathed. 'They *killed* him, damn it. He was ten.' Tears swelled in his eyes. 'I held his body. It was cold...'

He clearly couldn't continue. Putting one hand against the phone box, he inhaled deeply to steady himself.

'My wife,' he said finally, in a coarse, cracked voice. 'She's dying too. The Elixir is the only thing that's keeping her alive. If I hand it over to them–' his frown deepened '–I'll lose her too.'

Pat Dolan wasn't a religious man. Hell, after days like this, he wondered if he was even a moral man. But as he stood in that street, listening to this tale of horror and remembering the terrified face and brutalised body of Dr Rachael Leo, he saw something with absolute clarity.

'You can't sacrifice that woman, Tom,' he said. 'Not for money, not for family, not even for–' he couldn't quite believe he was saying this '–not even for eternal life.'

There was a silence between the two men. Pat found himself suddenly moved by the agony in Tom Shaw's expression. He could tell he was in the presence of a man being ripped apart by impossible emotions. 'What would your wife tell you to do, Tom, if she was here now? Would she ask you to let a young woman die so that she can live? Would she tell you to let your son's death be the first of many? Is that what she'd say, Tom, do you think?'

No reply. Just that continued look of a man in turmoil.

Time check. He'd been gone exactly an hour. He *had* to get back. From his jacket he pulled a pencil and a scrap of paper, on which he wrote an address.

'She's there,' he said. 'So is your Admiral Windlass, or whatever you said his name was. Don't bother calling the police.

If there's a government figure involved, it'll do nothing but flag up that you're on to them.' He looked at his watch again. 'I'd say you've got two hours before they waste her. The decision's yours, Tom. I can't do any more.'

And with that, Pat Dolan handed over the piece of paper and, without looking back, walked straight across the road and into the Lotus Flower, where he ordered bags of food to take back to the farmstead.

When he left the restaurant, Tom Shaw was nowhere to be seen.

Pinned to her upturned chair in the darkness, Rachael could hear voices in the room above. Her body ached. Her head throbbed. She was shivering and dizzy. And yet, through all this, she managed to distinguish at least three different voices. Someone else was here. The thought made her heart fall into her stomach.

She was not a suspicious woman. The scientific method was too engrained in her thinking for that. But in her confused state, it was not lost on her that the Elixir, her discovery that was intended to bring life, had so far brought nothing but death. She could not rid herself of the memory of Jack, bleeding and perplexed as the life ebbed from him. She hoped he had not suffered too much, but she realized, deep down, that it was a vain hope. And she also knew that she would soon be experiencing what Jack had experienced.

Because she would not reveal the formula to these people. And if that meant they were going to kill her, then so be it. The secret would die with her. Rather that than let it fall into the wrong hands.

Light. It blinded her, and sent a shock of pain through her skull. Her eyes were still closed as she felt the chair being righted, and she prepared herself for more violence.

It didn't come. Just a pregnant, threatening silence.

She opened her eyes.

There were indeed three men standing there. At first, because her vision was compromised, they looked like silhouettes. Gradually, though, they came into focus. Rachael recognized two of them: the government agent from the Roosevelt Room and one of the men who had been tormenting her since she had arrived in this basement. But the third man's face was unfamiliar. It was tanned. Handsome, she supposed, with a thick head of black hair that was neatly slicked back. Very few lines on his face, and those few that existed did so on account of the thin smile on his lips.

'Good afternoon, Dr Leo,' he said quietly. 'It's a great pleasure to have you here. I do hope Tony hasn't been unduly heavy handed with you?'

Rachael's only reply was a look of poison. Its only effect was to make the smile on the man's face broader.

'Forgive me,' he said. 'I've been very rude and failed to introduce myself. My name's Theodore Croft. I'd shake hands, only…' He gave a helpless little shrug at Rachael's inability to move from her chair.

Croft took a step forward. His head was at an angle, and he was examining Rachael like she was an exhibit at a zoo. 'A genius,' he said, '*and* beautiful. What a great shame it would be to dispense with you. You are precisely the type whose longevity would improve the gene pool rather than sully it.'

'Go to hell,' Rachael breathed.

'Oh, I'm sure I will, Dr Leo. But not for a long time yet.' He walked round the back of Rachael's chair, then leaned over so his lips were just an inch from her left ear. She could feel his hot breath on her skin, and it made her shudder. 'Would you like to know how Peter Wright and Sylvia Lucas died, Dr Leo? Would you like to know how they squealed and squirmed and begged for mercy? Or would you just like to tell me how to make the Elixir, and we can all avoid any unnecessary unpleasantness?'

Rachael closed her eyes again. She wished it could just be over. She thought of her mother, of how brave she had been at the moment of her own death. She swallowed hard.

'You might as well kill me, Mr Croft,' she said. 'Because I will die before I tell you.'

A pause. All Rachael could hear was her own breath, and the beating of her heart. She sensed Croft standing up straight. When she opened her eyes again, the two others were looking anxious. Croft himself, however, was standing between them and her, his face expressionless.

'I'm disappointed, Dr Leo,' he said quietly. 'I confess myself disappointed. I had hoped we might avoid this tedious negotiation.'

'I'm not negotiating with you,' Rachael whispered back. It was all she could do to keep the fear from her voice. 'So you might as well get it over with.'

For a moment, Croft didn't respond. He stepped forward, and lightly brushed the back of his hand against Rachael's cheek. The touch of his skin sent a shiver down her spine, but not so much as the look in his eyes: a gleam of such madness that she briefly forgot the courage she had hoped to display, and whimpered.

'What makes you think I'd want to kill you, Dr Leo, when there is so much information I require inside that pretty little head of yours. If you'd only tell me now. We could grow rich together, you and I…'

'Some things aren't for sale,' she breathed.

'Everything's for sale, Dr Leo,' Croft snapped with sudden impatience. 'I can do things to you that will make you sell me the secret of the Elixir for just a few moments of relief. Do you understand what I'm saying?'

Rachael understood only too well. But she didn't let it show. 'It's not for sale,' she repeated, and she let her chin fall to her chest.

There was another period of silence. In a corner of her petrified brain, Rachael found herself remembering the Irish man, and she briefly wondered if he'd managed to contact Tom. But as soon as that thought entered her mind, it flitted away. What could Tom do, anyway? He would be surrounded by police and poleaxed with grief. And perhaps it was better this way. Better that Rachael's secrets should die with her…

She heard Croft's voice again. 'Tony,' he said. 'Do what you need to do, but keep her alive and conscious. Those are your only parameters. Understood?'

'Understood, Mr Croft,' said Tony. 'Leave it to me.'

'Excellent,' said Croft. He looked at his watch. 'Young Mickey Connor should be back any minute. I don't mind admitting I'm ravenously hungry, and it's been a long day for you too, Admiral Windlass. No doubt you could do with a bite to eat.'

The two men left the basement, closing the door behind them and leaving Rachael in the company of Tony. He was looking at her like an artist in front of a painting, wondering which precision stroke would best suit his purpose and achieve the effect he wished to achieve.

Tom Shaw drove blindly.

His world was caving in. In a matter of weeks he had gone from having everything to having nothing. Sitting in a Pure Industries warehouse there was enough Elixir stockpiled, thanks to Rachael Leo's hard work, to supply the US at least for years. Enough to make Tom wealthy beyond imagining, and powerful too. But what were wealth and power without his son?

And how could he handle the grief without his wife?

He thought of the Irish cop who'd just cornered him. Easy for *him* to say that he should hand over the formula. It wasn't *his* wife that the Elixir was keeping alive.

But as that thought passed through his mind, he remembered being at Jane's bedside. He remembered what she'd said. *For Jack. I'll endure it for Jack.*

And now there was no Jack. No reason for her to endure anything anymore.

He braked suddenly. He'd just approached a pedestrian crossing, where a harassed mother was ushering her two young children across the road. She looked up in fright as Tom's car screeched to a halt, and instinctively put her arms around the kids, before hurrying them to the other side of the road.

Tom's car didn't move. Other vehicles started to sound their horns at him, but he barely heard them. All his attention was fixed on the young mother, hugging her children. Protecting them.

Doing what he, Tom, was unable to do.

And for what?

He felt a crushing sense of self-loathing as he sat there, waiting for the mother and children to disappear from sight, and wondering one thing: who would want to play God, when it meant choosing who was to live, and who was to die?

Pat Dolan pulled up outside the farmstead. His car stank of the Chinese food in bags on the passenger seat. It nauseated him. How could the men in this building even think of eating at a time like this? He turned off the engine and sat quietly for a moment, trying to gather his thoughts. Agent 2's instructions had been explicit. He was to do whatever was necessary to keep his cover. And if that meant following an instruction to kill Rachael Leo...

There was no way he could do it. He knew that, deep down. He guessed that it was the difference between being a CIA spook and a cop. The essence of being a police officer was to protect life, even if it meant putting your own in jeopardy. The idea that he might sacrifice an innocent to protect the big picture was abhorrent to him. But he also knew that if he refused, his skull would be the first to receive a bullet.

So why had he come back? What the hell did he think he could do? Play the action hero? Rescue the damsel? He hissed quietly at his own stupidity, and it was only then that he saw Theodore Croft. He had emerged from the farmstead and was standing in the doorway smoking a cigarette. Some more of his heavies – four of them that Pat could count – stood at a respectful distance. Pat could see, from the bulges about their clothes, that they were all armed.

Croft had noticed Pat. He was fixing him with a dead-eyed stare. Jesus, the guy gave him the creeps. Despite his Californian accent, he spoke like a polite English gentleman. It only made the lack of feeling in his expression and the horrific nature of his actions all the more monstrous.

Pat grabbed the bags of food and exited the vehicle. He walked up to Croft, who was now stubbing out his cigarette with his heel. 'I thought we'd lost you, Mickey,' he said lightly.

Pat gave him an arrogant shrug. 'You want to eat this while it's still hot?' he asked.

They walked in silence to the sitting room where Admiral Windlass was waiting for them. He looked impatient. 'You should let me get one of my guys on her,' he said. 'They're trained in interrogation techniques. They'll have her squealing in no time.'

Croft smiled. 'I have every confidence in Tony's abilities,' he said. And, right on cue, a scream sounded from down below. Pat, who knew how hoarse and exhausted the poor woman was, was surprised at its intensity. He didn't even want to imagine what Tony Foreman had just done to Rachael Leo.

There was something monstrous about the way Croft tucked into the food Pat had supplied. Even Windlass seemed revolted by it, though Pat noticed that the Admiral barely flinched at the occasional screams of agony that emanated from below.

'Not eating, Mickey?' Croft said through a mouthful of noodles during one of the silences that were almost as sinister as the screams.

Pat shrugged. 'Not hungry,' he muttered. One hand was in his pocket, sweatily fingering his BlackBerry. He glanced anxiously out of the window on to the driveway where his car was parked. There was no sign of anyone approaching.

No sign of Tom Shaw.

Time was running out. So were his options.

He glanced over at Admiral Windlass. Now that he knew who he was, he fancied he remembered seeing him on TV, standing just behind the President's shoulder, a constant face in the entourage of the most powerful man in the world. He couldn't even begin to imagine why the President's man had teamed up with a scumbag like Croft, but he had and the thought brought Pat out in a cold sweat.

Another scream. Croft continued to eat.

'I need some air,' Pat said. Nobody paid him any attention. He walked outside and stood in the main doorway, staring at his BlackBerry which was out of his pocket now and in the palm of his hand.

He remembered his handler's words: *Press 5 twice on that phone ... You do that, we'll be able to locate your position using its enhanced GPS chip. As soon as we get that contact, we'll send the troops in.*

Only with Windlass sitting in that room, complicit in these crimes, Pat didn't know if he could *trust* the troops.

But what choice did he have?

He stared hard at the BlackBerry.

And then he pressed 5.

When we come, we'll come in hard – like, Special Forces hard – so keep your head down and be prepared for things to go noisy.

Noisy for whom, he wondered.

His finger hovered over the 5 button.

He made to press it.

And then he stopped. A car was approaching up the long, bumpy driveway. It moved slowly, but even from a distance of 50 yards, Pat recognized it. He'd seen it just an hour ago, after all, in a run-down suburb of Laguna Niguel, on the opposite side of the road to a Chinese restaurant.

He dropped the BlackBerry back into his pocket, narrowed his eyes and turned back into the house.

As he walked into the sitting room, both Croft and Windlass looked up askance at him. They could clearly sense he had something to tell them.

Pat cleared his throat.

'We've got company,' he said.

18

There was a heavy rap on the door, and a tense silence in the sitting room.

'Who is it?' Croft asked finally, having slid his Chinese food to one side. 'Who the hell knows we're here?'

Neither Windlass, nor Pat, replied.

'Get him,' Croft hissed. 'I want him here. Now!'

Pat nodded. He removed his handgun from his jacket and, brandishing it obviously, headed to the front door. He opened it to see Tom Shaw standing there. He looked terrified, and he had good reason.

Pat raised one forefinger to his lips just as he pointed the gun at Tom's forehead.

'Inside,' he said.

Tom Shaw gave him an uncertain look, and stepped over the threshold. Pat nodded in the direction of the sitting room. Ten seconds later they were both inside.

Croft looked wary. He clearly wasn't expecting visitors, and he equally clearly didn't like surprises. His louche manner had disappeared.

'Who the hell are you?' he demanded.

Tom sniffed. 'The Admiral can make the introductions,' he said.

Now all Croft's attention was on Windlass.

'Tom Shaw,' said the government man.

Croft moved with a speed Pat would never have expected of him. He pulled out a gun and pressed it hard against the side of Windlass's head. 'You tipped him off.' Not a question; an accusation.

'Don't be stupid, Croft.'

Croft didn't take kindly to the insult. He cracked the weapon around the side of Windlass's head, but the sturdy Admiral absorbed the blow without even a flinch.

'I should just let him kill you, shouldn't I, Admiral?' breathed Tom. 'Just let him do to you what you did to my son?'

Croft looked between the two of them. He obviously didn't know what to think.

'How did you know where to find us?' he shouted suddenly at Tom. 'How the *hell* did you know?'

Pat held his breath, but kept his weapon pointed firmly at Tom. More than anything now, he needed cover, and he couldn't be sure this guy wasn't about to blow it...

'Where's Dr Leo?'

Croft didn't need to answer, even if he intended to, because at that exact moment, a shrill, piercing scream sounded from the basement below.

'Let her go,' Tom Shaw instructed.

Croft sneered. 'Is that what you came here to say, Mr Shaw? Was that your heroic little plan?' He strode forwards, looked Croft up and down, then spat on his shoes. '*How did you know where to find us?*'

'You think I'd let an asset like Rachael Leo wander around where just anybody could get their hands on her? She's electronically tagged. Don't try to find it. It's beneath the skin.'

Pat felt a moment of relief. It was short-lived.

'Kill him,' Croft said.

There was a nasty silence. Pat felt the sweat running down his back.

'*I SAID KILL HIM!*'

And then Tom Shaw spoke again.

'I'm here to give you the formula,' he said. 'But you have to let Rachael go first.'

The two men were face to face, Tom with his chin jutted out, Croft plainly considering his next move.

A scream from down below.

'Hold your fire,' Croft murmured. He thought for a moment, then continued to issue his instructions. 'Take him to the cellar. Tell Tony to stand down. I'll be there in five minutes.'

'You heard him,' Pat growled at Tom. He nudged him in the back of the head with the gun. 'Move.'

They didn't speak as they descended the stairs to the basement. Pat wished he could offer Tom, who was shaking with anxiety, some words of comfort. But even if he had them, he couldn't have risked it. As they entered the cellar, he braced himself for a scene of horror; but it was worse than he could have imagined.

Tony was standing in front of Rachael Leo with an old baseball bat in his hands. It was stained with fresh blood, as was the woman's face. There was purple swelling around the eyes; her lips were split and bleeding; teeth were missing. She was taking short, sharp breaths, clearly in great pain, and her eyes were rolling. But she was alive, and conscious. That, he supposed, was something.

'Stand down,' Pat said.

Tony looked over his shoulder. His eyes shone with violence. 'Last time I checked, Mickey Connor, I took my orders from Croft, not you.' And, to emphasise his point, he quickly raised the baseball bat in the air and slammed it down on Rachael Leo's right forearm. Pat heard the crack of a bone; a fraction of a second later, he heard Leo's almost-silent scream. It sounded like she had no more shout left in her.

Tom Shaw sprang forward, hurling himself at Tony Foreman and knocking him to the floor. But Shaw was no fighter, and Tony was. Within seconds he was back on his feet and pummelling the baseball bat into Tom's stomach.

'For Christ's sake, Tony,' Pat shouted. '*Croft* said to stand down!' And when Tony turned, red faced and angry, to look at him, Pat said: 'He wants them alive and talking…'

'Quite right, Mickey Connor,' said a soft voice from the doorway. 'I want them alive, and most definitely talking.'

Pat turned. Croft was standing in the doorway, leaning casually against the frame with a cup of what Pat supposed to be coffee in his hand. Behind him was one of his goons, who was carrying something – a large, plastic bowl, which seemed to be half filled with water. The goon placed the bowl gently on the floor by the doorway, then stepped outside the room. Croft, meanwhile, started to tut when he saw the state of Rachael Leo.

'Tony,' he muttered. 'Tony, Tony, Tony… is that any way to treat a lady?' He stepped forward until he was standing right in front of Rachael, where he bent down and placed his coffee on the hard concrete floor before standing up again and sneering at the battered woman. 'Your good looks have quite deserted you, sweetheart. A shame, because a pretty, intelligent thing like you would make excellent breeding stock. How fortunate for us all, then, that Mr Shaw has gallantly arrived to rescue you. Your knight in shining armour!'

He turned to the crumpled heap that was Tom Shaw.

'Time to start talking, Mr Shaw,' he said.

Tom's abdomen was bruised and throbbing. He gasped for the breath that the thug with the baseball bat had knocked from his lungs; and his veins pulsed with hatred.

'What do you know?' he whispered painfully.

Croft sniffed. He pointed at the Irish cop, Windlass and the thug called Tony. 'You three,' he said curtly. 'Get out.'

The three men were obviously reluctant. Windlass started to speak. 'I hardly think…'

'GET OUT!' Croft roared, and Tom could hear the madness in his voice.

They filed out, like chided children.

Only when the door was closed and Tom and Rachael were alone with him did Croft speak again. Now his voice was trembling slightly. Anticipation, Tom surmised.

'The Legum compound is treated with Dragon's Blood,' he stated. 'It is baked at a temperature of 150 degrees centigrade for 1 hour, and UV cured at an irradiation level of 365 nanometers.'

Tom listened carefully, and despite the pain he was in, a smile crept across his face.

'A temperature of what?' he asked.

Croft repeated himself.

'Peter Wright told you that? Tell me, Mr Croft, what did you have to do to him to force that information out of his head.'

Croft walked up to Tom and bent down. He spoke in a quiet, threatening voice. 'I put him through so much pain, Mr Shaw, that he was glad to give it up.'

With difficulty, Tom pushed himself up into a sitting position, and stared straight into Croft's eyes. 'He was glad to *lie* to you, Croft. Maybe you can't bully people the way you think you can. Peter Wright told you the wrong thing.'

And to himself, he thought: Peter Wright was a goddamn hero. Funny how you find them in the most unlikely places.

Croft didn't try to hide his anger. He grabbed Tom by the throat and squeezed; but Tom wasn't going to be bullied either. He swiped Croft's arm away and pushed himself to his feet.

'The correct temperature, Mr Shaw,' Croft said through gritted teeth. 'Now. Otherwise our pretty little companion gets a bullet in the forehead.'

Silence. Tom took a deep breath. He glanced over at Rachael. Her eyes were shut, her head hung. The only way he knew she was still conscious was because of the way her body shook.

'120 degrees,' he whispered. 'You bake the compound at 120 degrees. That's the only piece of information you need.'

Croft barely moved for a full thirty seconds. He was impossible to read. When he finally stepped back, the old arrogance had returned to his face.

'If you're lying to me, Shaw, you'll regret it. You know that.'

'I'm not lying to you,' he said. 'Now let Rachael go.'

'What do you think I am, Mr Shaw? An idiot? I'm afraid neither of you are leaving this room until I'm sure I have the correct formula. Oh, don't you worry. I have a laboratory waiting. I'll know very soon. But first...'

Croft walked over to the door, opened it, and beckoned his three accomplices inside.

'Restrain this idiot,' he said.

Immediately, Tony was striding up to Tom. With brute force, he grabbed his left arm and twisted it almost to breaking point behind his back. Tom hissed in pain, but watched as Croft turned his attention to the bowl he had brought into the cellar with him.

'I wonder, Dr Leo, if your formidable intelligence extends to a knowledge of creatures of the deep.' He walked towards her, carrying the bowl with all the reverence of a priest carrying a chalice of wine. Rachael was in no state to answer. Her body was still shaking, but she just managed to raise her head and see Croft approaching her.

'The Irukandji jellyfish,' he said quietly. 'One of evolution's most remarkable creatures. Tiny. No bigger than a thumbnail. They have no brain and so they are neither able to be aggressive nor passive. And yet...' He placed the bowl at Rachael's feet. 'And yet, they are so very deadly, Dr Leo. So very, very deadly. One sting is enough to bring about Irukandji syndrome. Have you heard of that Dr Leo? Most unpleasant. Often fatal. And more than one sting, of course…'

Tom struggled, but it was no good. Tony just tightened his arm and, poleaxed by pain, Tom fell still again. All he could do was watch as Croft placed one finger under her chin and gently raised her head a little higher.

'Is he telling me the truth, Dr Leo?' he breathed.

No reply.

'*Is he telling me the truth?* Or would you like to become more intimately acquainted with my little pets?'

Rachael's eyes rolled. She spoke, but her voice was so weak that Tom couldn't hear what she said. 'I'm telling you the truth!' he shouted at Croft. 'For God's sake, leave her alone.'

Croft made no indication that he'd even heard him. He bent down and slowly removed Rachael's leather slip-on shoe, and the ankle-length sock that was beneath it, to reveal the bare skin of her foot.

She started speaking again. Whispering. Over and over. Tom had to strain his ears to hear what she as saying; even then it took a few seconds to work it out. '*He's telling the truth … he's telling the truth…*'

A look of serenity crossed Croft's face. He still had Rachael's bare foot in his hands and he held it there, hovering over the bowl of Irukandji jellyfish.

'Let her go,' breathed Tom. 'You've got what you want, Croft. Now let her go…'

But Croft did not let her go. With a sudden jerking movement, he plunged Rachael's foot into the bowl and held it there, his strength more than a match for the feeble struggling of her leg. Rachael gasped; still Croft held her foot in the bowl, his eyes feasting at the sight of what was going on inside. Tom tried to escape Tony's grasp again, but the thug pressed his arm up so far he knew that another millimetre would break it.

Rachael's foot was in the water for thirty seconds before Croft pulled it out again. Even from a distance he could see that there were several red welts on the skin. She hadn't just been stung once, but several times.

Croft released her foot and stood up again. 'My scientists are on standby at a location not far from here,' he announced. 'They estimate that it will take three hours for them to establish whether or not you've told me the truth. *I* estimate that it will take Dr Leo four hours to die.' He gave a nasty smile. 'Not quite the 400 years she was hoping for, I'm afraid. But don't look so distraught, Mr Shaw. I'm happy to tell you that there *is* an antidote to this nasty little venom. I'll be more than happy to administer it, once I'm sure that you've been straight with me.'

He strode quickly up to Tom and stood inches away from his face.

'So if there's anything you want to tell me, Mr Shaw – anything you might have omitted – then now would be a very good time to do so.'

'You know everything I know,' Tom breathed.

'In that case, I see no reason for Tony to keep you in this undignified posture.' He nodded at the thug, who released Tom's arm and pushed him towards the center of the room.

Tom rushed up to Rachael. She was whispering again. Something else this time. '*Jack… I'm sorry about Jack … I couldn't stop it…*'

Croft was talking over her, issuing his instructions to Tony and the Irish new boy. 'Watch them,' he said. 'One of you in here with them all the time. The others will guard the door. If either tries to escape, kill one and leave the other alive. Do you understand?'

They understood.

Croft swept out of the room, not even looking back at the scene of devastation he had left in his wake.

A long, uncomfortable silence followed, punctuated only by Rachael's gasps. Tom started to examine her – pulling open her eyelids, feeling the strength of her pulse. He was no medic, but he felt he had to do something.

'I'm alright,' she breathed. '*I'm alright…*'

But she didn't sound alright, she didn't look alright and somehow her stoicism made Tom's anger bubble over. He punched the air – a gesture of impotent fury – then turned to Pat Dolan.

Pat, however, spoke before Tom was able to say anything that would break his cover. 'I'll watch them,' he announced, turning sharply to Tony. 'You mark the door…'

If Tony was in any way suspicious of Pat's suggestion, he didn't show it. It was with a nasty leer in Tom's direction that he left the room, closing the door firmly behind him. Tom heard a key turn in the lock.

They were alone. Incarcerated. His son was gone. He had given up the Elixir that was saving his wife. And Rachael Leo was hours from death.

He turned to Pat Dolan. For some reason all his anger and all his despair was directed to the undercover Irish cop who had brought him here. Tom strode up to him and grabbed him by the front of his shirt.

'I'm not going to lose another person today,' he hissed, 'and I don't trust Croft to bring us that antidote any more than I could throw him. So you'd better have a plan, my sneaky little friend. You'd better have a goddamn plan to get us out of here...'

Pat Dolan had no plan. Just a mass of confused ideas in his head. Jesus, he'd suspected Croft was a psychopath, but those jellyfish had taken even him by surprise.

'Get away from the door,' he whispered. 'To the back of the room. In case Tony's listening...'

The two men hurried over to the back wall.

'We need to untie her...'

'No,' Pat said firmly. 'The arm's obviously broken and the rope's keeping it immobile. And besides, if Tony sees we've freed her...'

'Then what the hell do we do?'

'Listen carefully,' Pat said. 'We've got two options. Option one, we try and fight our way out. But she's too weak to move, and there's at least six armed men out there, not including Tony.'

'Option two?' Tom asked.

Pat pulled out his BlackBerry. 'If I press this button twice, and assuming I've got some signal in this damn basement, my handlers will be able to locate our position and send in a team to extract us.' He raised his hand to stop Tom speaking. 'But it's a risk. I'm working for the CIA . If the spooks are taking their instructions from the White House – and it's got to be a possibility with that Admiral fella hanging around – the only thing my distress call's going to do is blow my cover. I'll be dead by teatime. And if Croft has his way, so will you.'

'And if you don't?' Tom's eyes were dead.

And if I don't, Pat Dolan thought to himself, *what then? Do I stand here and watch these people die?*

No. He wouldn't do that. He *couldn't* do that. To hell with Agent 2. To hell with the CIA and the LAPD. This was about lives, and he was a human being before he was a cop.

He nodded at Tom, then examined the BlackBerry. There was a single notch of service indicated on the screen. Would it be enough?

It would have to be.

He pressed the '5' button. Twice.

'What now?' Tom asked.

'Now?' replied Pat. 'Now we wait.' And pray, he added silently in his head. We wait and pray.

For Dr Rachael Leo, the pain was all-consuming. Her arm was limp, and the agony that pulsed through it was shrill. When the jellyfish had stung her, she'd felt very little: vague discomfort in her veins. But now, a strange and unpleasant sensation was creeping through her. It was nausea, but more than that. Her blood was hot one minute, cold the next. The room was spinning.

And her mind was starting to wander.

She had moments of lucidity. Moments when she almost managed to get her thoughts together and speak. But these thoughts were soon shrouded in a fog of confusion that pushed them away like oil repelling water. When this happened, the room started to spin; her surroundings started to change. She was no longer in that cold, concrete basement, but back in the lab, staring in horror at the sight of Jack's wounded, dying body. Or she was with Kyle, their lips brushing together lightly. She was looking into his eyes…

The venom continued to surge through her body and a sudden jolt of intense pain caused her eyes to ping open and she inhaled sharply. There was a shadow on the edge of her vision, and though she couldn't make out his face, she knew it was Tom, watching over her.

She tried to speak, but the words she breathed sounded garbled even to her.

Tom approached. He put one hand on her shoulder. 'Help's coming,' he whispered. 'You're going to be OK…'

But she shook her head.

'You need…' It took all her concentration just to form the words. 'You need… to know something…'

'Don't talk,' Tom said. 'Save your energy. Help's coming…'

It wasn't just Rachael's head that was shaking now, but her whole body, out of frustration. He needed to listen to her. *Why wouldn't he listen?*

'Elixir,' she breathed.

'Forget about the Elixir, Rachael. We've lost it. Croft has the formula...'

'No. *No he hasn't...*'

She sensed the door opening. Tony's voice. 'What the hell's going on in here?'

The Irishman replied. 'Don't worry about it, Tony,' he said. 'Just a touching little farewell scene between our two friends here.'

The thug grunted and shut the door. By the time he had done so, however, Rachael's lucidity had disappeared again. She was dizzy. Elsewhere. Transported from the cellar to her mother's bedside. Holding her thin hand as the life drained from her. Just like it was draining from Rachael herself...

Tom's voice, hissing urgently. 'Rachael! *Rachael!*'

Her eyes opened again. How long had she been away? She didn't know. Impossible to say... 'Elixir...' she breathed again.

'What do I need to know?' Tom was asking. She felt him squeeze her right shoulder in reassurance, but it caused a shooting pain down her arm and she winced.

'Fifth component,' she breathed.

'What are you talking about, Rachael? What do you mean?'

'Listen to me... There is a fifth component... I kept it secret... in case... in case...'

But she suddenly cried out loud. A crippling, cramping sensation had passed through her whole body, and for a few seconds she was paralyzed with unimaginable pain that she found herself almost wishing that death would take her. When it subsided, it felt like it had taken the remnants of any energy she had. Her head slumped listlessly on to her chest and she was only vaguely aware of Tom's urgent whispers.

'What fifth component, Rachael? *What are you talking about? What is it?*'

She wanted to tell him.

She wanted to speak.

Because if she didn't give him the information now, it would very soon be too late.

The secret would die with her.

But Rachael Leo's body would not do what her confused mind was telling it. No matter that every ounce of her being was focussing on the attempt, to such an extent that she was unable to hear the sound that was increasingly clear to her companions.

It was faint at first. So faint that for a few seconds Pat Dolan dismissed it as his hopeful, desperate imagination playing tricks on him. But after a minute or so he realized that there was no doubt, even in the deadened, insulated acoustic of this grisly basement.

And when the ventilation grate on the far wall started to vibrate slightly, Tom Shaw looked askance at him. Pat nodded. It *was* what he thought it was. It *was* the sound of a chopper approaching.

And they weren't the only one to hear it.

The door burst open. It was Tony and he looked alarmed. 'What the hell's that sound?' he demanded. '*What's going on?*'

He pulled his handgun and strode to the far side of the room, where he looked up towards the vibrating ventilation grate.

Pat moved quickly and silently, ignoring the voice in his head that told him this could be the last thing he ever did if it went wrong, and that he wasn't built for fighting. He removed his own weapon and, checking that the safety was on, brandished it by the barrel and crept up towards Tony.

The thug turned. He clearly knew something was wrong because his eyes narrowed and he raised his gun hand at the sight of Pat bearing down on him.

But too late.

Pat used all the force he could muster to slam the butt of his weapon down on Tony's head. There was a thump as metal met skull, and a flash of blood. Tony, though, was made of solid stuff. He staggered back against the wall, but he remained conscious.

He fired his gun.

The retort echoed against the concrete walls of the cellar, and for a moment Pat thought he was hit. But the round ricocheted harmlessly off one wall, splintering the concrete, and Pat knew he had just one more chance to down the shooter.

His second strike was even more brutal than the first and this time, when his gun made contact with Tony's head, the thug crumpled to the ground. Unconscious, but for how long, Pat didn't know.

'We need to untie her,' he said. 'Quickly.'

Tom Shaw didn't look as if he'd even heard. He was bent over, whispering urgently at the girl.

'*Untie her!*' he repeated. And then, cursing under his breath, he approached the chair himself. The ropes that bound

Rachael's hands were sturdy and firmly tied. It took Pat at least thirty seconds before he could even loosen the knot. All the while, Tom was whispering.

'What is it, Rachael? *What the hell is it?*'

The question meant nothing to Pat. He just kept untying, and after another thirty seconds, the rope fell to the floor. Rachael's broken arm, which the rope had been holding in place, swung limply to her side. She gasped in agony, but Pat knew there was nothing he could do about it. She'd just have to put up with the pain until he got them out of here…

'Help me lift her!' he shouted. '*For God's sake, man, help me lift her!*'

Tom nodded, and together they lifted Rachael – as gently as they could – from her seat, each man holding beneath one shoulder. She was heavy for such a slight creature, because her body was limp and she was unable to support herself. Pat panicked briefly that they might not be able to get her up the stairs; and what if Croft's men got to them before the SWAT team; and what if the SWAT team's instruction were not to rescue them, but the opposite…

Footsteps. Outside the cellar. Pat froze. He struggled for his gun, but two figures arrived at the doorway before he was able to engage it. He recognized them. Broad-shouldered. Mean-eyed. Alarm on their faces.

Which doubled when they saw Tony unconscious on the floor and their prisoners trying to escape.

Of Croft's two men, one was squatter than the other. He was also quicker off the mark. He raised his gun and pointed it directly at Pat.

And for the second time in as many minutes, the sound of a round being discharged echoed off the concrete walls.

Tom's whole body shook with the sound of it. He braced himself, ready to take the weight of Rachael's body when Pat Dolan fell to the floor.

But Pat didn't fall.

Croft's heavy, the one who was aiming his gun, could never have known what hit him. There was a gruesome explosion of blood and skull as a round entered the back of his head. The man was thrown two yards forward and landed with a sickening thump on the ground, face down and with the catastrophic wound to the back of his head on full show.

He felt his knees buckle.

The second man was raising his gun and spinning round.

The light – that single bulb hanging from the ceiling – went out.

Total darkness.

And then, sudden and unexpected, a blindingly bright flash of light, and an ear-cracking bang that disorientated Tom. He felt Rachael slide to the floor – not because anything had hit her, he thought, but because in the mayhem he and Pat had let go.

And voices. Sharp, brutish voices.

'*HIT THE GROUND!*' they shouted. '*ARMED POLICE! HIT THE GODDAMN GROUND!*'

Rachael Leo had never known such pain, or even that it could possibly exist, as the weight of her body crushed her broken arm against the concrete floor. But there was no energy left in her to scream.

She was aware only of snippets. The cup of coffee, now cold, that Croft had left on the floor by her chair, knocked over and spilt over the concrete. Thin beams of light shooting from the sights mounted on the weapons which the men who were now flooding into the room were brandishing. The acrid stench of whatever had caused that short, sharp explosion. The shouting: '*HIT THE GROUND! HIT THE GROUND!*'

Another gunshot, and more shouting. '*CLEAR!*'

The light returned, but it brought with it no illumination for Rachael Leo. Her vision was clouded. She knew she was losing consciousness.

Perhaps permanently.

She tried to speak, but the only sound that came from her throat was a strangled, gasping noise.

The fifth component. She had to tell Tom. *While she still had strength, she had to tell him…*

She stretched out her hand, and her fingertips touched the pool of cold coffee.

Weakly, her arm numb and her hand shaking, she forced her wet fingers to locate a dry patch of concrete. And although unable even to see the letters she was forming, and with chaos and shouting exploding all around her, she started to write.

Pat Dolan counted five men. They were dressed in black, but their body armour was a navy blue. Their faces were obscured by helmets and bulletproof visors. They carried short assault rifles – Pat didn't know what they were, but he knew he didn't like being at the business end of them. Which he was, because he was still carrying his own handgun.

'Drop the weapon! *Drop the weapon!*' The gunmen advanced, pace by pace. They weren't shouting. They were screaming, their voices tinged with the panic that Pat felt.

'Hold your fire,' he yelled at them. He bent down and laid the handgun on the floor.

It all happened so quickly. The moment he'd let go of his weapon, the gunmen advanced even faster. Pat started to straighten up, but at a bark from one of the men he hit the ground again.

They continued advancing. Pat was aware of Rachael Leo moving on the floor; and of the bowl of jellyfish – the surface tension trembling with the impact of the new arrivals. It was just a metre from his position, and he could see that one of the gunmen was going to kick it.

'No!' he shouted.

But too late.

A heavy leather boot knocked the edge of the bowl. As if in slow-motion, it tipped. The water sluiced out, and its deadly occupants slipped across the floor in Pat's direction.

It was a reflex action, the way he jumped up to avoid contact with the creatures. And it was a sudden movement that the gunmen clearly misinterpreted.

He saw one of them raise his rifle. Just as Pat had beaten Tony with the barrel of his handgun, the gunman crashed the hard metal down on Pat's head.

The shock of the impact resonated down his spine. The room turned upside down. Pat Dolan hit the concrete, unconscious and suddenly unaware of the chaos that was raging around him.

Suddenly there was silence.

Tom's breathing was heavy. Five men had him at gunpoint. Pat was motionless on the floor, the upset jellyfish just inches from his skin, but not moving.

And then there was a sound from where Rachael Leo was lying, crumpled. It was long. Rattling. Like something was escaping from her body.

Tom looked at the men. 'I need to go to her,' he said. Without waiting for a reply, he stepped over Pat's body, crouched down and cupped Rachael's head in her hands.

'Rachael,' he whispered. 'Wake up! *Wake up!*'

But she didn't wake up. Nor did she breathe. Tom held two trembling fingers to the side of her neck. There was no pulse.

One of the gunmen approached. He had removed his helmet and ditched his weapon. 'Move aside,' he instructed, and as Tom shuffled numbly out of the way, he squeezed Rachael's nose and started administering rescue breaths and chest compressions.

Thirty seconds passed.

A minute.

Silence in the room.

More rescue breaths.

More chest compressions.

The gunman continued his resuscitation techniques long after it was clear they were in vain. When he finally stood up again, his head was bowed and Tom was cold with shock.

He shuffled on his knees back towards Rachael. Like Jack, she didn't look peaceful in death. Far from it. Her pale, cold face was a picture of pain. In his mind, Tom remembered the Friday evening, not so long ago, when she had called him into the lab to reveal her astonishing discovery. He remembered the look of bright excitement in her eyes; the way her face shone and her voice trembled with the thrill of it all. Rachael Leo thought she was going to live forever. But it wasn't that which had excited her, Tom knew, but the thought of the gift she was giving humanity.

But Rachael *hadn't* avoided death. Death had taken her in the most abominable way it could contrive. And it had taken Jack. The thought was like a needle going through him.

And all for nothing. Because Rachael was dead, and the secret of the Elixir had died with her.

Two more gunmen arrived in the room. 'House clear,' stated one of them.

The man who had tried to resuscitate Rachael had turned his attention to Pat Dolan. 'He's alive,' he said. 'But only just. He needs a medic fast.'

'Extract,' said a third voice. 'You!' Tom looked round to see one of them addressing him. 'On your feet. We need to get you out of here.'

Tom nodded, but he turned back to Rachael and laid one hand gently on the side of her face.

And then he saw it.

It was very faint. Barely there at all, and covered by Rachael's right hand. Tom lifted the limb – it was already cold, but not yet stiff – and moved it out of the way to check he wasn't making it up. But there was no mistaking it.

Rachael Leo had attempted to write something on the concrete floor.

Tom squinted, trying to make it out.

Two letters, feebly formed in childlike writing:

T . . . H . . .

What followed, though was indecipherable. An E, maybe? It was impossible to tell. There was just a sequence of unreadable symbols: evidence of the dying Rachael's weakness and confusion. But at the end of that illegible scrawl were two letters he *could* make out:

I . . . S . . .

He stared at the writing for a few more seconds. It was fading, as the liquid in which they had been written evaporated. But then Tom became aware of two of the gunmen standing over him. They bent, and yanked him sharply up underneath his arms.

'Wait!' Tom shouted. Another man had lifted Pat Dolan over his shoulder. '*Wait!*'

Nobody paid him any attention. They dragged him, struggling, from the room, up the stairs on to the ground floor of the house and outside. The helicopter had touched down just yards from Tom's own car and its rotary blades were spinning fast, blinding him with their downdraft. The men pulled him in the direction of the chopper, and by now it was clear to Tom that there was no point in fighting. He was being rescued, whether he wanted it or not.

As he was bundled into the waiting aircraft, so many images swam around his head. Jack. Rachael. Theodore Croft and his cold, hard eyes. The scenes of horror he had seen that day, both in the lab and in the basement of his house.

And the letters, scrawled on the concrete floor by a dying woman with a secret she wanted to reveal.

What had Rachael been trying to write? As Pat Dolan's unconscious body was loaded up and the helicopter lifted off, Tom's brow was furrowed in concentration. The indecipherable letters. What could they be? In his mind, he scrutinised what he had seen, and a sentence formed: '*Th*e fifth component *is*...'

Is what?

Rachael had been trying to tell him, he realized as the chopper swerved over the farmstead and back towards Laguna

Niguel. She'd been trying to tell him the final component, but she had died before it was possible.

Which meant that once the stockpile Rachael had accumulated was gone, the Elixir was lost.

For ever.

PART FOUR

FOUR MONTHS LATER

19

Nurse Alison Davis had been on duty since 6 a.m., but a few hours on the high-dependency ward were enough to exhaust anyone. Yesterday two car-crash trauma victims had died on her – mercifully, in her opinion, given the horrific nature of their injuries – but it always unpleasant when it happened, and she found herself hoping today would be easier.

She went from room to room, checking on her patients. Two cancer sufferers, in for palliative care; a triple bypass gone wrong. Born just a few months too late, she thought to herself as she checked their blood pressure and their catheters – at least, they were if what everybody was saying about this new wonder drug was true. Elixir, they called it. The country had gone mad for it. Even Alison herself had put in an application for herself and her family. Two days ago, a letter had come back. 'Dear Mrs Davis, we are delighted to inform you that your application for Elixir has been approved…' It didn't seem real, somehow. When she'd first heard about it, she'd imagined herself whooping with elation should she be allowed a supply of the drug. But now she'd gained approval, nothing seemed so different. She still came to work. She still kept house for the family. There was something both exciting and depressing in knowing there was no end in sight to the reassuring drudgery of her life.

She had initially decided not to take the Elixir, as her husband was out of work and they couldn't afford to pay for two doses. But then, gradually, she was worn down by the increasing awareness of her own mortality and the news of her friends and family that were deciding to take it, the final straw being when her mother announced that she made an application. So, she signed up and, after her husband left her, made an application for one of the new fangled 'two hundred year mortgages' that Pure Financial were offering, to buy a brand new three bed apartment just off Pacific Highway.

It cost me my marriage, though, she thought as she refilled the water jug of an old man, blinded by age and kept alive only by dialysis. *But there's now time to meet someone else.*

She walked along the hospital corridor and came to the private room of the fifth patient on her rounds. Two men were standing outside. Two men were *always* standing outside. Not police officers – she had gleaned that much – but there to protect the occupant of this room. Why were they there? Who was paying them? These were questions that had been asked – and not answered – by all the nurses on this ward. And even though they recognized Alison, they insisted on checking her identity card before they allowed her to enter.

Each of these rooms had a small television on the wall. The patients seldom turned them on, because they were seldom in a position to. This room was the exception to the rule, but it wasn't the patient with the once-broken nose who had turned it on; it was the doctors. When someone is in a deep coma, they said, stimulus was good. And as nobody ever came to visit this man, TV was the only stimulus he was likely to get: that and the regular beeping of the life-support machine by his bed.

She picked up the notes hanging at the end of his bed. Name: Patrick Dolan. Age: 32 Alison scanned the list of drugs that were keeping his body alive, even if his mind was shot to pieces. All of them to be administered intravenously, including food and water. And the Elixir – though why this man should have got his hands on it earlier than anyone else was a mystery to her. She shook her head. Wouldn't it be kinder just to let him slip away peacefully? Was there really any chance that he would ever wake up again?

Alison was just pulling back the covers to give him a bed bath when her attention was caught by what had previously been nothing more than a babble from the TV. She stopped what she was doing and turned to watch it.

Her eyes widened. *It was him*. She looked around for the remote control. When she found it on the armchair which nobody ever used, she turned the volume up a little and stood, transfixed.

The screen showed the President of the United States, smartly suited and smiling for the cameras that flickered and flashed. A text banner at the bottom of the screen indicated that he was in the Roosevelt Room at the White House. But it was neither the President, nor the building that she stared at. It was the unassuming man standing, slightly uncomfortably, next to him, holding a brown A4 envelope and frowning, as though he would rather be anywhere but here.

The text banner at the bottom of the screen offered more information:

Tom Shaw, CEO of Pure Industries, makers of the new wonder-drug Elixir, is honored by the President of the United States...

Tom Shaw. There wasn't a person in the country – in the world – who didn't know that name. It was this man who, just four months ago, had announced the Elixir to the world; who had promised that, for a small fee that few people didn't think was worth paying, immorality was theirs. Tom Shaw who, in the small amount of time that he had been in the public eye, had made the leaders of the world seem insignificant.

She remembered well, a month after the announcement, how it had become common knowledge that a serial rapist with a life sentence had made an application for the new drug. There had been an outcry. Irate journalists had written at length on the moral dubiousness of allowing such a person to extend their life; hysterical TV anchors had shrieked their reports from outside the facility where this monster was being held. On Capitol Hill, the question was debated and argued; and the President himself appeared unwilling – or unable – to make a decision either way.

He didn't have to. Tom Shaw, without reference to anybody, had ordered that the rapist's application be rejected. Alison Davis didn't consider herself to be a particularly sophisticated or insightful person, but even she could tell that with this one action, Tom Shaw had demonstrated that his authority – his *power* – was greater than that of the President. And if he had more power than the President of the United States, he had more power than *anybody*...

No wonder that the sight of him on the television screen transfixed the hard-working nurse. No wonder that she was more interested in watching what was unfolding in the Roosevelt Room than in attending to her patients. She stared at the screen as the President tried to shake his guest's hand. But Tom Shaw refused it, and for a moment the President looked all at sea.

Alison blinked. The life-support machine that was beeping by the patient's side had suddenly beeped a little faster. But it immediately settled down again, and Alison turned back to the TV, and to the events that were unfolding before her eyes.

Tom Shaw stared at the President's hand, outstretched and awaiting his own. His eyes traced the shape of his fingers, and he thought about death.

Jack's death and Rachael's. Peter Wright and Sylvia's. They were not dead by this man's hands, but those slender fingers had blood on them nonetheless. How could he touch them? How could he shake hands with the man who had murdered his son?

Two Secret Service personnel approached, but they stepped back at a gesture from their commander in chief, who was clearly eager to avoid unpleasantness.

'Shall we begin, Mr President?' Tom asked briskly, blinking slightly at the camera flashes that illuminated both men, his eyes flickering towards the television cameras that were broadcasting this event to the nation.

'Yes,' the President replied 'Yes, of course. Let's begin.' He held out one hand to offer Tom a seat at the table. Tom nodded, and sat down. The President took his place next to him.

And then he spoke. Words directed at Tom, but meant for the camera. 'Mr Shaw,' he announced, 'it's more than a pleasure to welcome you to the White House. It's an honor.'

Tom didn't react. He was remembering the welcome he received on the occasion of his first visit to the White House, in this very room.

'The United States,' the President continued, 'has always been at the forefront of scientific research. Ours was the first nation to put a man on the moon. To transplant a human organ. And now, we have given the world perhaps its greatest gift. The gift of life.'

The President paused, allowing his dramatic statement time to sink in. Cameras flashed. Tom remained stony-faced, the irony of the President's words rolling over him.

'In the coming weeks,' the President continued, 'those citizens who have applied on behalf of their families for the Elixir will learn the result of their applications, and I am assured that none of these applications will be unreasonably refused.' He glanced over at Tom, who nodded his agreement. 'In the meantime, it is right and proper that we as a nation give Mr Shaw a token of our gratitude for the gift he has given us. Mr Shaw, it is with true humility for the scale of your achievements that I award you the Presidential Medal of Innovation, the highest honor we can bestow on one of our citizens.'

The President smiled a winning smile as an aide handed him a small box, which the President in turn presented to Tom.

Tom didn't take it. There were a few anxious seconds, and the President was obliged to place the box on the table in front of them.

More camera flashes. Worried looks being exchanged by the officials in the room.

Tom cleared his throat. 'Mr President,' he said. 'I have a gift for you too.'

The President's eyes tightened – a look of well-concealed anxiety. This wasn't in the script. He didn't know what was happening. And yet, with the cameras rolling and the nation glued to their sets, there was nothing he could do.

The silence in the Roosevelt Room was like a thick blanket. Tom took a moment to drink it in.

Strange, he thought to himself, and not for the first time that day. Strange to know you're about to kill a man. And strange to know that nobody – really, *nobody* – can touch you.

Tom's briefcase was by his feet. He bent down and removed a sheaf of paper from it. And as he passed it to the President, his eyes lingered for a moment on the front page.

It was very familiar. Indeed, it would have been familiar to almost everybody in America. The Pure Industries logo at the top. Just beneath that, the words: APPLICATION FOR THE PROVISION OF ELIXIR.

And beneath that: NAMES OF APPLICANTS.

The name of the President had been typed on to the document and the signature underneath, in a pale turquoise ink, was the President's own. It was somewhat obscured, however, by the overbearing black stamp imprinted at an angle across the paper.

Two words: **Application Rejected**.

The President took the document with a perplexed look at Tom. When his eyes fell upon it, the color drained from his skin.

'No...please...no!' he groaned. He didn't understand; by depriving him of the Elixir, Tom Shaw had sentenced The President to a living death, a cruel 'Sword of Damocles' which, as his family all busied themselves planning their extended future, condemned him to the fringes, destined as he now was, to become a fond but fading memory. A dead man walking.

But why?

Tom gave him no time to react any further. No time to argue or to beg. He scraped back his chair and, ostentatiously ignoring the little box that held the Presidential Medal of Innovation walked away from the table and out of range of the cameras. They remained fixed on the President, stunned into immobility. He stared at the paper, looked up, then back down again. He was clearly struggling to know what to do.

After 20 seconds that felt a lot longer to everyone in the room, he looked up again and said, with an unconvincing smile, 'God bless America.'

He too stood up, and as the TV cameras stopped running, the President was immediately surrounded by a crowd of advisers and secret service personnel. But all his attention was on Tom who, standing by the door, mouthed two words at him.

'For Jack.'

And then, within seconds, the President was swallowed into the chaos of the Roosevelt Room, and Tom Shaw was free to slip quietly out and negotiate the now familiar corridors of the West Wing.

He felt quite calm for a killer. But then, he told himself as he ignored the curious looks from White House staffers as he passed their offices, it was something he would have to get used to.

The power to give extended life, or condemn to an early death, was his. He would give generously, but, yes, sometimes he would have to take away.

And the politicians of the world, the men and women who considered themselves powerful, and just, and right, would simply have to get used to it.

Clint checked, then double checked, the Departures board for reassurance. His flight hadn't been delayed, it was on schedule, there was no problem. He tried to relax but the anxiety returned almost immediately and he found himself checking the Departure board again...then again.

During the attack on the Lab, he'd been in the storeroom when he first heard the unmistakeable sound of gunshots, then Ruth's muffled shouting. He'd turned the light off and cowered in a darkened corner of the storeroom and saw Rachael being dragged away, their eyes meeting for a second and that look of blind terror on her face was seared into his mind.

Unbelievably, he remained undetected and after slipping away unnoticed from the Lab, he'd kept on running, convinced that he'd be pursued by the thugs.

He'd spent most of his savings, paying for flights, meandering across the US, each time staying at increasingly seedy hotels. He needed to stay low-profile...but he could never escape the gut-churning fear.

Every look from a stranger was a potential threat, unsolicited conversations were terminated – often rudely - but the anxiety continued to grow.

But, after months of running and, with his savings almost all spent, Clint finally decided that he had to leave and seek sanctuary outside of the USA. And there was one place where he believed no-one would find him.

The voice over the loudspeaker system at JFK International airport reminded passengers to stay close to their bags and Clint's eyes flicked up to the Departures board again.

In ninety six minutes, he calculated, the plane would be taking off and he'd be leaving the USA for good.

Soon he would feel safe again.

The night chill of the desert made Lynda shiver but she maintained her slow pace back towards the tent, where Nat was sleeping, close enough now to hear the deep timbre of his snoring above the sound of the chirruping cicada.

Her shin struck a rock but she silenced herself immediately, swallowing the pain that spread all along her leg. She stood still whilst rubbing her shin, but a slight movement in the hessian sack she was carrying made her freeze to the spot. She waited for the creature within to settle, then, when satisfied, moved forward slowly towards the tent. Lynda realized that she was holding her breath, so permitted a small release of air through an open mouth, nothing more than a sigh.

'Nat would be proud of me remembering that old Special Forces trick', she thought.

Lynda loved her husband. Yes, he was your typical military type, strict, unbending, dedicated, hard-hearted in most matters...except when it came to her. He was strong, powerful man who was putty in her hands and that's why she loved him. It made her feel special that he was willing to bend the rules for her because she was his 'Princess'. He used those actual words, even when in company, causing her to feign embarrassment but, in truth, she loved it.

He looked after her, even when he was a relatively poor Navy Seal, nothing was too much trouble for him when it came to spoiling her. So to keep him company and to learn the ways of the desert and jungle during his 'hardcore' camping holidays was not too much of a sacrifice.

Through his tutelage, she had learnt a lot about the desert, what plants she could and couldn't eat, what cacti could produce unlikely sources of water and which creatures were particularly dangerous.

But, in truth, it was still an imposition and she had never really grown to enjoy sleeping in a tent, living off what they could forage from the land, however, she suffered in silence, as, after her, 'extreme camping' seemed to be his one only other pleasure.

So, when he came home from work early and suggested... no, not suggested, insisted that they 'disappear' for a few days to the desert, she agreed without much of a fight. The condition was, of course, that she would be dropped off at a five star resort for a bit of R & R afterwards.

But, last night, under the desert stars as they sat by the camp fire, he'd shocked her. He'd told her that he was broke and was probably about to be fired by the Government, he may even go to prison, as he'd done something wrong, very wrong. She didn't ask what he'd done - it was irrelevant as far as she was concerned - and, for the first time since they were married, she saw tears well in his eyes. She reached for him and she held him tenderly whilst the big bear of a man sobbed in her arms like a baby. In that moment, whilst she whispered soothing words, she decided what she had to do.

She had to kill him. And soon.

At first, her head spun at the enormity of the impending change in her lifestyle. No more five star holidays, the cars would have to go and they'd have to move to a smaller house. Yes, she loved Nat, but she hated poverty even more. Yes, he had to go and go quickly, as the window of opportunity would close quickly, if he was incarcerated.

She walked slowly towards the tent, her heart pounding so loudly, foolishly, she feared that it would wake her husband.

There was a slight stirring of the creature again and the weight shifted again in the sack which caused her to stiffen her arm and hold it far away from her body. The rhythm of her husband's snoring continued unabated and she squatted in front of the tent near the zip that would expose the end of his sleeping bag.

Slowly, with one hand, she unzipped the tent

Now came the tricky bit, but she was confident in her expertise. She had rehearsed this in her mind ever since she'd made her decision and, despite the pounding of her heart, she was surprised how calm she was. With the same hand she'd used to open the tent, she located the zip to the double sleeping bag and slowly, very slowly, created an opening. Despite Nat being a big man, she couldn't see his feet, as he had the habit of sleeping with his knees close to his chest, in the fetal position.

The moment of truth. Would the fearsome noise of the creature wake her husband? Would it, as she hoped, seek the safety of darkness to escape its confinement or would it turn on her and fight?

She took a deep breath and, whilst still holding the sack away from her body, she untied the top and then laid it close to the opening of the sleeping bag. Nothing at first, then a brief rattle before the sinuous movement of the snake indicated its desire to escape the captivity of the sack and find safe haven within the warm, cave like opening ahead.

The Mojave Rattlesnake is among the most venomous of all. Its poison is highly neurotoxic and interferes with transmission of nerve impulses which, without the early introduction of anti-venom, frequently proves fatal. Her husband had taught her what they look like, where they can be found and how to handle them safely. It has a bad reputation for being a particularly aggressive when riled, so it fitted her requirements nicely.

The sudden movement startled her so much that, she nearly fell over, but she recovered in time to see it dart out of the sack and enter the end of the sleeping bag. It undulated its way towards the top of the sleeping bag, skirting the back of her still sleeping husband and she quickly secured the zips on both the sleeping bag and tent.

She tried to imagine what would happen, whether her husband would wake first and how would he react to finding a deadly snake in his sleeping bag?

In fact, Windlass remained asleep as the snake slithered underneath his slightly raised knee, upwards along past his groin and may have even exited out through the top of the sleeping bag without incident - if Windlass hadn't snored.

The snake recoiled immediately, emitting a vicious rattle which woke Nat who, even though still half asleep and in the gloom of the tent, realized immediately that he was in grave danger. Instinctively, he palmed its head away whilst, at the same time, trying to exit the sleeping bag. Enraged, the snake struck immediately, plunging its fangs into Windlass's neck, injecting the deadly venom, then struck again and again, a fang piercing his eyeball, as Windlass lashed wildly in a desperate attempt to keep it away.

Lynda had just reached their 4 x 4 when a scream pierced the night that chilled her blood. She scrambled into the cab and gunned the engine but she could still hear the screams. She chanced a look over to the tent just in time to see the silhouette of her husband, still inside the tent, wriggling frantically as both animals partnered in a macabre dance in their desperate fight for life.

How many times would he be bitten before he killed the snake? she wondered. With no means of calling for help, one bite would be sufficient to kill him, albeit slowly. She'd made sure that the only anti-venom kit was safely tucked away in the First-Aid kit that was stowed in the trunk of the vehicle. How long would it be before he was found? Nat always selected the most remote of places for camping and regarded any human contact as an invasion of his privacy.

She didn't look back as she left the campsite. She loved her husband and didn't want him to suffer for too long. But there was an irony about his death that wouldn't be lost on his former comrades. Hopefully, some might say 'he loved the desert and the desert took him, he'd be happy with that'.

The thought of being married to him, tied to poverty for a couple of hundred years made her scrutinize the depth of her love for him and she found it wanting. But it was the realization that she mightn't even be able to afford the annual payments for the Elixir that pushed her over the edge.

No, she rationalized, this way was right. He would keep his unblemished reputation with the Marine Corps and might even be awarded a burial with full military honors. He'd be happy with that, as he would have been in the knowledge that she could live well after cashing in his two million dollar life policy. He would have wanted her to be comfortable.

As she found the track that would take her to the highway, she shivered, turned the heater on, and then prepared herself to play her part; first, shock at the sudden death of her husband, and then, the grieving widow. But not for too long.

Tom Shaw's car took him from the White House to a private airfield on the outskirts of Washington DC. His Learjet was waiting for him there. Already the trappings of immense wealth were commonplace to him. He barely noticed them, and he certainly didn't care about them.

The Learjet was airborne for five hours, coming in to land on the West Coast at midday local time. A helicopter was waiting for him. He transferred with a minimum of fuss, and twenty minutes later was being set down on a bespoke helipad within the compound that he now called home. It was set in the mountains, and protected by high walls and a small army. Luxurious, but again Tom didn't notice the luxury. He didn't care about it. He strode away from the chopper, which took off again almost immediately, and ignoring the armed guards that followed him at a discreet distance, stepped into that small corner of this immense compound that he and Jane shared. He hurried into her bedroom, nodded at the nurse in attendance to indicate that she should leave them, and sat by her bedside.

Her eyes were closed, but he could tell she was awake. The remote control to her television was lying on the bed, just next to her frail hand.

'I watched you,' she whispered.

Tom didn't answer.

'You did it?'

'I did it.'

'Then you're not the man I married,' said Jane.

The comment was quietly spoken, but it cut through him like a sabre.

'He killed Jack,' Tom replied.

Only now did she open her eyes. Six months ago, he would have said that she couldn't look any worse. He'd have been wrong. It wasn't just the gaunt, sallow skin or the thin, dull hair. It was the eyes. Haunted. Desperate. Barely an hour went by that Tom didn't remember the moment he'd told her. Didn't hear the feeble mewing of despair that came from her lips.

'You don't even look like you,' she said.

Tom's eyes narrowed and his hand involuntarily touched his hair. It was very short now. Almost army short. Occasionally he would catch sight of himself in the mirror and be surprised. Even to his own eyes he look ruthless, but he found that didn't worry him.

'I don't want to take it anymore. I want to die.'

Silence.

'There's nothing left for me to live for,' she continued. 'I've lost my son, and now I've lost my husband.'

'I won't let him die for nothing, Jane. I can't let that happen. I can keep you alive, until they find a cure…'

'You'll have to force me to take it, Tom. Would you really do that?'

Tom paused. Would he really?

'If I have to,' he said.

Another long silence.

'You should probably leave me now,' Jane breathed. 'I don't think there's anything else for us to discuss.'

Tom clenched his jaw, but nodded and stood up. 'I won't let you die, Jane. Jack wouldn't want me to. And you'll thank me, one day.' And then, more quietly: 'I've already murdered one person today. Don't make me murder you too.'

Jane turned her head, slowly and painfully, to one side. 'You're not God, Tom,' she said.

Tom felt the skin tighten around his eyes. He turned and walked out of the room.

Kyle Byng's flight from Miami landed at Bogata International Airport around midday and after passing through Passport Control, he made his way straight to the Arrivals Hall. It was his first visit to Colombia and, as his impression had been formed solely from TV news reports of various gang killings and assassinations, he was twitchy. However, he was pleasantly surprised by the sophistication of the procedures and, in particular, the smartness of the Colombian police officers. He was startled by the fact that he found himself staring at them and had to forcibly look away.

A driver was holding a card with his name on so, after identifying himself, he was escorted to a shining deep blue S Class Mercedes parked outside and took his seat in the rear of the vehicle. As they drove off, Kyle noticed four motorcycles, two at the front and two at the rear, apparently escorting them.

All had pillion passengers who were facing the rear, with their backs to the rider and the obvious bulges in the jackets made it clear that they were armed. Helmetless, their faces were impassive, but their eyes darted everywhere.

Kyle said nothing but sank a little deeper in his seat. 'So much for keeping a low profile', he thought.

The driver and the motorcyclists weaved their way through the heavy traffic expertly and soon they were on the Calle 50, passing through the occasional small village. After about forty minutes, the driver turned off the main road onto a smaller road then, after a few more turns, their way was blocked by a pair of ornate and impressive gates, which were opened automatically as the vehicle's sensor was detected. Kyle noticed that the motorcycle escort peeled off at this point and the limo proceeded up a sweeping drive towards the main house which, when it came into view, made Kyle catch his breath.

It was massive, with the central courtyard flanked by two wings. Three stories high, painted coffee cream with each window picked out and framed by brilliant white shutters. In the center of the courtyard were an array of large fountains and the sunlight shimmered and reflected off the spray creating miniature rainbows.

Croft was waiting for him at the massive entrance door. He was wearing skin tight cream jodhpurs, deep brown knee length riding boots and a brilliant white shirt. A broad smile creased his already deeply tanned face and he looked as though he didn't have a care in the world.

Whilst embracing Kyle in a bear hug, he whispered in his ear a warning that he didn't yet trust his servants, with the obvious implication that he wanted Kyle to keep quiet and wait until they were alone. Kyle was guided through the house, past massive marble pillars and huge doors with oak surroundings, out onto a large patio, where they were on their own.

'Kyle, my friend, would you like a drink?'

Ignoring him, Kyle turned to Croft and asked 'Have you heard?'

Croft overlooked the rudeness.

'Have I heard what?'

'Windlass is dead'.

'Yes, I know...so what? He was a muscle bound buffoon and there are plenty more of those for hire. Don't worry your pretty little head about it'.

Kyle stared at him for a few seconds as though he was debating whether, or not, he should put the next question, then, very quietly, asked 'Did you have anything to do with it?

Croft gave a little laugh. 'Look, Kyle. You may have a low opinion of me but, trust me, ordering snakes around is something I am not yet able to do. Give me time though...' He flashed Kyle his most brilliant white smile.

'It's not a laughing matter Theodore, it just seems too convenient timing for my liking. Someone must know what he did and order a hit. They could have injected him with snake venom for all we know. And, if they know about him, they could be coming after us next.'

'Calm down Kyle. Yes, I did some digging and, it seems that Windlass was off on one of his weird camping holidays with his wife, he left the door open to his tent and a nasty snake accepted the invitation, Windlass was able to throttle it to death but not after he'd been bitten five, or six times, mostly on his neck and face. They found the poor snake still in the tent. The shame was Windlass's wife had just left for a couple days pampering at a local resort and taken the truck, as she said that Windlass was always determined to hike out, as part of his holiday. The man was obviously crazy?!'

Croft shrugged his shoulders and carried on. 'She called the cops when he failed to show. Seems he lasted about two days after being bitten but with no phone and a fifteen mile hike to the nearest civilization, he didn't stand a chance. He should have known better...'

'What do you mean?'

'Snakes. Can't trust them'. Croft laughed then slapped Kyle on the back and walked over to the terrace bar and took a bottle of beer from the ice box.

Kyle, refusing the offer of a beer, said 'I can't believe you're cracking jokes at this time. Aren't you worried about what's happened?'

Croft shrugged 'Not at all. In fact, it's worked splendidly for us, as Windlass will take the rap for all the nastiness. Although Tom mightn't be convinced yet, the cops seems to accept that Windlass was the chief Machiavellian plotter responsible for all the violence – a rogue Government agent - and now he's dead, most of the heat is off for the time being. The only person who can identify you is the undercover cop who is in a coma in a hospital and can easily be disposed of, if and when it becomes necessary which, according to my information, will be highly unlikely. Tom doesn't know of your involvement so you can carry on working for him. See, leave it all to me and there's nothing to be concerned about...apart from one thing.'

'What's that?'

'The fact that we failed. That missing fifth component of the Elixir. Neat move by Dr Leo, keeping it to herself. I underestimated the little lady doctor. Very lax of me, which is as unusual as it is irritating'.

Kyle stuttered a little. 'But all those deaths, some friends of mine murdered. All for nothing. What about you, aren't you concerned. Tom knows who you are. Aren't you worried that he'll come after you, or tell the Cops at least?

Croft sat in a pine rocking chair and took a swig of beer. After thinking for a few seconds, he said, 'Tom's main focus was to find the killer of his boy, but is now being told by the cops that it was Windlass and he's dead. I am only a secondary target, less important but, yes, he may tell the police, I'm presuming that he will. So, that's why I'm taking sensible precautions and lying low for a while. In fact, I quite like Colombia, not as bad as its painted actually, the food is great, the women are feisty and the local police chief is already in my pocket. I have a date with an eminent plastic surgeon for a little 'nip and tuck'...I know, it's like trying to improve a masterpiece but needs must, and all that'. Croft's smile returned.

Kyle said 'What do you want me to do? Tom is locked away in his mountain fortress with all his scientists and now won't trust anyone with the details of the Elixir for fear of putting them in danger. All the research work is conducted in secret silos, with information shared only on a 'need to know' basis. In fact, although Tom still trusts me and we speak daily on the phone, I'm still based in LA managing the day to day business in

Tom's absence and working on the development of new Elixir businesses'.

Croft stood up, walked to the edge of his veranda and surveyed some of his thousands of acres of rich pasture land that stretched out in front of him. After a while, still with his back to Kyle. 'To be honest, for the first time, I think we have to accept that we've been beaten. Tom is practically untouchable now and getting stronger all the while, much as it hurts me to admit it'. He turned to face Kyle.

'However, it's not all bad, the drugs trade is flourishing here still, so I may turn my massive intelligence and famed organizational skill to that. Despite all the money they have here, it's still being run here like a cottage industry by the local village thug, so I think it needs the 'Croft Touch' to bring some sophistication to the operation. Yes, some here mightn't welcome my interference but, hey, that's life …I deem it a challenge worthy of my intellect.'

'So, what do you want me to do?'

'Keep your eyes and ears open. Sounds like you're going to be busy in Los Angeles but, you never know, you may hear a snippet worthy of my attention. You know how to contact me. Other than that, let's go our separate ways and enjoy our new adventures without rancor, or recrimination. Now, as you're only here for one night, let me show you to your room and after dinner I'll take you on a tour of the ranch'.

Croft took Kyle into one of the wings of the house and showed him into a vast bedroom, decorated pure white, complete with its own balcony. Kyle noticed that one of the servants had placed his overnight bag at the foot of the bed.

Croft made to leave, but stopped in the doorway.

'Oh, Kyle, if you want my continued support, there is one thing you must promise me'.

'Yes, what's that?' Kyle, though, was stung by the knowledge the Croft could actually withdraw his support and wondered what it would actually mean in practice.

He didn't have to wait long for an answer. Croft fixed Kyle in a cold stare, all sign of his previous good humor gone from his face.

'The undercover cop. If there's any suggestion that he's coming out of his coma, you must kill him immediately. I will contact you as and when it becomes necessary'. He didn't wait for Kyle to reply but turned and left the room, leaving the door open.

Kyle staggered a little and slumped onto the bed, then heard Croft's still loud voice coming from the passageway.

'Not just for my sake, of course, but yours Kyle. Because, if you don't...I'll have you both killed'.

Tom sat in near darkness and stared out of the window of his office at the stunning outline of the Saddleback mountain range silhouetted by the sinking sun. The door to the private veranda was open which allowed a warm breeze to flutter the papers on his desk and the screech of an eagle high above pierced the silence.

He'd made himself a sandwich and a coffee but his appetite had deserted him and the sandwich was left untouched on his desk, where it would stay until he decided to dispose of it. There was no one else to tidy up after him.

He hadn't replaced Ruth, he hadn't even considered it. The police had found her diaries, meticulously kept, in which she made it clear that she loved Pure Industries, it was her life, and the staff, all of them, were her family.

Her suspicion that Tom wasn't up to running the company was also well documented, as was her amateurish attempt to write a business proposal to bring in a new Board and management team. In text book style but twenty years out of date, she'd even prepared a few slides for presentation to venture capitalists in which she'd secured herself the position of 'assistant to the CEO', the exact same role she already held.

'Poor Ruth,' thought Tom 'she didn't even want a seat on the new Board, she just wanted to make sure that Pure would be in safe hands'.

The thought stung Tom and Jane's words also echoed in his head. *You're not God*. She was right. But in the absence of Him, the power to award life was Tom's alone...

For now.

He touched his temple absentmindedly and stroked it gently, whilst continuing to think.

Five years. Five years to study and research. With the income from the Elixir he would continue to employ the finest minds and spend whatever needed to be spent. And he *would* find it. He *would* find the missing ingredient. He *would* discover what Rachael was trying to tell him moments before she died.

He closed his eyes and, as he had so many times before, he remembered those terrible minutes in the basement of that farmstead. He remembered the look of unspeakable agony on Rachael's face. He remembered the words she had scrawled on the concrete floor.

'*The* fifth component *is*...'

He was not a man who allowed himself to be distracted by hunches, or gut instincts. But ever since that day, he'd had the uncomfortable impression that he was missing something.

Something important.

The eagle screeched up above. The sun continued to sink. It grew cold. Tom just sat there, his eyes closed, his stomach churned.

His brain active.

'*The* fifth component *is*...'

'*The* fifth component *is*...'

In his mind, he saw the coffee stains drying. Disappearing. The letters became jumbled. They rearranged themselves. They settled.

And Tom Shaw opened his eyes.

He remembered that Friday night when Rachael had summoned him to the lab. The story she had told him. How the Legum compound had become contaminated ...

It couldn't be that simple.

But it was.

He suddenly understood.

He suddenly knew what Rachael Leo had been trying to tell him.

If the eagle that was soaring above Tom Shaw's mountaintop eyrie had flown 200 miles South, it would have arrived at the hospital where Pat Dolan lay in his deep coma. It was dark in his room. The only light came from the machine by his bedside that was keeping him alive; the only sound from the regular pinging that announced it was successfully doing its job. He was as still as a corpse; but a corner of his mind, trapped by the coma, was active.

Lying there, unable to move, unable to communicate, Pat Dolan relived his last few seconds of consciousness, like a movie reel destined forever to repeat itself. He saw the SWAT team bursting into the room. He saw himself on his knees, laying down his weapon. He saw Rachael Leo, the young woman he'd being trying to save, close to death on the floor. It seemed ridiculous, but was she trying to write something. At a time like this, what was she trying to say?

She glanced at him. And... maybe it was Pat's fevered imagination, but did she try to say something? A single word, mouthed silently? Pat thought he understood her, but it made no sense. No sense at all.

He saw a boot upturning the bowl of deadly jellyfish. He pushed himself away. He felt a blow to the head.

And then the movie reel reset itself, and for the hundredth time, Pat Dolan relived the scene, unable to make any sense of the young woman's silent, desperate message.

'*The* fifth component *is*...'

But that wasn't what she was trying to say. Tom understood that now. The letters burned in his mind. He had studied all of Rachael's notes, looking for clues and a team of top scientists were, even now, working with her technicians, just to see if they could tease some new information that would help him in his quest for the missing component.

But now he had it. With the last vestiges of her strength ebbing away, Rachael had tried to tell him what the fifth component was and, in desperation, when she could talk no longer, wrote it on the cellar floor. Tom realized now that Rachael had started to write 'the fifth component is....' but her strength gave out very quickly.

T...H...

So, despite being consumed with pain and no doubt realizing that she was about to die, she found the strength to raise her arm one last time to write the final two letters that would, hopefully, give Tom the clue he needed to unlock the Elixir.

I...S.

This.

THIS..!

Rachael had been using the fifth component. Over the months of discussion, she had told him everything he needed to know. How the indigenous Indians used it in cases of snake-bite, helping to ward off the terrible coma and how it exerts a soothing action on the vascular system, preventing a too rapid wasting of the tissues of the body; its value in treating heart disease, ascites and pleuritic effusion which combines well with digitalis.

The answer had been staring him the face all this time, literally.

On a reflex, Tom removed his cell phone from his pocket and dialled a number. It rang once. Twice. Three times.

And a voice answered.

'Hi' said Tom. 'It's me.'

A pause.

'How are you, Tom?' The voice was soft. Full of concern. Like it always was.

'I know the fifth component,' Tom said.

More silence.

'You do?'

'I do.'

'What is it, Tom?'

t... h... i... s...

Tom picked up the polystyrene cup containing the now stone cold brown liquid and smiled in the near darkness, barely able to suppress his joy.

'It's...*coffee!*'.

24227856R30192

Made in the USA
Charleston, SC
19 November 2013